WINTER'S CRY

*Detective Meadows relives a harrowing past
in this gripping mystery*

CHERYL REES-PRICE

Published by The Book Folks

London, 2022

ISBN 978-1-80462-052-6

www.thebookfolks.com

Winter's Cry is the seventh title in a bestselling series of standalone mysteries set in the heart of Wales.

Prologue

The boy looked around the courtroom hoping that today he would see a friendly face. Everyone was standing and facing forward as they waited for the judge to take his seat. It didn't matter that he could only see the backs of heads. He knew what the faces were on the other side. Faces of disapproval, eyes that narrowed and radiated a deep loathing as they glanced his way. Again, there was no one here for him, he was alone and in a lot of trouble. He felt fear mingled with sadness shroud his body like a heavy cloak. It weighted him down, making him feel smaller. Some days he wished he would shrink and disappear.

The judge sat, and everyone took their seats. The boy sank into his chair and leaned forward, resting his arms on the wooden stall. He'd been told to sit upright, but he didn't think it mattered now. He'd been sat in the same place for days. The dock. He knew now that was what it was called. The first day he didn't know anything, the men in their wigs had made him laugh. Brian had told him off for that. Brian was his barrister, another word he had learned. Brian was supposed to be his friend and help him. The boy knew Brian didn't like him. No one in this room did. Brian had said the boy's grandad had paid a lot of money for him to help, but his grandad hadn't been to see him. Hadn't come to court. Ashamed, that's what Brian said. If he had been younger, he wouldn't have had to come to this place, but he was eleven years old. Old enough to know right from wrong, old enough to face the consequences of his actions. That had been said a lot.

The boy pulled at his collar, it was hot and stuffy in the room, and it smelt of polished wood. To him there seemed to be too much wood. It filled the room and crept up the walls, making you feel closed in. He hated this room and the people in it. He focused his attention on the front of the room like he had been told to do, but only at the back of Brian's wigged head. He didn't want to look any further because he would have to look at the judge who sat perched above everyone else. The judge scared the boy. A few times he had cast a steely glance his way making him shrink further in his seat. He wasn't the only one. To the boy's right the jury sat quietly listening. From time to time they looked his way, and it wasn't the type of look that anyone would welcome. Worse than the jury were the people that sat on the left. Some of them were journalists, he'd been told. They wrote down all the details so that everyone would know what he had done. Worse than the press was Craig's family. Craig had been the boy he had killed. Craig with his blond hair, blue eyes, and angelic face that everyone cried about. Little eight-year-old Craig, innocent, his life taken by pure evil, the prosecution had said. Craig had been a little shit, the boy thought.

The prosecution barrister was talking. Looking at the jury as he spoke. Brian had told him that this was the end of the case. The jury would decide if he was guilty. He didn't see the point. He did do it, but he didn't know why. The barrister was talking about that day, but the way he told it wasn't right. He wasn't there, the boy thought. There was only supposed to have been three of them that day; the boy, and his two friends, Gareth, and Alan. Craig was Gareth's younger brother and he always wanted to hang out with them. Gareth's mother said they had to take Craig with them. So really it was her fault. The memories started creeping in. The grotesque gash running down Craig's temple and through his eyes. Trying to dig a hole. He tried to block them out, but he couldn't stop the horror of that day playing out in his mind.

* * *

This was not the story that was being told now. Alan and Gareth had said they were afraid of the boy. They told the court how the boy had bullied and hit Craig that day. That he had dragged Craig to the quarry as he cried for his mother. That tried to stop him hurting Craig and that the boy said he would kill them if they told on him. He had never meant for Craig to die. That was the truth. He concentrated now on the closing speeches. When they ended, a prison officer led him to the holding cell and shoved him inside.

The boy didn't mind being shoved around. He'd had much worse off his father.

'I doubt the jury will be out long,' the prison officer said. 'Then the judge will decide how long you are going away for. You understand?'

The boy nodded.

'Are you afraid?'

The boy shrugged.

'Well, you should be. Evil little bastards like you are locked away forever. You'll be going to a place where no one cares what happens to you.'

The boy looked at the floor and fought back his tears. He wouldn't let the guard see him cry. He hadn't cried since he'd been arrested. He knew it would do him no good. He used to cry when his father hit him but learned that it only made things worse.

He sat and chewed at the skin around his nails, which he had already bitten down to the quick. He kept gnawing until the metallic taste of blood filled his mouth. The time stretched out before him and eventually he lay down and fell asleep. The opening of the door awoke him, and the guard took him back to the courtroom. One of the jury members stood up and said the word "guilty" in a clear and loud voice. The court filled with a triumphant roar. Then all was quiet. The boy's legs shook as he stood when the judge addressed him. It was only when the sentence was announced that he let the tears come.

Chapter One

DI Winter Meadows loosened the collar of his shirt as DS Tristan Edris placed a cup of tea on his desk.

'Thanks,' Meadows said as he picked up the cup.

'Can't the temperature on this air con go any lower?' Edris asked. 'I feel like I'm melting.'

'The air con is not the problem,' DS Stefan Blackwell said. 'It's like a greenhouse in here. If they had bothered to put up blinds, we wouldn't have this problem. I'm sure it's against Health and Safety to work in this heat.'

'I think it's supposed to be tinted glass,' Meadows said.

'Well, it bloody isn't,' Blackwell snapped.

'Stop bitching,' DC Reena Valentine said as she grabbed a cup from the tray Edris set down. 'You complain when it rains, complain when it snows, and then complain when we get a bit of sun.'

'It's not a bit of sun,' Blackwell said. 'It jumped from 15 degrees to 31 overnight. It would be alright if the weather gradually warmed up.'

'It will cool down soon enough,' Meadows said. 'These heatwaves never last long. Best enjoy it while we can.'

Blackwell huffed and returned his attention to his computer screen.

'Worse thing about it is it's only Tuesday,' Edris said. 'It'll probably be chucking it down by the weekend.'

'Well, Paskin picked a good week to take her holiday,' Valentine commented. 'She's probably sunning herself on the beach.'

Meadows wouldn't have minded a swim in the sea or even dipping his feet in a cold mountain stream. He pushed his chair back and walked to the window. Outside he could see the river Amman running past the building.

'We could always take it in turns to jump in the river,' Meadows said. 'That would cool us down.'

'Yeah, I'm up for that,' Valentine said.

'I'm not getting my kit off in front of the whole station,' Blackwell said.

'Spoilsport,' Valentine said. 'Well, as soon as I'm out of here I'm going to the beach. Why don't you pop home at lunchtime, grab your trunks and a towel, and come with me?'

'And roast in the car all evening, no thanks,' Blackwell said.

'We'll be on Pendine Sands in an hour at most,' Valentine said.

'I'll come,' Edris said.

'Yeah OK, you can buy the chips.'

'Well, I'm not sitting on a beach with him,' Blackwell said.

Valentine turned to Meadows. 'You coming?'

'Love to,' Meadows said, 'but Daisy is picking up Mum on her way home and we're going to chill in the garden.'

'Just you and me then.' Edris winked at Valentine.

Valentine shook her head. 'Great.'

Their conversation was interrupted by the appearance of Sergeant Dyfan Folland.

'How come you look so cool?' Edris asked.

'Trees shading my window,' Folland said. 'We've also got all the fans which push the heat up here.'

'You can send some of those fans up here,' Blackwell said. 'Why should you get all the perks?'

'You don't have to be in uniform all day.'

'Yeah, but I'm not in bloody shorts and flip-flops,' Blackwell snapped.

Folland laughed and turned to Meadows. 'Got something for you. Farmer digging up one of his fields has found human remains. Hanes has been to take a look and says they are definitely human. The farm is just outside Rhandirmwyn.' Folland handed Meadows the address. 'Hanes had some difficulty finding it, but you shouldn't have a problem. It's close to where you come from. Isn't it?'

Meadows looked at the address. 'Bryn Coch Farm, yeah, it's right next door.'

'You want me to take this one?' Blackwell asked.

Meadows laughed. 'And miss an opportunity to get out of the office? Edris and I'll go. If nothing urgent comes up in the next couple of hours, you and Valentine can take off early. Make the most of it when it's quiet.'

'Great,' Valentine said. She turned to Edris. 'Sorry, looks like you're going to miss out on the beach.'

Edris groaned.

'Never mind,' Meadows said. 'We'll be crossing over the Tywi. You can jump in when we've finished.'

* * *

They left Ystrad Amman Police Station and took the road over the Black Mountain Pass with the windows down and the wind ruffling their hair. Meadows breathed in the fresh mountain air that mingled with the smell of melting tarmac. Sheep grazed lazily on the side of the road not flinching at the passing car. At the top of the mountain the ice cream van was doing a roaring trade with sightseers licking at dripping cones as they admired the view. As tempting as it was to stop, Meadows drove on, following the road as it twisted down the side of the mountain. By the time they reached Llangadog, Edris was cranking up the air con.

'It'll be worse when you get out of the car,' Meadows said as he hit the button to close the window. 'You need to acclimatise yourself.'

'Acclimatise?' Edris laughed. 'Can't you see the heat rising off the road? I'm going to end up with sweat patches on my shirt.'

'We're going to a farm, I don't think anyone is going to notice. I thought you'd be more worried about what you might step in,' Meadows teased.

Edris wrinkled his nose and waggled his feet. 'I just got these shoes.'

'You can always wash them off in a stream,' Meadows said and laughed at the look of horror on Edris' face.

They passed through Llandovery then in and out of villages, some with just a cluster of houses and a post office which doubled as a shop. The distance between the villages widened with stretches of open farmland and forests. Hills rose above the farms with the grass turned hues of yellow and brown in the heat.

'Cwm Rhaeadr.' Meadows pointed to the left. 'If you look carefully, you can see the waterfall coming down between the hills. Highest one in Carmarthenshire.'

'Oh yeah, I see it,' Edris said. 'Wouldn't mind sitting under there.'

'It's quite a hike. I used to go up there as a kid. There's a small pool at the bottom. Great for cooling off.'

'Unnamed road.' Edris pointed at the satnav. 'We really are in the middle of nowhere.'

'Yeah, that's what makes this place so special. You can forget about the rest of the world when you're here.'

Meadows turned off the road and onto a track that led to a farmhouse. A police car was parked in the yard and PC Matt Hanes was talking to a man dressed in green overalls.

Once out of the car Meadows could see that Hanes was struggling in the heat. His face was puce and sweat trickled from beneath his hat.

'This is Jim Hughes,' Hanes said. 'He owns the farm.'

Meadows introduced himself and Edris.

'I understand you were working in one of your fields when you made the discovery,' Meadows said.

'Yeah, I was taking down some trees with my son, Louis,' Jim said. 'We were uprooting a trunk. We'd chained it and Louis was reversing the digger while I guided him. The trunk came up and there it was. A skull. Made me jump, I can tell you. Not the sort of thing you expect to see.'

'No,' Meadows agreed. 'It must've been a shock. What is the land used for?'

'Mainly sheep, but we decided to do some work there and turn it into a caravan park. Plenty of walking around here and people like that sort of thing. Get away from things. We were taking down the trees to extend the area.'

'So, the land hasn't been disturbed for some time?' Meadows asked.

'Not by me,' Jim said. 'Or my father who owned the farm before me. We only reclaimed the land about a year ago. It was taken over by that lot.' He indicated an area to the right.

'You mean the Peace Valley Commune?' Meadows asked.

'Yeah, that's what they call themselves. They crept into our land over the years. Just kept taking it. My father was too soft with them. They took the piss, that's what those types do, they want everything for free. Don't work – most of them are on benefits.'

Meadows didn't rise to the comment. Although he could say plenty to defend the commune, he needed to remain impartial. He usually found that people who held strong views and prejudices couldn't easily be swayed. Mostly it just saddened him.

'So did you just take the land back or did you go through the courts?' Meadows asked.

'It was done properly if that's what you mean,' Jim said. 'Solicitor's letters were sent. They ignored them at first. Then when it escalated, they gave in, so it didn't get as far as court. They knew they were in the wrong.'

'OK,' Meadows said. 'Would you mind showing us the paperwork. It would be useful to have a clear picture of the boundaries, the use of the land, and who has access.'

'Yeah, that's no problem. Although I don't see how that will help. It may be my land, but this has nothing to do with me or my family. You're best off asking questions to that lot. They get up to all sorts of things. Festivals and strange rituals.'

'We will need to establish how old the remains are,' Meadows said. 'It's possible they are ancient and were there long before the commune was established. In the meantime, if you could find any paperwork pertaining to the land while PC Hanes shows us where the remains were found, that would be helpful.'

'Just make sure you close the gates after you. I don't want any of my animals escaping,' Jim said.

'Don't worry, we'll make sure that doesn't happen.'

Meadows and Edris followed Hanes through the fields with Edris watching where he was stepping.

'He doesn't care much for the commune,' Edris said.

'No,' Meadows said, 'there's no love lost between the local farmers and those that live on the commune. They've protested several times over the years. Tried to get them removed. I guess the farmers felt that there could be a better use for the land. What they don't see is that the commune is self-sufficient. They eat what they grow and sell the surplus. They keep bees, handmake furniture, and other crafts to sell. Generally they have a low carbon footprint, and I don't know anyone that claims benefits.'

'You should have put him right,' Hanes said.

'Everyone is entitled to their opinion.'

They came to a large gap in a dry stone wall and stepped through. A digger was parked with its bucket hanging in the air.

'It's just in here,' Hanes said.

They walked about thirty foot in from the wall, passing upturned tree trunks until they came to an area that had been cordoned off with tape wrapped around trees.

'I called forensics. They should be here soon,' Hanes said.

'Thank you,' Meadows said. 'I think you need to get out of the heat for a while. Collect the paperwork from Jim, take his statement then head back to the station. There's no point in you hanging around here.'

'Great, I'm only on shift for another hour and a half,' Hanes said.

'Valentine is going to the beach,' Edris said. 'If you hurry you can go with her.'

'Might just do that,' Hanes said. 'See you later.'

Meadows stepped under the cordon and looked at the upturned tree trunk. Thick roots stuck out while the smaller ones bowed under the weight of the earth. Two of the larger roots encased the skull. It was as though the tree had respectfully grown around the remains. He crouched down as Edris came to stand next to him. He could see more bones had been disturbed. The roots had scattered them as they were yanked up from the ground. There was a sweet powdery aroma in the air and as Meadows looked at the surrounding ground he saw the source of the smell was clumps of small purple flowers. He returned his attention to the skull.

'Well, an adult, but that's as much as I can tell,' he said.

'Yeah, looks like the tree was planted on top of the body,' Edris said. 'These trees are probably hundreds of years old judging by the size.'

'No, I don't think so,' Meadows said. He stood up and looked back at the stone wall. 'Jim said the land was used by the commune and he's right.' An uneasy feeling crept over him. 'Wood is the main source of fuel for the commune, heating, cooking, and even building homes. Whenever a tree is taken down at least two more are planted in its place. I planted a few of these myself. I remember the wall. The woods didn't always come this close to the boundary. Over the years it's expanded. We weren't allowed near the wall and were strictly forbidden to cross over it. We planted on the edge of the woods to expand it.'

'But the body could have already been there,' Edris said.

'I guess but it doesn't look like it was buried that deep,' Meadows said.

'You know there is no law against burying someone on your own land. There are certain environmental issues to be considered and it has to be marked on the deeds. Perhaps it's nothing sinister – a natural burial,' Edris said. 'It would fit. Is that generally what happens in the commune?'

Meadows would've liked to think that was the answer, but he doubted it would be that simple.

'Not that I have heard of,' he said. 'Never in my time there. Plenty of ashes scattered. Besides, the location is too close to the neighbour's boundaries, and an open field where crops are likely to be grown. I doubt permission would have been granted.'

A movement in the woods caught their attention.

'We're being watched,' Edris said.

Meadows could see a man half hidden by the trees. He waved but the man didn't return his greeting, instead he turned and walked off.

'It looks like Haystack,' he said.

'Haystack?' Edris asked.

'Yeah, that's what he's always been called, don't know his real name. I don't think anyone does. He's a recluse.'

'Isn't everyone living on the commune a recluse?' Edris asked.

Meadows smiled. 'No, it's a group of people with a common purpose. They just live an alternative lifestyle. Haystack lives in the woods. Doesn't mix with those in the commune unless he has to.'

Their conversation was interrupted by the arrival of Mike Fielding and the rest of the forensic team.

'Interesting,' Mike said as he peered at the skull. 'It's not going to be an easy job to excavate all the bones, especially if the remains were lying prone. Some could be trapped under the neighbouring tree.'

'The farmer is pulling down the trees,' Meadows said. 'I'm guessing he won't mind if a few more have to be pulled down.'

'That will make things a little easier,' Mike said. He crouched and peered in the hole left by the tree trunk. 'What's that?' He pointed down. He looked over his shoulder and called out to one of his team. 'Rhys, pass me a brush please.'

'I can't see anything,' Edris said peering over Mike's shoulder.

'Yeah, well, I'm trained to see things you miss,' Mike said. He leaned over and started brushing away at the earth.

Meadows watched and saw the edge of a semicircle appear. As Mike scraped and brushed, the object became clearer.

'What is it?' Edris asked.

'Looks like some sort of purse,' Meadows said.

'A woman then,' Edris said.

'Or it could be a man's coin pouch,' Mike said. 'It's leather which takes about fifty years to biodegrade which should narrow things down for you.'

Mike stood up and with gloved hands gently opened the pouch.

'There's some coins inside,' Mike said. He gave the pouch a gentle shake and the coins slid onto his hand.

'They don't look ancient,' Edris said.

'Can you see a date on any of them?' Meadows asked.

Mike moved out from the shade of the trees and looked at each coin in turn. '1985 on this two-pence piece,' he said.

'How long has the commune been here?' Edris asked.

'Well I was born here in 1982,' Meadows said.

'Oh,' Edris said. 'If the coin is dated 1985, then...'

'Yeah, this poor soul could've been put in the ground when I was living here.'

Chapter Two

Meadows could sense Edris' excitement as they walked the track into the commune. He knew Edris had wanted to visit for a long time. Like for many others who had heard of the place, it was curiosity. A different lifestyle. Some even viewed it as a cult. To Meadows it had been his childhood home. Nothing out of the ordinary. Life was a bit more simplistic, but people worked, children learned, and it rained on them the same as it did the neighbouring farms. People fell in love, children were born, people got sick and died. Life went on the same as it did anywhere else. There was nothing secretive or magical about the place. They were just ordinary people who wanted to be left alone. Yet people viewed them as different, wanted to look inside and ask questions. He'd always kept his life here separate from his work. Now that was about to change.

'When were you up here last?' Edris asked.

'Last Tuesday evening for the summer solstice. I only came up for a couple of hours.'

'They'll be surprised to see you back so soon.'

'Yes, but it's not a casual visit. We're going to have to tread carefully. Some that have been here a long time have suffered years of prejudice and are not big fans of the police.'

'Yeah, I figured that much,' Edris said.

'Just think of it as if we were investigating remains found in Bryn Bach or Dan y Coed. You went to school with a lot of people from that area.'

'Yeah, and a lot of them don't invite me to the pub because of my work.'

'Exactly and I'm guessing they wouldn't be comfortable with you questioning them. Particularly the older generation who knew you when you were the village bad boy.'

'I'm happy to ask all the awkward questions,' Edris said. 'Or we could just call in Blackwell.'

'No, not yet. Can you imagine?'

Edris chuckled. 'Yeah, he's not the most tactful of people.'

They walked past the old farmhouse that was now just a shell. Its roof had caved in long ago. A track led them by an orchard and a large vegetable garden. Several people, carrying watering cans, greeted them as they moved in the opposite direction. One man stopped and set down the cans. He smiled as he wiped away the sweat that ran down the side of his face.

'Hi, Martin,' Meadows said.

'Winter, what are you doing here? And dressed like that, in this weather,' Martin asked.

'I'm on duty,' Meadows said.

'Oh.' The smile slid from Martin's face. 'So just in the area and you thought you'd pop in.'

'Something like that,' Meadows said. 'This is my colleague, Edris.'

Martin looked at Edris and gave him a brief nod before picking up the cans. 'I better get on. We're trying to keep the crops hydrated. They're drying out as fast as we are watering them. We can't afford to lose them.' He walked off.

'I see what you mean about not liking the police,' Edris said. 'Maybe I should've waited in the car.'

'Don't worry about Martin, he never liked my choice of career. Come on, I'll introduce you to Jerome, he'll give you a warm welcome.'

'Is he like the leader or something?' Edris asked.

Meadows laughed. 'There is no leader. He's one of the olds, that's what they call themselves, short for older generation. He was like a father to me when mine left.'

They walked a little further and came to the first field where various dwellings were dotted around, a mix of yurts, tepees, and caravans.

'It's much bigger than I imagined,' Edris said. 'More spread out.'

'They don't live on top of each other. There are also buildings for showers and toilets, storerooms, and a cabin that's used for drying herbs and making essential oils. As well as gardens and polytunnels for growing food,' Meadows said. 'Oh and beehives, a couple of cows, and a fair few chickens.'

Edris looked around. 'It does look very organised, and everyone looks busy.'

'What did you expect? People sitting around smoking weed all day?' Meadows laughed. 'It's hard work. They're just a group of people that reject mainstream culture, doesn't mean everything comes free. They use the land to survive and whatever skills they have to make enough money for additional food.'

'Do you ever feel like giving it all up and just staying here?'

'No,' Meadows said. 'It's good to come up here for a break and it's like visiting family but I enjoy my job.'

They reached the centre of the field which was marked by a large pagoda covered with vines. Inside, a woman with short grey spiky hair and an angular face was reading aloud to a group of children.

'Hi, Jenny,' Meadows called.

She stopped reading and a smile lit her face. 'Winter, how lovely to see you.'

'You too,' Meadows said. 'Is Jerome around?'

'I think he's moving some compost. Either that or he's gone for a nap.'

'Thanks, I'll let you get back to your lessons.'

There were more greetings as they walked through the field and although Meadows felt out of place wearing a suit, no one else questioned it. Most were too busy with chores to stop and talk.

'Is it just this field or is there more?' Edris asked.

'Much more,' Meadows said. 'There's a lot of land so the commune is spread out across the fields. There are more homes in the next field. Everyone has plenty of space and privacy.'

As they neared the far end of the field a man appeared from the side of a yurt. He wore only jeans and sandals and was pushing a wheelbarrow piled high with compost. He had long grey hair tied back, and a white beard trimmed into a point. His bare chest and arms had a leathery look of someone who had spent their life outdoors. He dropped the handles of the wheelbarrow and looked at Meadows and Edris. Then recognition dawned on his face.

'Winter, my boy. What a lovely surprise.'

'Jerome.' Meadows stepped forward and hugged the older man.

Meadows introduced Edris and the men shook hands.

'Any friend of Winter's is welcome here,' Jerome said. 'You look like you are about to collapse, son. No wonder in that suit. I've got some spare shorts if you want to change and jump in the stream to cool off.'

'Erm, I'm OK, thanks,' Edris said.

'Actually I'm afraid I'm here in an official capacity,' Meadows said. 'We were called out to Bryn Coch Farm. Jim Hughes was working in one of his fields and found human remains.'

'Bloody hell,' Jerome said. 'That must've been a shock for him. He's not the nicest of guys but still, that's awful.'

Meadows nodded. 'The thing is the remains were found on land that up to a year or so ago was used by the commune. It's the edge of the woods.'

'Right,' Jerome said.

'I'm sorry I'm going to have to ask you a few questions,' Meadows said.

'Don't be sorry, my boy. It's your job. Come inside, have a drink and cool off.'

'Thanks,' Meadows said. He took his shoes off and followed Jerome inside.

'It's much cooler in here,' Edris commented.

'Yeah, most people are surprised. Cool in the summer and warm and cosy in the winter,' Jerome said.

Meadows took a seat on one of the large floor cushions and watched Edris' eyes travel around the yurt. A lattice wooden frame supported the canvas. On one side was Jerome's bed which was covered in a brightly coloured throw. On the other side was a free-standing shelving unit with crockery, books, and Tupperware boxes.

Jerome opened a small fridge, took out some ice and popped it into two cups and a glass. He then uncovered a jug and filled the glass before handing it to Edris.

'Lemonade. Mina makes me a fresh jug every morning.'

Edris took a sip. 'It's lovely, thanks.'

'You look surprised,' Jerome said.

'I didn't expect you to have ice,' Edris said.

Jerome laughed. 'The beauty of solar panels. Runs the fridge, the lights and charges my phone.' He pointed to two large batteries that sat in wooden casing. 'I can go up the top field and get internet access. We're not that far removed from the world.' He seated himself next to Meadows who noticed that he struggled getting down on the floor. 'So, what would you like to ask me?' Jerome asked.

'I remember planting trees where the remains were found. There's a dry stone wall that marks the border. I can't see that the wall was moved at any point in the past. My point being is that I don't think that land belongs to Jim Hughes.'

'You're right,' Jerome said. 'We never took his land.'

'Then why not fight for it?'

'For what? A lot of expense and trouble. You know people's views of us. We wouldn't have won. It was easier to let him have it. Keep the peace.'

'Who owns this land?' Meadows asked.

'We all do.'

'Edris thought that you may have had a natural burial on the grounds.' He looked at Edris who nodded. 'Has anyone, to your knowledge, been granted permission to do something like that?'

'No, you know how things here work. We always have a discussion. I would have known about it. You know there are a lot of cairns in the area. Could it be something like that.'

'We don't think the remains are that old,' Meadows said. He didn't want to tell Jerome about the coins at this stage.

'Is this going to come back on us?' Jerome asked.

'I hope not,' Meadows said. 'It will all depend on exactly how long the remains have been in the ground.'

'How long have you lived here?' Edris asked.

Jerome thought for a moment. 'I came here in 1981. Don't ask me the exact date,' he said with a smile.

'And can I take your full name?' Edris asked.

'Jerome Gwyn.'

'Thank you.' Edris wrote in his notebook.

'Previous address?'

'I can't help you with that. I last lived with my parents over fifty years ago.'

'You've probably been here the longest,' Meadows said.

'Yes, me, Iggy, Mina, and of course your mum and dad. Jenny came not long after, then Cosmo. Oh and Haystack has been here a long time.'

'Who owned the land before?' Meadows asked.

Jerome shrugged. 'No idea.'

'That's OK. We can look into it.'

'So what happens now?' Jerome asked.

'We'll call in a specialist to look at the remains. We'll know more when we have a sex, age, and the remains are dated. Meantime there will be police activity in the woods as well as here. It will be a case of collecting names and how long the various families have lived here. Also, we'll need to track down previous residents. It will just be general questions for now,' Meadows said.

'A lot here aren't going to like that.'

'I know, that's why I'm counting on you to smooth the way. The quicker we get answers the faster we can leave you in peace.'

Jerome nodded. 'I'll do my best. Is there anything else you want to know?'

'You must've seen a lot of changes over the years. People coming and going,' Edris said.

'Change is the natural order of things, whether good or bad. I've met some amazing people.'

'Were there any problems? Arguments, violence, that sort of thing?' Edris asked.

Jerome shook his head. 'Any disagreements are talked through. We've had some people come that didn't fit in. An amicable solution was usually found. If not, they were asked to leave. There was a couple of occasions where people turned up, thinking it was a place to drink and freely take drugs, they got into fights. We had to be a little forceful, but they got the message and didn't come back.'

'What do you mean by forceful?' Edris asked.

'We packed up their things and dumped them outside the gate. Refused to share our food with them. We all have to work for what we've got. No one freeloads. Other than that, then no, there have been no problems.' He looked at Meadows. 'In your time here can you ever remember being scared, unloved, or threatened by someone?'

'No,' Meadows said. 'It was always a happy place. Still is. Can you think of any time when someone left suddenly, maybe left all their stuff?'

'You know more than most that people move on without a goodbye to the ones they propose to love.'

Meadows knew who Jerome was referring to. Edris gave him a curious look. 'Yes, but anything completely unexpected?'

'No, not that I can think of.'

Meadows drank the last of his lemonade. 'I think that's about it for now. Thank you.' He stood up.

'It's no problem,' Jerome said. 'I hope you find your answers.'

'We'll have a chat with Iggy then we'll be on our way,' Meadows said.

'You'll probably find him with his feet dangling in the stream. He never copes well in the heat.'

They left Jerome in his yurt and walked across the fields until they came to a wide stream. There were three people there. One was a portly bald man with a jolly face, who sat on the bank with his feet in the water. He was carving a piece of wood that was wedged between his legs. Another man was sitting in the stream letting the water flow over him. He had long hair and a beard, both a mix of brown, ginger and grey. The beard trailed his chest. With his small stature, serious brown eyes, and fine features, it made him resemble a garden gnome. Talking to the two men was an elderly woman dressed in a tie-dyed rayon dress. She had long dark hair streaked with grey. Her hands rubbed away at clothes that she held under the water.

'Iggy,' Meadows said.

The portly man stopped carving and turned to look at Meadows. A smile lit his face. 'Hello, kiddo,' he said.

Meadows smiled. It didn't matter how old he got he was always referred to as 'my boy', 'kiddo' or 'lad' by the older generation. He introduced Edris then turned to the woman. 'This is Mina and that's Cosmo cooling himself.'

'Alright?' Cosmo said. 'Why don't you c-come in and join me?'

'It's tempting,' Meadows said. 'Oh why not.' He sat on the bank and took of his shoes and socks. 'Come on,' he said to Edris.

'I haven't got a towel,' Edris said.

Mina laughed. 'You don't need one. The sun will dry you in no time.'

Meadows rolled up his trousers and waded into the stream until he was positioned between Iggy and Cosmo. Edris sat on the bank with his feet dangling in the water.

'So what are you two handsome boys doing here? You don't look like you've come for a break,' Mina said.

Meadows filled them in on what had been discovered at the farm. Iggy listened without comment, the colour drained from Mina's face, and Cosmo sat up straight.

'I didn't do anything,' Cosmo said. He spoke in a slow deliberate voice. Each word sounded out.

'Of course you didn't, Cos,' Iggy said.

'It's OK, Cosmo,' Meadows said. 'We are just collecting information. Just names and how long everyone has been here. Are you alright, Mina?'

'Yes.' She continued scrubbing at the clothes. 'It's just a bit shocking. I go into the woods by myself.'

'No one here is going to hurt you, dead or alive,' Iggy said. He looked at Meadows. 'Do we have to answer your questions?' He spoke in clipped tones which was at odds with his attire and surroundings. Meadows often thought that Iggy wouldn't be out of place living in a stately home.

'Not if you don't want to, but you have nothing to worry about,' Meadows said.

'Yeah, that's what they all s-say then you are dragged off to a st-station and locked up,' Cosmo said.

'You've had experience with the police, have you?' Edris asked.

'There was a time when they were always raiding us. Looking for drugs. They'd find one little bit of weed and that was it, we were treated like criminals,' Iggy said.

'That was years ago, Iggy,' Meadows said. 'I promise you that no one is going to be looking for weed or any other substance for that matter. We just want to find out about the poor soul that's been buried in the woods. They've probably got a family somewhere that was looking for them. Imagine not ever knowing what's happened to a loved one.'

'Yes, I can see that would be a rotten business,' Iggy said. 'I'll help if I can, but I honestly don't know anything about it.'

'Great,' Edris said. 'So can I take your name?'

'Iggy.'

'And that's short for…?'

'Just Iggy. Everyone knows who I am and where to find me.'

'How long have you lived here?' Edris asked.

'I landed here sometime in the eighties and haven't moved since.'

'And you?' Edris turned to Mina.

'Much the same. I'd rather not give you my full name. I left that life a long time ago.'

'Was there any trouble here that you can remember?' Meadows asked. 'Threatening behaviour, that sort of thing?'

'The only trouble came from the farmers. They wanted us off the land,' Mina said.

'People d-didn't like us much in the village and then there was…' Cosmo screwed up his eyes in concentration. 'You know, Iggy.'

'I don't,' Iggy said.

'That one, he did all that funny s-stuff in the tent. I can't remember his name.' Cosmo knocked the side of his head with his fist.

'Don't worry, it will probably come to you later,' Meadows said. 'Write it down when it does.'

Edris looked at Cosmo. 'I don't suppose you are going to give me your real name.'

'No he's not,' Iggy said.

Cosmo smiled. 'I've been Cosmo for a long time.'

'OK,' Meadows said. 'I could happily stay here with my feet in the water, but we better go. If any of you remember something, even if it doesn't seem important, let me know. I'll come back up when we have some more information.'

'It was good to see you,' Iggy said. 'Give my love to your mum. Will she be coming up soon?'

'Yeah, in a couple of weeks. Enjoy the sun,' Meadows said.

'Nice to meet you,' Edris said.

They walked back through the fields until their feet were dry enough to put on their shoes and socks. Back at the car Meadows opened the door and got a blast of boiling air.

'I'm not getting in there,' Edris said.

'I'll put the air con on and let it cool down for a few minutes,' Meadows said.

Edris sat on the grassy verge and pushed back his blond hair which had clung to his forehead. 'They all seem very nice but not that helpful.'

'That's perhaps because they really don't know anything about the remains.'

'Mina looked a bit shaken,' Edris said.

'Yeah, I did notice her reaction. It could be more than the fact that she'd been unknowingly passing a body in the woods.'

'And Cosmo was… well, odd.'

Meadows laughed. 'He's always like that. He's had a speech impediment since childhood. So he talks slowly, he also tends to just say what he's thinking. He is bad-tempered but a lot of that is to do with frustration when he stutters or can't find the right words. The "I didn't do anything" comment is a normal response from him.'

'Erm, Jerome mentioned you'd know about people going missing. Do you mind me asking what he meant?'

'I thought you'd pick up on that,' Meadows said. 'He was talking about my father. He walked out on us when I was seventeen.'

'And you haven't seen him since?'

'No.'

'You don't think that—'

'No,' Meadows said. 'We weren't living here at the time. We were in the cottage where I live now. He walked out and never came back.'

'That must have been hard on you and your brother.'

'It was harder on Rain. He's three years younger so it wasn't an easy time. Right, let's get going.'

Meadows was glad to move the conversation away from his father. It had been years since he had thought about him. The last time they were together wasn't something he wanted to think about. He just hoped their paths wouldn't cross during the investigation.

Chapter Three

Jerome sat at the back of the pagoda and listened to the discussion going on around him. News had spread fast about the remains in the woods, and he could understand the concern it caused. He knew he needed to remain calm and reassuring even though he didn't feel that way himself. His insides churned and he felt sick.

'How long are the police going to be here?' asked Martin, a father of four who had grown up in the commune.

'They didn't say,' Iggy said. 'Obviously they are going to be buzzing around the woods. If we stay away from that area they shouldn't bother us.'

'But they're going to be asking questions,' Callie, a middle-aged woman, said. 'What if they want to search our homes?'

'They are not going to search our homes,' Jenny said. 'Your weed is safe.'

The group laughed and the tension dispersed.

'We don't have t-to worry. Winter is one of us,' Cosmo said.

'Yes,' Jenny said, 'but he is still a detective. His priority will be his job.'

'And so it should be,' Iggy said. 'He's worked hard to get where he is.'

'Well we've got nothing to hide,' Martin said. 'My main concern is reporters. Once they hear about this they will come. They'll be the ones asking stupid questions. Taking pictures.'

'Then we'll make a sign for the gate. "Keep out" or "No trespassing" – something like that,' Jerome said.

'Maybe we should put a lock on the gate,' Mina suggested. 'Just until this blows over.'

'Good idea,' Iggy said. 'All those in favour?'

There was a show of hands.

'Good,' Jerome said. 'So that's settled.'

The group dispersed leaving Jerome, Iggy, Cosmo, Mina, and Jenny. They waited until they were alone and were sure no one could hear them until they spoke.

'I think we have a lot more than the press to worry about,' Jenny said.

'What do you mean?' Mina asked.

'Some of us would rather not have our whereabouts known or the past raked up.'

'Well it looks like it's just been dug up, I told you back then something was wrong,' Mina said.

'I don't know what you are talking about,' Jerome said.

'Yes, you do. You said I was overreacting.'

'Don't bring that all up again,' Iggy said.

'You're not going to leave us, are you?' Jenny asked. 'Like last time.'

'No,' Mina said. 'It's just you wouldn't listen before.'

'But it turned out OK in the end,' Iggy said.

Mina nodded.

'As long as we don't give our names then we will be OK,' Iggy said.

'Too late, they've already got mine,' Jerome said.

'Why would you tell them?' Cosmo asked.

'It's OK,' Jerome said. 'They have to dig pretty deep to find my past.'

'We just have to be careful,' Iggy said. 'Cosmo nearly told them about Jonah.'

'That's his name,' Cosmo said.

'Well, you need to forget it again,' Iggy said.

Jerome noticed Mina's discomfort. She sat with her eyes downcast and fiddled with the hem on her dress.

'Are you OK, Mina?' Jerome asked.

'Yes, he's just one person I don't want to think about,' Mina said.

'None of us want to think about him,' Jenny said.

A memory came to Jerome's mind. He was in the big tent that they used for communal meetings. Fern Meadows was on her knees. Her arms wrapped around her body as she sobbed. Jonah stood over her, his lips twisted into a satisfied smile. He shook the memory away. That's all in the past. What matters is the people sat around me now, he thought. They were his family, the people he loved.

'We'll be OK,' Jerome said. 'Let the police come and ask their questions. We haven't done anything wrong. What's important is to protect Winter. He's like a son to me.'

Jenny took his hand and gave it a squeeze. 'We all love him.'

'Yeah,' Cosmo said.

'So we mustn't talk about Jonah,' Iggy said.

They all nodded their agreement.

Chapter Four

Meadows felt happy to walk through the door of his cottage. All he wanted was a cool shower, to change into something comfortable, and forget about work for a couple of hours. It was quiet in the cottage and Meadows guessed that Daisy Moor was on her way to pick up his mother, Fern.

He hurried up the stairs and stepped into the shower, turning it to cold. It didn't have the desired effect. His mind was still whirring from the day's work and no amount of water could wash away the feelings of foreboding he felt. He tried to reason that it was because the commune was his place of escape, where he went to recharge. Particularly after a difficult case. Now he was mixing the two and by asking a few simple questions it felt as though there was a divide between him and those that he was close to. Worse than that was the fact that he would have to speak to his mum about it. They rarely mentioned his father and it may be the case that he would have to bring him back into their lives.

'There you are,' Fern said as Meadows stepped into the garden.

Meadows gave his mum a hug before turning to Daisy and kissing her. 'Good day?' he asked.

'It was OK until some pain-in-the-arse detective sent me a pile of bones to assemble,' Daisy said.

Meadows laughed. 'Yeah, sorry about that.' He poured himself a glass of elderflower water from the jug on the table and sat in a chair between his mother and Daisy.

He'd met Daisy while working a case. She had taken over from the retired pathologist and within a year they were dating. Now he couldn't imagine his life without her. He loved everything about her; her long black hair, mischievous blue eyes, and wicked sense of humour, but more than that it was her compassion for the victims and the families she dealt with.

'This sounds interesting,' Fern said.

Meadows knew his mother liked nothing better than to hear about his cases. She had been his sounding board over the years, and she was always discreet. She's going to find out sooner than later, he thought. Better hear it from me.

'Human remains were found on Bryn Coch Farm.'

'You mean Will Hughes' place?' Fern asked.

'Well it's his son, Jim's, now. The thing is the remains were in the woods that border the farm. On land that, up until a year ago, was used by the commune.'

Fern shook her head. 'You think someone from there is responsible?'

'I have to look at that possibility. It's going to be difficult if not impossible to get the bones identified,' Meadows said.

'I called in a forensic anthropologist,' Daisy said. 'It's going to be a few days until they can get here. Then we'll have some idea of how long the person has been buried.'

Meadows nodded. 'From items we found we're looking at 1985 onwards. Once we narrow down the date it will be a case of talking to those that were there at the time, tracking down those who have left, and maybe that will turn up a missing person. Someone must know something. I've talked to the olds today, but they couldn't help.'

'Well I don't think I can be of any help. We left years ago,' Fern said.

'This could've happened when we were there,' Meadows said. 'How many were living there when you joined?'

'Not as many as there are now.' Fern smiled and took a sip of her drink. 'Six of us, but not for long.'

'Why did you join the commune?' Daisy asked. 'I can imagine you in a long dress, flowers in your hair, and staging some protest.'

Fern laughed. 'No, it wasn't quite like that, but I was a free spirit.'

Meadows had heard some of his mother's story, but he was happy to sit back and listen.

'I met Jerome first. He was volunteering on a project.'

'What sort of project?' Meadows asked.

'I'm not sure which one. He was involved in all sorts. Homeless shelters, community gardens, young people who had got into trouble, that sort of thing. We got talking and he invited me to go to the commune. I went and never left.'

'You could have got yourself into all sorts of trouble. Going off with a strange man,' Meadows said.

'I'm a good judge of character,' Fern said.

'What about your family?' Daisy asked.

'I didn't have any family. I grew up in care. Once I turned sixteen, I was on my own.'

'That must have been hard,' Daisy said.

Fern shrugged. 'I got by.'

'So were you and Jerome together back then?' Daisy asked.

'Not exactly together,' Fern said. 'We had some good times.'

'I don't think I want to know,' Meadows said. He looked at his mother. Even in the autumn of her life she was beautiful. Her long blond hair threaded with white came down to her waist. She had vibrant blue eyes and had kept her petite figure. The only thing that gave her age away was the arthritis that gnarled her fingers.

'I didn't bring you up to be a prude,' Fern said and laughed. 'Anyway, Jerome and I became good friends, and we still are. Just because we're a little older doesn't mean we don't have needs.'

'Good for you,' Daisy said. 'Everyone needs a little love from time to time.'

Meadows shook his head. 'OK, enough about your love life.'

'If you want to know what went on in the commune then expect to hear a lot more about people's needs,' Fern said. 'We all fell in and out of love, changed partners, some had more than one, even shared the responsibility of children.'

'That must have caused some jealousy,' Meadows said.

'Yeah, I suppose it did, but it rarely lasted and mostly we all got along.'

'Was Dad there at that time?'

'Yeah, he was there before me. He was close friends with Jerome,' Fern said. She looked at Daisy. 'Kern was the best-looking man I'd ever laid eyes on. Tall, with dark curly hair, and green eyes. That's where Winny gets his looks.'

Meadows could feel himself blush. 'Everyone thinks the same of their child.'

'Don't be so bashful,' Fern said. 'Everyone used to comment what a beautiful child you were.'

'I can see that, you still are,' Daisy said.

'Alright enough of the flattery,' Meadows said. 'Anyway you can't have all got along all the time.'

'No, we had our ups and downs,' Fern said. 'More people came and sometimes it took a while for them to settle down. Some stayed for months, years, or never left.'

'Can you remember any incidences where there was violence?'

'No, nothing like that.'

'What about Dad? He had a temper.'

'Not back then. He was happy in the commune. He changed when we left. Are you going to have to speak to him?'

'It looks like I might have to. Do you have any idea where he is?'

'No, he could be dead for all I know. No one would tell us. I think it's likely he set up home in another commune somewhere. I did miss him when he left, and I hoped he'd come back. In the end I guess he didn't want to. He knew where we were. It wouldn't surprise me if he had another family. How do you feel about seeing him?'

'I don't know.' Meadows sighed. 'It will be strange after all these years. I'm not sure I would know what to say to him. Things between us weren't good when he left.'

'We're all different people now,' Fern said. 'I forgave him years ago. I needed to move on. If you do see him, keep an open mind. He must've had his reasons for leaving. If he wants to get to know you, give him a chance.'

'I will but it's not easy to forget how hard things were for you when he left. You were alone with two children and a mortgage to pay. I remember how hard you used to work.'

'I was never alone,' Fern said. 'Don't you remember how often Jerome or Iggy would visit? They used to bring food and anything they thought we needed. Then just when I thought I'd lose the house a solicitor's letter turned up. The mortgage had been paid off and the deeds were in my name.'

'You never told me that. So Dad paid off the mortgage?'

'No. I don't think it was him. He wouldn't have had the money. It was done anonymously. I suspect someone from the commune. Just because they choose to live a simple life doesn't mean they're poor.'

'No I guess not, still it's a huge sum of money.' Meadows would have liked to ask more questions but didn't think it was fair on his mother or Daisy. They'd both expected a pleasant evening in the sun. 'OK, enough work talk. Let's eat.'

* * *

Meadows was in the office early next morning. He'd already sent off emails to all the communes that could be contacted asking about Kern Meadows. He knew it could be some time before he received a reply. Most had websites set up, but he suspected they would only check emails sporadically.

It was forecast to be another hot day, but he had managed to persuade Sergeant Dyfan Folland to give him some fans which now whirred in the background. Valentine was first to come through the doors. She wore a green sleeveless dress and strappy sandals. Her onyx hair was pushed back with a pair of sunglasses.

'How was the beach?' Meadows asked.

'Heavenly,' Valentine said. 'I stayed until the sun went down. Shame Edris missed out. I'm going back again after work.'

Blackwell was next in, already looking hot and bothered, then came Edris.

'I wouldn't mind wearing sandals,' Edris said.

'Nothing stopping you,' Valentine said.

'Yeah, I'd look a right prat wearing them with a suit.'

'Wouldn't make a difference,' Blackwell said. 'You are a prat.'

'Yeah, well I bet you're one of those who wear socks and sandals to the beach,' Edris said.

'OK, shall we start?' Meadows said. He'd found that distraction was the best way to stop Edris and Blackwell bickering. He walked over to the incident board and the team gathered around.

'As you can see we don't have a lot of information yet. I've pinpointed the location of the discovery on the map.' He pointed. 'At the moment we are looking at any date after 1985. Priority is identification. People come and go in communes, but no one can completely vanish without leaving a trace. Someone knew this person. Someone buried them. Our unidentified could well have a family that has been missing them all these years. They deserve answers. They may have been reported missing. I think that's a good place to start – a general search of missing persons in the area.'

'What? That's over thirty years,' Blackwell complained.

'Start with the local area,' Meadows said. 'Carmarthenshire is a big enough area although I can't see there being that many missing persons. Once we know more, like age and sex, we can widen the search.'

'This is where we miss Paskin,' Valentine said. 'Shame she is on holiday.'

Meadows nodded his agreement. 'I've talked to Folland this morning. If we need more help, uniform can assist. Next, we need to establish ownership of the land. It could be collective. I want to know who owned the land before it was taken over.'

'I'll look into that,' Blackwell said.

Meadows nodded. 'That brings us to the commune itself. From information we gathered yesterday it was set up in 1980 or 81. Some of the original members still reside there.' He pointed to the names on the board.

'Iggy? Cosmo? How are we supposed to work with those names?' Blackwell asked.

'They weren't very forthcoming,' Edris said.

'So who runs this place?' Valentine asked.

'No one,' Meadows said. 'Decisions are made by consensus. There is no hierarchy. There are olds, or the older generation. Those are the names on the board. They are respected for their knowledge and wisdom, but they only give advice if asked. Not one of them is seen as a leader, nor would they claim to be. There are around thirty families that have a permanent residence on the commune then there are those who just pass through. Over the years there have been raids by the police and problems with the neighbouring farmers and the wider community. They have a distrust of outsiders, particularly the police, so we are going to have to tread carefully.'

'Everyone was friendly yesterday,' Edris said.

'Mutual respect is the only way we are going to get information,' Meadows said. 'Edris and Valentine, I'd like you to look into any raids, and arrests. I'll concentrate on old photos and footage that's been posted online. I know a documentary was made some years ago. Not everyone took part, but it could help identify those that were there.'

'Don't you think that this is all a bit too close to home?' Blackwell said. 'I'd be happy to take the lead on this one.'

'I think I can manage to remain unbiased,' Meadows said. 'Over the years we've all had to interview people that we know. It goes with living and working in these tight-knit communities. Yes, my family lived there for a number of years, but I think that will work in our favour. I know the people and they trust me. The commune is a bit like a village. It can accommodate up to 300 people. In the past there has been that many. It's not like I or my family are directly involved. Of course if that changes or if any of you have concerns about me working this case I'll step aside.'

'I haven't,' Edris said.

'Me neither,' Valentine added.

Blackwell shrugged. 'OK fine, I just thought I'd mention it.'

Meadows smiled. 'No problem.'

* * *

They worked quietly through the morning. Meadows found a documentary from 1989 posted on YouTube.

Residents of the commune, together with local farmers, shopkeepers, and people from the community, had given interviews. There was a clear divide between them. Each one was eager to give their views. Some of them weren't nice to listen to and it saddened Meadows to hear such prejudice. More so that these opinions of the commune were still held by some.

Edris poked his head around the side of his computer. 'You found anything interesting?'

'Lot of accusations of stealing made by the farmers. One claims his house was broken into by one of the commune members. Another talks about missing chickens. The shopkeepers say they come in and frighten away customers. Wild, dirty, and uncivilised seems to be the general consensus. There's talk of wild parties, rituals, and sacrifices.' Meadows laughed. 'I can't say I recall any of that sort of thing when I was growing up. I think you're likely to find a lot of filed complaints.'

'I've seen some footage of the raids. Reports of cannabis plants being dumped all over the place so blame wouldn't be pinned on one person. Didn't stop several arrests though.'

'I haven't come across any of the olds on camera,' Meadows said. 'Looks like they just wanted to be left in peace. It may be worth talking to the farmers, see what reaction we get. It could be that one of them decided to take matters into their own hands.'

'Wouldn't someone from the commune have reported it?' Valentine asked.

'There wasn't a good relationship between the commune members and the police back then,' Meadows said. 'They're still wary of the police.'

'They could've said something yesterday,' Edris said. 'If there had been threats or violence from the farmers, you'd think now would be a good opportunity.'

Meadows shook his head. 'They wouldn't point the finger. Especially without evidence. They like to live a peaceful existence, which means letting go of the past and not being vindictive.'

'Well I've found the owner of the land,' Blackwell said. 'Jerome Gwyn.'

'We spoke to him yesterday,' Edris said. 'He didn't say he owned the land. Why would he lie?'

'I'm not sure he did lie,' Meadows said. 'He said the land belonged to all of them. That's how he would view it.'

'Maybe he gave the land to the commune, or he purchased it on their behalf,' Valentine said.

'It wasn't purchased,' Blackwell said. 'It's a deed of transfer.'

'From whom?' Meadows asked.

'Caradog Llewelyn. I checked. He died in 1979. Nothing suspicious.'

'See if you can find out what the relationship was between Jerome and Caradog. It may be nothing but maybe someone else thought they were entitled to the land.'

Meadows hated that everyone he grew up with was now a potential suspect, but he said he was going to be unbiased, and he needed to prove that not only to the rest of the team but to himself. He checked the time.

'Right, come on, Edris, we need to get over to the morgue. With a bit of luck there will be something to help us identify this poor soul.'

Chapter Five

It was eerily quiet in the basement of the hospital. The only sound came from their footsteps as they walked down the corridor. Meadows admired Daisy working in this environment all day. The smell of the chemicals, the harsh lighting, and the various medical instruments seemed to give you a sense of distorted reality.

'Well this shouldn't be too difficult,' Edris said.

'What makes you say that?'

'It's just a pile of bones. Nothing gruesome.'

'Still a person,' Meadows said. 'They have a story to tell and need justice just the same as if they had died yesterday.'

'Yeah, you're right,' Edris said.

Daisy was waiting for them and led them into the morgue where the bones had been arranged on a metal gurney.

'As you can see, Mike and the team managed to excavate all the bones, so you are looking at a complete skeleton,' Daisy said. 'Male, forties, or fifties is my best guess. You'll have to wait for the expert.'

'Well that's a good start,' Meadows said. 'Any obvious injuries?'

'There's a hairline fracture to the skull. See here.' Daisy pointed. 'Given the tree roots and the weight of the trunk and earth then it's possible that it's post-mortem. So nothing definite there. What is of interest are the ribs. There is a notch on the third and fourth ribs on the left-hand side.'

Meadows stepped closer and looked.

'A stabbing?'

'That would be my guess,' Daisy said. 'I've seen these types of marks on a fatal stabbing victim before. The notches here are symmetrical.' She pointed. 'I think we're looking at a single stab wound with a double-edged weapon.'

'Anything else?' Edris asked.

'He had a couple of missing teeth. Lower canine and a molar. Evidence of dental work. We can use dental records to confirm identity when you have some leads.'

'Well, so far we have nothing,' Edris said.

'Mike may be of more help,' Daisy said. 'He said they had recovered some interesting bits in the earth.'

'Great,' Meadows said. He turned to Edris. 'We'll stop by before we go to the commune. See you later,' he said to Daisy. He always felt awkward when they were in a work setting. The natural thing would've been for him to kiss her, but he felt it wasn't appropriate.

They drove to the forensics office and found Mike in the lab.

'I hear you've got something for us,' Meadows said.

'I was about to photograph the finds and send them over to you,' Mike said. 'As you're here, you may as well take a look.'

Overhead air con units hummed as they pumped out cold air. It made the temperature feel comfortable despite the heat generated by the computers and other machinery.

'We are still sieving through the earth so we may find more. The pouch we found was a leather mix. Foreign made, I can't make out a manufacturer's mark. Even if we could, I doubt it would be of much use. Probably mass-produced. The coins inside had various dates. The latest one being 1990.'

'That narrows it down a bit,' Edris said. 'But only to about thirty years.'

'Well you don't expect me to do all the work for you, do you?' Mike said with a smile. 'Also inside the pouch was some sort of ticket. Could be a bus or cinema ticket. We're trying all sorts of tests to try and see if we can get some lettering from it. I won't bore you with the details.'

'If you can get something from it that would be good,' Meadows said.

'Now which one of you can tell me what these are?' Mike picked up a tray and rattled the tiny metal pieces.

'Are they studs from jeans?' Meadows asked.

'Yep, the denim is long gone. We also found remnants of canvas and plastic, so the body was likely to have been wrapped. I've kept the best until last. I've cleaned it up the best I can.' Mike picked up another tray and handed it to Meadows.

Meadows looked down and his stomach flipped. For a moment it felt like the floor shifted beneath his feet. A coldness crept over his body. He stared at the object. It was a metal disc engraved with a continuous line interweaving around itself. There was a hole on each side of the disc which was threaded with leather string.

'Looks like it was worn as a bracelet. You can touch it,' Mike said. 'It's been tested and there's no fingerprints or DNA, which is to be expected given where it was found.'

'We could get a photo out in the media. It may give us a lead. That pattern might mean something,' Edris said.

'It looks handmade,' Mike said.

Meadows didn't trust himself to speak for a moment. He tried to steady his breathing. 'It's a symbol for eternal spiritual life or the unity of family. There's a tree on the other side.'

'That's right,' Mike said.

Meadows turned the disc. 'It's my father's.'

'What!' Edris' eyes widened. 'Are you sure?'

'Yes.' Meadows put the tray down and pulled up the cuff of his shirt. 'See, the same as mine. Except I have a snowflake.' He flipped the disc of his bracelet. 'There's the tree. My brother made them for us. Design and technology was his favourite lesson. He was good at it. He stayed after school to finish them. I remember he was upset because the other boys... well, you can probably guess what they said. Kids can be cruel. We told him we would put them on and wear them forever.' He smiled. 'That's what we did. They match our names. Rain's bracelet has three drops of water, my mother's has a fern. There was no symbol for my father, so he used the infinity symbol. They all have matching trees. The tree of life.'

'I'm so sorry,' Mike said.

'I don't know what to say,' Edris said.

'I'm going to have to go,' Meadows said. 'I can't be involved in this case.'

Chapter Six

Meadows had just ended a call with his brother when Daisy walked through the door.

'Mike called me,' she said. 'I'm so sorry.' She put her arms around him.

'I'm OK,' Meadows said as he hugged her. 'It's just a bit of a shock.'

'Of course it is,' Daisy said. 'It's one hell of a way to find out, and then to think I was discussing my findings with you. A relative should never have to experience that. If I'd had any idea…'

Meadows could see the compassion in her eyes. 'It's alright,' he said. 'I don't want you to give it another thought. You were just doing your job, as was I. I mean what are the chances?'

'What's going to happen now?'

'I've spoken with DCI Lester. Obviously, I'm off the case. He's put me on compassionate leave. Blackwell will be SIO overseen by Lester. I'm not to have any contact with the team.'

Daisy smiled. 'I guess you're not going to sit around feeling sorry for yourself.'

'No, I can still ask questions. I'm probably in the best position to get answers from those in the commune. It will be accessing information that's a problem.'

'I'm sure your team are too loyal to leave you completely in the dark. I can't see Edris staying away.'

'That's what I'm banking on, although I don't want him to get into trouble. There's not a lot I can do at the moment. Blackwell will no doubt be going up to the commune, so he'll be the one to break the news there. I've just got off the phone with Rain. He's catching the next available flight home. That just leaves Mum. I've been putting it off but I'm going to have to go and see her before she hears the news from someone else. I've delivered bad news to so many families you'd think I'd be used to it.'

'This is different,' Daisy said. 'Do you want me to come with you?'

'No, it's probably best I go on my own. Thanks anyway.' While Meadows would've liked to have Daisy's support there were some memories he wasn't ready to share. There was also a scenario plaguing his mind. It had started when he saw the bracelet. He needed to talk to his mother about it before his brother arrived home. He had no idea how he was going to bring the subject up, but it had to be said. It was going to be far worse than telling her that her absent husband was dead.

* * *

Meadows hated being the one to have caused the look of shock on his mother's face.

'Are you sure?' Fern asked.

That was usually the first question Meadows got when breaking bad news. The doubt and hope. At least his mother wasn't devastated. She wasn't sobbing or drained of colour. Just shocked.

'Right age range and it's the bracelet Rain made. He wouldn't have given that away. We'll have to wait for

DNA results. It may take a while as it has to be extracted from the bones. They'll look at dental and medical records, but I'm fairly certain.'

'All this time I thought he'd left us,' Fern said. 'To think I felt so angry with him at that time. He was dead and no one noticed. That's awful.'

'We weren't to know,' Meadows said. 'Did you know he went back to the commune after he walked out?'

'No, but I guess it would make sense. Do you know when he died?'

'No, he could have gone back up there at any time. Can you think of anyone who would want to hurt him?'

Fern shook her head. 'No. Could it have been an accident? Or maybe he took his own life, and he didn't want us to know so left instructions for someone to cover it up.'

'What makes you think that?'

'I'm sure he tried to kill himself before he met me. There were scars on his wrists. I asked him about it, but he wouldn't open up to me.'

'I never noticed that,' Meadows said.

'He always wore long sleeves,' Fern said.

'I don't think it was anything like that. We found evidence of a stab wound.'

Meadows carefully watched his mother's reaction. It didn't take long for it to come. That moment the thought strikes you. That sick feeling. He'd experienced it himself only hours ago.

Fern remained quiet for a moment then she folded her hands on her lap and looked at Meadows with a determined expression.

'No, I can't think of anyone who would want to hurt your father.'

Meadows nodded. It was clear Fern wouldn't voice her fears. It would be up to him. If she knew something, he had to know.

'I called Rain. He's coming home.'

'No, he mustn't,' Fern said. 'What if…'

'What if?'

'Nothing.'

'I know what you're thinking. I thought the same.'

'Then you know he can't come home. He's your brother. You have to protect him no matter what. He was just a child.' Fern picked up her phone. 'I'll call him, tell him not to come.'

Meadows stood and gently took the phone out of his mother's hand. 'It's too late. He's probably on a plane or at least in the airport. You have to let him come. We need to know the truth.'

'We don't know that he…' Fern shook her head.

'Exactly, we don't know.' Meadows laid his hand on his mother's shoulder. 'It will be OK, try not to worry. We mustn't bombard Rain with questions when he gets here. He'll tell us in his own time.'

Fern nodded. 'I'll make us some tea.'

'You sit there. I'll make it. Camomile, I think.'

In the kitchen Meadows took two cups from the hooks and filled the kettle. As he waited for it to boil, he thought about the notches he'd seen in his father's ribs earlier that day. He gazed out of the kitchen window into the courtyard. It was quiet and peaceful in the house. Not like it had been the night his father left. He sighed and allowed himself to remember.

He was sitting in his bedroom, his CD player turned to full volume as he studied for the upcoming exams. It was late and he was cramming as much information as he could before his mother came up to insist he turn off the music and get some sleep. As the song came to an end, he heard raised voices drifting up the stairs.

Great, Dad's pissed again, he thought.

He put down his textbook and opened the bedroom door. Rain was on the landing peering over the banister.

'Go back to bed.'

'No.' Rain looked defiant. 'He's been drinking again.'

'All the more reason to stay in your room.'

A crash followed by a scream sounded from below. Rain ran down the stairs, Winter followed, his heart thudding in his chest. In the kitchen he quickly took in the scene. A smashed plate on the floor, his father's face contorted with rage, his mother cowering by the sink.

'Win, take your brother upstairs.' His mother pleaded with her eyes.

'Rain, go upstairs now!' he ordered before stepping in front of his mother. He pulled back his shoulders and glared at his father. 'Why don't you leave her alone and go and sleep it off?'

Kern Meadows narrowed his eyes. 'Get back to your room, you moody little fucker, before I teach you a lesson.'

'Please, Win,' his mother begged as she stepped forward, eyes darting wildly between her husband and her son. 'Look after Rain, I'll be fine.'

Winter stood his ground. He could feel his body trembling and he clenched his fists. 'No, Dad, I think you better leave.'

Kern lurched forward before Winter had a chance to react. He could hear his mother's screams as he felt his father's fist impact his jaw, the metallic taste of blood filled his mouth as a second blow hit his stomach. As his muscles contracted he felt the air leave his body and he struggled to draw in a breath. He sank to his knees as his father continued to punch and kick him.

'Kern, stop!' he heard his mother scream.

A crack rent the air and Winter pulled his head up in time to see his mother crash to the floor. Rain stood, his eyes wide with shock.

'Run! Go and get help,' Winter shouted.

Rain looked from his brother to his mother then pulled a knife from a block on the kitchen counter and waved it at Kern. 'Get away from them,' he shouted.

'Rain, no!' Winter struggled to his feet, pain shot through his head, his body was on fire.

'Are you threatening me, boy?' Kern laughed. 'You put that knife down now or you'll get a hiding you'll never forget.'

Rain lunged forward and as Kern held up his arm in defence, his son plunged the knife into it.

Kern yelped as blood spurted from the wound. Winter stood paralysed as Rain dropped the knife and ran. He watched his father take chase.

'Go after them,' his mother sobbed.

Meadows brought himself back to the present. Was that how it happened? he thought. Or had Rain still been carrying the knife when he ran out. It had been days after that when Rain returned home. Jerome had brought him back. Rain had been scared back then. Scared and angry. But angry enough to plunge a knife into his father's chest? If that was the case, then was Jerome the one to help bury his secret? Meadows was sure Rain couldn't have done it alone. Despite their father leaving, Rain had grown up into a good man. Devoted his life to helping others. Was this out of some sort of guilt? Meadows sighed. If Rain confessed, would he keep his brother's secret or turn him in?

Chapter Seven

Meadows watched as Fern fussed around in the kitchen. She placed cups on a tray then removed them.

'I've got some nicer ones somewhere,' she said. 'And I've baked some cakes.'

'Just come and sit down,' Meadows said.

'I can't, I'm too wound up. I couldn't sleep last night and when I did, I woke at five. I just kept thinking through things.'

Meadows knew the feeling. He'd lay awake for hours watching the clock pass from Wednesday to the early hours of Thursday morning, then time sped up and now Blackwell was due to arrive any moment. 'Try not to worry.'

'I can't help it. What are they going to ask?'

'We've been through this. I don't want it to look like I've prepared you. Honest answers. If anything sounds rehearsed, then it will make them suspicious.'

'I'm more worried about you,' Fern said. 'You're their boss and they are going to hear things about your family. How your father behaved. How are you going to feel about them knowing about your childhood?'

Meadows smiled. 'Well I guess it's just karma. I've had to dig into other people's lives. Ask them to tell me things they're ashamed of. Divulge information about the people they love. I'm sure they felt the same. I'll be fine. I'm not ashamed of my background and I have nothing to hide.'

'What about Rain?'

'It will be up to Rain what he tells them when he gets back. Anyway, I don't think it will be that easy for them to ask the questions. Valentine will probably feel uncomfortable; Blackwell, I'm not too sure about.'

A knock on the door put an end to their conversation. 'I'll get it,' Meadows said. 'You go and sit down.'

He walked slowly to the door, opened it and welcomed in Blackwell and Valentine. Blackwell appeared to be his usual self while Valentine gave him an awkward smile.

'Kettle's on and Mum's made some cakes,' Meadows said as he led them into the sitting room where Fern was standing.

'Stefan, Reena,' Fern said. 'How lovely to see you both.

Meadows expected Blackwell to correct his mother, maybe ask her to address him formally, but he just smiled.

'I'm so sorry for your loss,' Valentine said, she looked at Meadows. 'For both of you.'

'Yes,' Blackwell said. 'I can't imagine how you must be feeling, especially given that it was your case.'

Meadows believed that Blackwell's comment was genuine. 'Thank you. I'll make us all some tea then we can start.'

Meadows could hear them exchanging pleasantries from the kitchen. Work, family, love life. The usual things. It felt strange being on the other side of the investigation. He put the tea on a tray with the cakes and carried it to the sitting room. He handed out the cups then took a seat in the armchair.

Blackwell took a sip of his tea and set the cup down. 'You know how this goes. I'm going to have to ask some awkward questions. DCI Lester is happy for me to take over the investigation, but if you are at all uncomfortable then I've no problem passing it over to another team.'

Despite Blackwell's gruffness and their ups and downs over the years, Meadows knew that Blackwell was a good detective, and the team would work hard to solve the case.

'I'm more than happy for you to continue,' Meadows said. He looked at his mother.

Fern smiled. 'Of course, Stefan. I'm glad it's you two.'

'Maybe not a good idea to use first names,' Meadows said. 'This is an official visit.'

'Nonsense,' Fern said. 'I don't expect them to call me Mrs Meadows.'

Blackwell smiled, which was something Meadows didn't see often. He nodded at Valentine who took out her notebook.

'I have a couple of items for you to look at,' Blackwell said. 'I know Meadows, erm, Winter, saw the bracelet yesterday, but a ring was also found.' He handed two small evidence bags to Fern.

Fern looked at the items through the plastic. 'Yes, the bracelet is Kern's, he never took it off. It matches mine.' She held out her wrist. 'The ring is also his. We both had Celtic bands, I haven't worn mine in years.'

'When was the last time you saw your husband?' Blackwell asked.

'Erm… years ago,' Fern said.

'1999,' Meadows said. 'End of April, beginning of May. Sometime around then. I can't give you the exact date.'

'Are you sure of the year?' Blackwell asked.

'Yes,' Meadows said. 'I was still in school.' He turned to his mother. 'It was just before Bethan Hopkins was murdered.'

'Oh yes,' Fern said. 'Yeah, he wasn't around when that happened. She went to school with Win, it's not something you forget.'

'So you weren't living on the commune at the time?' Blackwell asked.

'No we'd left two years before that.'

'We were living in the cottage that I live in now,' Meadows said.

'I couldn't find a missing person's report,' Blackwell said. 'Had you separated?'

'No,' Fern said.

'My father walked out on us,' Meadows added.

'Had there been problems? Arguments?' Blackwell asked.

'Yes,' Fern said.

'Violence?'

Fern nodded. 'On a few occasions.'

Blackwell looked at Meadows. 'Was your father violent towards you?'

'On one occasion, yes,' Meadows said. He could see Valentine scribbling away in her notebook and wondered what she must be thinking.

'What about your brother? Rain, isn't it?'

'Not that I'm aware of. You'll have to ask him yourself.'

'Where is he?'

'In India but he's getting a flight home. As soon as he arrives I'll let you know.'

'OK,' Blackwell said.

'So, the last time you saw Kern, was it after one of these violent incidents?' Valentine asked.

'Yes, we argued, and he left,' Fern said.

'What was the argument about?' Blackwell asked.

Fern sighed. 'I don't know. The usual, lack of money, and living the life he hated.'

Blackwell addressed Meadows. 'Were you a witness to this fight?'

'I was home, yes.' Meadows hoped Blackwell was going to move on.

'Weren't you worried when he didn't come back?' Blackwell asked.

'No, I thought he had gone back to the commune,' Fern said.

'You didn't check?' Blackwell asked.

'No, I thought he needed some space, time to figure things out. Then I assumed he didn't want to come home. Went off to join another commune. The months turned into years.'

'You have a lot of friends at the commune,' Blackwell said.

Fern nodded.

Meadows knew exactly where Blackwell was going with this. He would be thinking along the same lines.

'Anyone you're particularly close to?'

'No, I have a lot of good friends there.'

'And you regularly go up to stay?'

'We both do,' Meadows said.

'Did your friends know that Kern had a temper? That he was violent towards you?'

'No,' Fern said. 'He was never violent when we lived in the commune.'

'When did you start going back to the commune?'

Fern shrugged. 'I suppose a year or so after Kern left. Jerome used to check on me and he asked us to come and stay. He thought it would be good for the boys.'

'So your friends knew Kern had left you?'

'Even though we lived away they would still come and visit so they found out not long after he left. I told them we'd had an argument, nothing more.'

Meadows thought his mother had answered the question well. She had avoided mentioning Rain's involvement without lying.

'What about Kern's family. Did they have any contact with you after he left?' Valentine asked.

'Kern didn't have any family. Well, none he spoke about. There was no contact during the whole time we were together.'

'What about other people outside the commune, friends he grew up with?' Valentine asked.

'There was no one. Our lives were inside the commune.'

'What about when you moved?'

'Not really. He'd talk to whoever was in the pub, but there was no one he was close to.'

'Did anyone turn up looking for him around that time? Someone you hadn't met before?' Blackwell asked.

Meadows wondered where Blackwell was going with this.

'No, no one,' Fern said.

Blackwell looked at Meadows.

'No,' he said, 'I don't remember seeing him with someone I didn't know or anyone asking about him.'

'Were you aware that your father had a prison record?' Blackwell asked.

'No.' Meadows looked at his mother.

'No, he never said anything to me,' Fern said.

'I guess it's not surprising,' Meadows said. 'He did like a smoke and probably took some other drugs when he was younger. It was the seventies.'

'This wasn't for possession,' Blackwell said. 'Your father was convicted for manslaughter in 1969. He drove head on into another vehicle and killed four people. He served eleven years.'

Chapter Eight

Meadows was still reeling from Blackwell's revelation. As soon as Blackwell and Valentine left, his mother retrieved her tobacco tin, rolled a joint, and lit it. He didn't blame her and was tempted to join in.

'Are you OK?' Meadows asked.

'Yeah, it's just... well, I'm wondering if I actually knew the man. All the years we were together, and he never mentioned it. It's one hell of a secret to keep.'

'Perhaps he was ashamed.'

'We've all done things we are ashamed of. He knew everything about me. I didn't keep anything from him. It wouldn't have mattered. I still would have loved him. If he kept that a secret, what else was he hiding?'

Meadows nodded. 'I think we have to prepare ourselves for the fact that he had a whole different side. From Blackwell's questions I gather he thinks the past caught up with him. Serving eleven years he would have met some dubious characters who he may have stayed in touch with.'

'I suppose he could have. We weren't together twenty-four hours a day,' Fern said. 'He could've met up with someone without me knowing.'

'Do you think the others knew about his past?'

'I don't know. He was very close to Jerome and Cosmo. He may have told one of them.'

'I need to speak to them. Blackwell's next move will be to go to the commune for information. I'll wait until he's been and go up in the morning.'

'What if someone remembers Rain being up there that time?' Fern asked.

'I doubt it. It was a long time ago. The only person who knows is Jerome and maybe the other olds. They wouldn't say anything to Blackwell about it.' Meadows sighed and rubbed his eyes. 'I've been thinking about that night.'

'You and me both,' Fern said.

'I'm sure Rain dropped the knife before he ran out.'

'No I don't think he did. I was terrified at the time thinking what would happen if your father caught up with him.'

'Why didn't you call the police?'

'I was going to but then Rain could outrun your father and he was smart. He would've hidden from him. I didn't want the police coming here, seeing the state we were in. Then there was Rain running around with a knife. I had no family, no one to turn to. I thought I'd be seen as an unfit mother, unable to control my children. I was afraid to lose you boys. I know now it was stupid. But I was young. If I had called the police, then none of this would have happened.'

'You can't think like that.'

'Rain had already used the knife on your father. We know now they both ended up back at the commune.'

'I just can't believe that Rain would do something like that,' Meadows said.

'Not deliberately, but if he was scared…'

'Even then, I think he would've told us. We need to believe in him. In any investigation the family always comes under suspicion first. If Rain tells Blackwell about what happened in the house that evening he'll become a suspect, innocent or not. We need to think carefully about who else could've done this, even if it means suspecting our friends.'

Fern nodded. 'You're right. I've been thinking the worst before even asking your brother. He couldn't have done it. I know what lives in his heart. He was a kind loving boy.'

'And he still is,' Meadows said. 'Think, was there anything that happened just before Dad left?'

'Nothing,' Fern said. 'I thought he'd gone off with Mina.'

'Mina? Why would you think that?'

'He was with her when I joined the commune. I didn't intentionally split them up. It just happened. She didn't want to share him and neither did I. Your dad chose me. She wasn't happy about it. The next time I went to the commune after your dad left, Mina had gone.'

'Why didn't you tell me?'

'I didn't want to upset you at the time. It was bad enough that he'd left us. Think how you would've felt if you thought he was with another woman. Then Mina came back so obviously he wasn't with her.'

'Blackwell said Dad served eleven years which means he must've got with Mina as soon as he came out of prison. Dad was the same age as you, wasn't he?'

'Yes, born the same year and rhyming names. We used to say that it was a sign we were born for each other. Stupid really.'

Meadows did a quick calculation in his head. His father would have been too young to be driving in 1969. He didn't want to say anything to his mother. She's heard enough deception today, he thought.

'Mina might have known about his past, may have even been connected to someone he knew inside. Then there's Jerome. You said they were close. So how did they meet?

You and Jerome were also close, he knew what Dad had done to you. What if they argued?'

'I don't like this,' Fern said. 'You're talking about people I've known all my life.'

'I know but as Dad died and was buried in the commune, we have to face the fact that one or more of them knows something about it. Jerome owns the land of the commune. What if he also has money? Someone paid off your mortgage. Was it out of guilt?'

'He's always looked after us,' Fern said. 'But so has Iggy.'

'What do you know about Iggy?'

'He was already there when I joined. Good friends with your father and Jerome.'

'Do you know his real name?'

'No, he's always been Iggy. Always has a smile for you. Even when we had storms that blew down some of the tepees, and we were cold, wet, and hungry, he was cheerful. Had us all sleeping in his caravan until we got sorted. I don't think I've ever heard him say a bad word against anyone, never raised his voice in anger.'

'What about the others?'

'Jenny and Margaret came next and Cosmo about a year later.'

'Did he just turn up?'

'Yes, well, I think Jerome met him first and invited him. I was a bit wary of him at first.'

'I can understand that. He comes across as serious at times and I don't think the speech impediment helps.'

'No, he's always had trouble. You know what he's like when he can't find the right word. He gets frustrated.'

'Did something happen to him?' Meadows asked.

'I don't know. It's not the type of thing you ask. Anyway it's just Cosmo, he's a real sweetie when you get to know him.'

'What about Haystack?'

'He came after me, I think. He always kept to himself. I can't see any of them harming Kern.'

'No,' Meadows agreed. 'There were plenty that came and went over the years. It's just a case of finding out who was there in 1999 that isn't there now. Can you think of anyone? Maybe they turned up and Dad behaved differently, out of character? Or a feeling you had that something wasn't quite right?'

'He used to take off for a couple of days every year. Around about the same date. He never explained. I followed him once. It wasn't easy. He caught three buses. I'd put my hair up under my hat and put on sunglasses. I think he could've easily have spotted me if he wasn't so distracted. I thought maybe he was going to see his family, but he went to a cemetery just outside Cardiff. I couldn't get too close, or I would've risked him seeing me. He was in there for hours. After he left, I went inside. I thought I'd easily pick out the grave he'd been visiting but I didn't recognise any of the names close to where he was standing. No Meadows.'

'Did you ask him about it?'

'No, then he would've known I had followed him.'

'My guess is that it was one of the people that died in the collision. Without the file I can't get the names and check. That's the sort of thing we're looking for. Is there anything else? I remember life at the commune as being the best time of my life. We were so happy. Things only changed when we moved. Have I got it wrong? Did things go wrong before we left?'

'I suppose he did change then. He didn't want to leave the commune.'

'But you had to because Rain became ill.'

'No, well yes, Rain was suffering with asthma, so that was sort of the reason, but it was mainly because of Jonah.'

Something stirred in Meadows' memory. Walking past the big tent, people chanting, someone crying. 'I remember Jonah, he used to run meditation classes. That's why we had the big tent and built the pagoda. All those people came to join him. He'd strut around and the women would swoon over him. He was OK though.'

'Jonah was not OK,' Fern said. 'He had some strange ideas. He'd travelled a lot or so he said. Europe, India, and America. There were rumours that he was part of a cult, broke away and wanted to run his own. He'd invite people to come to our celebrations. One time a couple of hundred turned up for the summer solstice.'

'I remember that,' Meadows said. 'Some of them got loud but I don't recall any fighting and certainly nothing cult-like.'

'Jonah was clever. He was a good-looking man and charming. He had a way of making you feel at ease. He turned a lot of women's heads. Slept with a fair few. He wanted to be the leader, have people adore him. Those who didn't follow him he tried to convert. He would find their weakness. He'd always be slithering around, whispering in your ear when you were alone. Then the tent became a place for other things.'

'What sort of things?'

Fern shook her head. 'I got caught up in it. Thought he talked sense. I didn't realise how toxic he was until we left. All you need to know is that your father was scared of him. So scared he left the only place he called home.'

Chapter Nine

Meadows and Daisy knelt in the attic of the cottage, searching through boxes. Dust motes moved around in air that was thick with heat. Meadows could feel his hair sticking to his forehead. He didn't think he could stand to be up there much longer.

'Look, photos of you as a boy. You were so cute,' Daisy said as she handed him one.

'They may be useful,' Meadows said. 'Most of them were taken in the commune. There could be pictures of people that were around before we left. It could help jog some memories. Maybe I can find one of Jonah.'

'Your mum wouldn't say what he got up to?'

'No, it must be bad because you know how open she is about things. No subject is taboo.' He took a lid off another box and pulled out a pile of papers.

'What have you got there?' Daisy asked.

'Looks like old deeds.' Meadows scanned the words as he flipped the pages. 'Yeah, it's the deeds to the commune land. They're in Jerome's name. Why would they be here?'

'Maybe he gave them to your father for safekeeping.'

'Yeah, not much room in his yurt. I'll ask him about them. See if he wants them back.' He opened the last box and shuffled through the contents. 'Nothing.'

'What exactly were you hoping to find?'

'I don't know. Something, anything that would give me an idea of who my father was. Something from his past he held on to. The very least his birth certificate. He walked out that night and never came back so he didn't take anything with him.'

'Maybe things got lost when you moved from the commune,' Daisy said.

'He didn't have a passport, so a birth certificate would've been his only form of identification.'

'You should be able to get a copy.'

'Yeah, I'll do that. I just wanted to check something. Blackwell said he was convicted in 1969. He was born in 1955 so that would've made him thirteen or fourteen when he crashed the car.'

'It has been known for teenagers to joyride,' Daisy said.

'Yeah, but back then? It was the sixties. I doubt he'd know how to drive. Maybe a sixteen- or seventeen-year-old.'

'So you think he lied about his age?'

'Either that or Blackwell got the dates wrong. Why lie?'

'Why don't you call Blackwell and ask him? He'd know from the records what age your father was when he was convicted.'

'I should have asked him at the time. I guess the conviction took me by surprise. I just want to find evidence of his date of birth. Then I'll talk to Blackwell, see if he made a mistake or…' Meadows ran his hands through his hair. 'I don't know.'

'I think you're looking for answers when there are no questions,' Daisy said. 'Your brain is getting fried up here.'

'Yeah, come on, let's go down. We'll take the photos and sort through them.'

As Meadows was climbing down the ladder there was a knock on the door.

'You can get that,' Daisy said. 'I'm going to have a shower and get the cobwebs out of my hair.'

When Meadows opened the door he was surprised to see Edris.

'What are you doing here?'

'I came to see how you're doing,' Edris said. 'And I've brought you some information.' He stepped inside. 'This is a copy of your father's file. Blackwell will have my balls if he finds out, but I thought you should see it.'

Meadows took the file. 'I could kiss you.'

Edris laughed. 'Please don't.'

'I really appreciate this,' Meadows said. 'You know you could get into a lot of trouble, and I wouldn't want that.'

'Don't worry, I was careful, and it was my decision. If it was my father, I would want to know. Anyway all I'm doing is visiting a friend. I'm officially off duty for the evening.'

'Come and have a seat,' Meadows said. 'Daisy will be down in a minute. We've been up the attic looking to see if we can find anything of my father's.'

'Any luck?' Edris plonked down in an armchair.

'No, just some old photos.' Meadows sat down and opened the file. The first thing he did was check the dates. 'According to this, Kern Meadows was convicted in 1969 when he was seventeen.'

'That's right,' Edris said.

'My father's date of birth was 27th of July 1955.'

'We did notice the date of birth on the court records differed from the one you gave us,' Edris said. 'We checked through the registry of birth and deaths. There was no other Kern Meadows born in the fifties.'

'Another thing he lied about,' Meadows said.

'Maybe he thought it would throw off the police if they looked him up.'

'Yeah, I guess that makes sense. Databases weren't that good back in the day.'

'How did your mother take the news?'

'She's OK, a bit shocked but I left her baking. She wanted to be alone for a while.'

Meadows opened the file and started to read. Daisy came downstairs and made Edris a drink and then they both sat quietly while he absorbed the information. He got to the end of the file and closed it.

'It's worse than I imagined.'

'Yeah, it's not good,' Edris said.

'What happened?' Daisy asked.

'He stole a car along with his brother Patrick, and two friends, Nicolas and Lee. They'd all been drinking and taking drugs. My father drove the car at speed down a single-lane road. He hit a car coming the other way head on. The driver of the other car, Anne Parry, was driving home with her three children after visiting her parents. Anne and her daughter Donna were killed. The other two children were seriously injured. Patrick and Nicolas also died in the collision.'

'There are transcripts from the court case. I can try and get you a copy,' Edris said.

'I think I've read enough,' Meadows said. 'I take it Blackwell is checking out the families of the victims?'

'Yes, Anne Parry's husband, Ray, has been dead for twelve years. The other daughter, Christine, was nine at the time of the accident, and is paralysed. Her brother, Steven, who was seven at the time had head injuries, we haven't been able to contact him. That leaves Lee Morris and the family of Nicolas Llewelyn to track down. Lee Morris was the youngest of the boys in the stolen car. He was also badly injured. Kern Meadows admitted to stealing the car and, in a statement, says Lee Morris played no part in the theft, so he was never charged. Both of your father's parents have since died. They only had two sons.'

'It's a lot of guilt to live with,' Meadows said.

'He didn't intentionally kill those people,' Daisy said.

Meadows nodded. 'A moment of madness or rather an evening of madness. Young and stupid. That wouldn't have been any consolation to Anne Parry's husband. You can understand why he might want to seek revenge. He lost his wife and child and was left to care for two injured children. When did he die?'

'Sometime in 2010,' Edris said. 'Blackwell spoke briefly to Christine. He doesn't think there is anything in it. She said that while her father was devastated at the time, he was happy with the sentence your father received and he concentrated on making their lives as comfortable as he could. She doesn't believe that he would've had anything to do with your father's death. Blackwell doesn't want to waste too much time on that line of enquiry. He thinks that thirty years after the incident is too long for someone to act out of revenge. Besides there's no evidence and the suspect has died.'

'He was in prison for eleven years then lived in the commune. He wouldn't have been easy to track down,' Meadows said

'Or maybe it has nothing to do with the accident,' Edris said.

Meadows thought of his brother, who was now on a plane. He had hoped that his father's murder was some sort of revenge for the accident. If that was the case, Rain would be in the clear.

'What are you going to do now?' Edris asked.

'I'd like to talk to Christine Parry.'

'I can't give you her details,' Edris said, 'but she's married; she's Williams now, lives in Penarth.'

'Thank you. She may not want to talk to me but it's worth a try. In the meantime I'm going up to the commune. Someone there must know what happened and has kept quiet for over twenty years. I can't believe my father was murdered and buried there with no one hearing or seeing something.'

Chapter Ten

Meadows walked through the graveyard that his father had visited. The sun hadn't long risen and already the warmth gave the promise of another hot day. He hadn't slept well again so he decided the best thing to do was to keep moving. He'd been walking up and down the rows of headstones looking at the names and dates. He had expected at some point to see Anne Parry and her daughter's grave or even Nicolas Llewelyn's but so far he hadn't spotted the names or any other names that would have some meaning to his father.

Why visit this graveyard? It had to have some meaning. He finished browsing the last rows then got back in his car and headed for the commune. When he arrived he found the gate locked and a "no entry" sign hanging from a post. That should deter the journalists, if they can find the place, he thought as he jumped the gate. He was wearing a pair of cropped trousers, a cotton short-sleeved shirt and sandals, but this wasn't enough to keep him cool. He could feel the heat of the sun on his arms as he walked past the orchard, the rich smell of fruit lingering in the air.

He found Jerome sitting outside his yurt, talking to Jenny as they ate from a bowl of strawberries.

'I'm so sorry, my boy,' Jerome said as he stood up and hugged Meadows.

When Jerome released him, Meadows could see the deep sorrow in the older man's eyes. He looked like he had aged in the last couple of days.

'Thank you, it must have been a shock for you. From what Mum tells me you were good friends.'

Jerome nodded.

Jenny was next to hug him. She was a tall woman with a stern face. She had home-schooled most of the children on the commune, including Meadows. He remembered her no-nonsense attitude, and discipline only took a look of disapproval. Meadows could feel her ribs through her clothes. He hadn't seen her close up for a while and was shocked to realise how much weight she had lost. He looked at her now and saw she had a pallor to her face. She must be in her seventies, he thought. Always such a strong woman and now she looks frail.

'We're all devastated by the news,' Jenny said. 'You, your mother, and brother have been in my thoughts since we heard. How is Fern?'

'She's OK,' Meadows said.

'I take it from your clothes you are not here on official business,' Jerome said.

'No, I'm on leave but there are some questions I want to ask.'

'I'm sure there are,' Jerome said. 'I'll tell you anything I can remember although I'm not sure it will be anything more than I told you already. I spoke to that detective, Blackwell. He's an uptight character. Needs to chill out a bit.'

Meadows laughed. 'Yeah, he can come across as a bit gruff.'

'The girl was nice,' Jenny said.

'Valentine?'

'Yeah, I got a good vibe from her,' Jerome said.

'Would you like me to leave you two to talk?' Jenny asked.

'No, stay,' Jerome said. 'It's not like we have any secrets from each other.'

'You may be able to help,' Meadows said. 'Did either of you know about Dad's prison record?'

Jenny shook her head. 'First I heard about it is when the detective asked.'

'I did,' Jerome said. 'He didn't talk much about it. I know there was an accident, and he lost his brother and a friend. A mother and child died. He felt guilty about it. He could never forgive himself. If he didn't tell you then it was because he didn't want to taint you with his past. He was so proud when you were born. He once told me he didn't deserve to be happy. He worried that karma would take you from him.'

'How did you meet him?'

'I used to do voluntary work with the homeless. I got to know him and invited him here.'

'Jerome used to collect all lost souls,' Jenny said.

'Is that what you had in mind for this place?' Meadows asked. 'Somewhere for the homeless to live.'

'What do you mean?' Jerome said.

'I was looking up in the attic for any paperwork Dad may have left behind. I came across the deeds for this land. They were in your name.'

'Yes, it was left to me by my grandfather. I gave the deeds to your father for safekeeping. Back in the seventies I was into all that anti-capitalist crap. When I say crap, I mean that you can't change the world by a few demonstrations and ranting. I used to get so riled up. It didn't do me or anyone any good. I wanted to get away from it all, so I started up the commune. It was meant to be a place for likeminded people. I didn't really know what I was doing. Along the way I met people I clicked with. Some had no place to live, some wanted an alternative lifestyle, and some worried about the effect that the world was having on the environment and what would be left behind. I never think of this place as mine. It belongs to us all. Everyone here works hard to make it what it is. I would appreciate it if you kept this information to yourself. I wouldn't want anyone to think I'm in charge.' Jerome smiled. 'I like things the way they are. Keep hold of the deeds. They will be passed on to someone who feels the same as me when I leave this life.'

Meadows wondered who that may be. Jerome had no children of his own as far as he knew.

'I won't tell a soul,' Meadows said. 'I wanted to ask you about the time you brought Rain home when he ran away.'

'Shouldn't you be asking him?' Jerome asked.

'I will be, but that was the last time we saw Dad. I know Mum told you what happened between the two of them. All I can say is it will be helpful to hear your version of events before I speak to Rain.'

'I didn't get involved,' Jenny said. 'Rain didn't speak to me about it, and I didn't ask him.'

'All I can tell you is that Rain was very upset when he arrived here,' Jerome said. 'He was tired and hungry... well, exhausted. He'd walked a long way alone. I gave him something to eat and let him sleep. I called your mother from the phone box in the village to let her know he was safe. I thought it was best to wait until he was ready to tell me what happened. He didn't say a lot. If you're thinking that something happened between Rain and your father here, then you're wrong. Kern turned up a couple of weeks after Rain went home. He didn't want me to tell Fern he was here. He took off again after a month or two. I didn't see him again after that.'

There was something in the way that Jerome spoke, and Jenny shifted, that made Meadows think that something was being left unsaid. Would Jerome cover for Rain? Most likely, he thought. Or maybe Jerome took matters into his own hands. He tried to shake these thoughts away. These people were like his family.

'Mum told me they left the commune because Dad was afraid of Jonah. Do you know why he was afraid?'

'Was Jonah still around then?' Jenny asked. 'The years kinda blend.'

Jenny smiled and Meadows thought that it looked forced. It was clear by her mannerisms that she was uncomfortable with the mention of Jonah's name.

'Kern didn't say anything to me,' Jerome said. 'They weren't friends, but I wouldn't say he was frightened of him.'

'Tell me about Jonah,' Meadows said.

'He came here with some others, or more like they followed him. He had a group that he would hang out with. They all sort of dressed the same.'

'He ran classes, meditation, that sort of thing,' Jenny added.

'So nothing out of the ordinary. Nothing that made you feel uncomfortable?' Meadows asked.

'No,' Jerome said. 'Some people here looked up to him. He liked that, thought himself a bit of a guru, a leader or whatever you want to call it. I think Kern was concerned that he would try and turn us into some sort of cult. Anyway he left in the end.'

'When?'

Jerome shrugged.

'Where did he go?'

'I've no idea,' Jerome said. 'I suspect he tried to set up his own commune somewhere. His followers went with him.'

'I found some pictures taken here from the eighties and nineties. I know most of the people but there are some faces I don't recognise.' He handed the photographs to Jerome.

Both Jerome and Jenny looked through them. Their faces lit up as they started pointing out people.

'Oh look there's me and Mags,' Jenny said.

'You can keep that one if you like,' Meadows said.

'Thank you.'

'How young we all look,' Jerome said.

Jenny laughed. 'Well, we were once.'

Jerome looked at one of the group photos. 'That's Cosmo, and Iggy with hair,' he said. 'That's Seren, I don't know if you remember her. Lovely woman. Stayed for about ten years. That one there is Jonah.' He pointed.

'I thought it might be,' Meadows said. 'I have a vague memory of him. Was Jonah still here after Dad left us?'

'I'm pretty sure he was,' Jerome said. 'Yes, because I saw them together a few times when Kern came back. It was odd given that Kern used to stay away from him.'

'What were they doing?'

'Erm, just talking, I think. They could have been arguing but if they were they weren't shouting at each other. Nothing like that.'

Meadows turned to Jenny. 'Did you see them together?'

'On a couple of occasions. I saw them coming out of the big tent. I can't be certain if that's before you all left or after. There was nothing odd about it. Maybe your dad had taken up meditation.'

'He was very down when he came back,' Jerome said. 'I remember that. He was sorry for what had happened with Fern. He didn't drink while he was here. He never was a drinker until you all left. He was working hard. I think he wanted to make amends.'

'So who left first, Dad or Jonah?'

A fleeting look passed between Jenny and Jerome.

'I think it was Kern that left first,' Jenny said. 'Yes, because it was the year my son, Carl, died. Kern came back here just before I left to nurse him. He had cancer. It was the first year I missed the summer solstice celebrations. Jonah was still here when I got back.'

Meadows looked at Jerome. 'Do you remember Dad being here for the summer solstice?'

Jerome thought for a moment. 'Yeah, I'm sure he was. There was a lot of people that year if I remember correctly.

Yeah, because I thought Kern must've left with them. Maybe got talking to someone and went off to another commune. All the while he was still here with us.' Jerome's voice cracked and he cleared his throat. 'Sorry, it's been such a shock. Even though I hadn't seen him for years I guess I always thought he would turn up someday.'

'We thought we'd have a get-together tomorrow evening to celebrate his life,' Jenny said. 'It would be lovely if you'd come with Rain and Fern.'

'That's a nice idea,' Meadows said. 'I can't speak for Mum or Rain, but I'll definitely come.'

'Good,' Jerome said.

'I'm going to catch up with the others before I have to pick up Rain from the airport. I'll see you tomorrow,' Meadows said.

'Give our love to your mother,' Jenny said as he walked away.

There was a gentle breeze in the field, but the movement of warm air did little to make Meadows feel any cooler. He hoped that the others would be down by the stream so he could jump in and cool off, but he found Iggy sitting in a deckchair outside his caravan.

Iggy was chiselling a piece of wood and next to him Cosmo sat smoothing the edges of a sculpture with sandpaper. They looked a comical pair. Iggy, round, jolly and hairless, and Cosmo, small and serious with a wild tangle of long hair and a beard. Around them cats of various sizes and colours snoozed in the sun.

'Hi, guys,' Meadows said.

Iggy put down the wood and stood up. 'I'm so sorry, kiddo.' He pulled Meadows into a hug.

'Thank you,' Meadows said as he looked down at Iggy's shining pate. He pulled away and saw Cosmo was standing and staring at him.

'I can't... I can't talk to you,' Cosmo said. He took off before Meadows had a chance to respond.

'He's upset,' Iggy said. 'I expect he can't find the right words and you know he gets frustrated. I guess sometimes there are no words.'

Meadows nodded and took Cosmo's seat, picking up the wooden mouse he had been sanding. 'This is cute.'

'They sell well at Christmas fairs,' Iggy said.

'It's only the beginning of July,' Meadows said.

'Got to start early.'

A ginger cat jumped on Iggy's lap and curled up.

'Is that a new one?' Meadows asked.

'Yes.'

'How many is that?'

Iggy smiled. 'Number twelve. Puss just turned up a couple of months ago.'

Meadows laughed. All Iggy's cats were called Puss. 'I guess he heard it was a good place to come. It must cost you a fortune to feed them all.'

'That's why I make all these wooden animals to sell. I wouldn't be without my cats.'

Meadows leaned down and stroked one of the cats. 'Were Cosmo and my dad close?'

'We all were back then,' Iggy said. 'I think you'll find that Cosmo is more upset for you. He feels deeply for others. Everyone here is upset by the news. Even the ones that didn't know your father know you. Then there's the police, they were here most of yesterday asking questions. They were in the woods with a metal detector. Don't know what they are hoping to find.'

'A murder weapon,' Meadows said.

'Oh, right. Well, on top of that, journalists turned up. One lot jumped the gate. Martin and some of the other men marched them off. I think they got the message that we don't want to talk to them.'

'And now you have me asking questions.'

'That I don't mind, kiddo, but there's nothing I can tell you. I wish I could help.'

'You'd be surprised what people notice without realising its importance,' Meadows said. 'Jerome thinks the last time he saw my father was summer solstice 1999.'

Iggy laughed. 'That's going back some. My memory is not that good.'

'Jonah was here at that time and a lot of other people he brought along.'

'Jonah, yeah I remember him.'

'Did you get on with him?'

'I get on with most people. Jonah was OK. Had some funny ways but don't we all? No harm in him.'

'What about what went on in the big tent?'

Iggy picked up his wood and started whittling. 'Meditation and all that isn't for me. I didn't get involved. I prefer to keep busy.'

'I did hear that he wanted to become a sort of leader for the commune.'

'Well, not everyone took to him. Whatever his plans were, they didn't work out because he left.'

'Mum said Dad was afraid of him. Do you know why that may be?'

'No, maybe she didn't mean afraid, like fear. I don't think he trusted the guy. A lot of the ladies liked him, and your mother was a looker, still is.' Iggy smiled. 'Perhaps Kern thought there was a danger that Jonah would try and take Fern from him. Jonah was charming and a terrible flirt.'

'Can you remember the last time you saw Dad? Was there anything different about him? Maybe acting out of character?'

'I know there had been some trouble between him and Fern. He didn't talk to me about it, but he was unhappy. I thought he had just moved on. A fresh start. I never imagined, well…' Iggy shook his head.

'It's what everyone thought,' Meadows said. But someone knew that he didn't leave, he thought. 'I'll leave you get on with your work. If you do remember anything…'

'You'll be the first to know,' Iggy said.

Meadows walked through the second field. It was slow progress as many stopped him to offer their condolences. He asked some of them questions, particularly if they had been around at the time his father was murdered. While Kern was well liked, getting people to remember when they last saw him was a big ask. So far he only had Jenny, Jerome, and Iggy's word that Kern had been alive after Rain had run away and returned home. It wasn't much comfort. People's memories were even more sketchy when it came to Jonah. Meadows got the impression that they were all choosing not to remember him.

He kept walking until he came to the lavender field. Mina was sitting in the middle of the vast purple blanket, cutting the stems. Two baskets sat either side of her. As he walked towards her, brushing against the plants, they released the wonderful relaxing scent that Meadows remembered from his childhood pillow.

Mina stood up and put her hands on either side of Meadows' face. This single gesture was enough to cause Meadows' throat to constrict with emotion. He remembered that Mina had that effect on people.

'It's OK to be sad,' she said.

Meadows covered her hands with his for a moment then let go. She's right, he thought. He was sad. He'd been too busy trying to pretend it was just another case. All this time he thought his father had abandoned the family. He never got the chance to come back and say he was sorry. Things could have worked out. They could have been happy. It had been the only time his father had hit him. Something had tipped him over the edge, and someone had taken his life. There would never be a chance to put things right.

'It will get better,' Mina said then returned to cutting the lavender.

'You've got a good crop this year,' Meadows said.

'We've been expanding. Natural remedies are popular now.'

'You still making your own oils?'

'Yes, along with soap and remedies. You must take some home with you. I have a batch of geranium oil. Good for uplifting the spirits.'

'I'll give it a go,' Meadows said. 'I want to ask you a few questions if that's OK.'

Mina nodded. 'You can help fill the baskets. I'll cut.'

Meadows knelt beside her. 'Mum told me that you and Kern were close at one time.'

Mina smiled. 'Is that your polite way of asking if he was my lover? He was once, a long time ago. Before he got together with Fern. I promise you there was nothing but friendship between us after that.'

'Did you know about his past?'

'Prison? Yeah, I guessed by the way he was.'

'What do you mean?'

'You should know that people can have difficulty adjusting to the outside world, particularly if they have served a long time. He was unsettled. Always watching over his shoulder at first. He barely left the commune. It was like he still had invisible boundaries. I asked him about it, but he wouldn't give me any details. He eventually found his peace and we were happy. Then your mother came to join us. They fell in love. I was hurt at first, but I forgave them.'

'Did Kern ever talk about friends or acquaintances from his past?'

'No, and no one came to visit him.'

'Can you remember the last time you saw Kern?'

'Yes, it was the summer solstice.'

'Are you sure?'

'Yes, I wouldn't easily forget that night.'

'Did something happen?'

Mina nodded. 'I can't talk about it so please don't ask me.'

Meadows could see the look of fear in her eyes.

'If there is someone here you are frightened of, I can help you.'

'It's not that simple.'

'Please, you cared for Kern. He's been lying in an unmarked grave all these years. Don't you think he deserves some justice?'

'I can't be sure, and I have no evidence. It's just I knew something was wrong, but no one would listen to me.'

'I'm listening,' Meadows said.

'When Kern came back after the fight with Fern he was depressed. He was so cut up about what he had done. I told him it would be OK. He just needed time to get himself together then he should go and apologise. He said he couldn't, that he was a monster and that would never change. I asked him what he meant by that, but he wouldn't tell me. He said he was going to ask Jonah for help as he couldn't see any other way. It was odd because he never liked Jonah. He spent a lot of time with him after that. It did seem to be doing Kern some good. I think Kern was doing some sort of meditation or therapy in the big tent, although I did hear them arguing once.'

'What about?'

'I don't know but it was clear that Kern didn't want to do something. He seemed OK though. He was happy building the bonfire for the celebration. A lot of people came that year. You know, to us it is just a celebration. A time when things are good, the weather is kind, and we have plenty of food growing. Yes, we still put the ashes of the bonfire over our doorway for protection but the majority of us aren't heavily into spirituality. Jonah was different. Midsummer to him was a time the veil between this world and the next is at its thinnest. He was talking a load of crap and chanting with a large group. The rest of us were just enjoying ourselves and we were spread out, so I didn't notice when Jonah left the group.'

She stopped talking for a moment, put her hands to her face and took a calming breath.

'I had drunk a little too much that night and was going to the woods for a pee. It was a clear night so it wasn't that dark, and I could see well enough without a torch. As I got nearer the woods, I saw Jonah coming out. He had blood over his clothes. I asked him what had happened. He said he'd fallen over but he was fine. I offered to help him, but he said he was just going to clean up and I should go back to the celebration. There was something off about him. I didn't think much more of it at the time. The next morning I woke up late. There was no sign of Kern. He usually brought the ashes around with Jerome. Most of the visitors had left by the afternoon. I asked Jerome and he said that he hadn't seen Kern since the celebrations. When there was no sign of him by the evening, I was worried. I told the others what I had seen. They laughed it off. I suppose the idea that Jonah had done something to Kern seemed a bit far-fetched. Iggy said Kern had spent a lot of time talking to the visitors and likely had taken off with them for a few days.'

'What about Jonah?'

'I didn't speak to him. He gave me a strange look when I passed by, but he didn't say anything, then he left the commune. I think that night. He came back just before the winter solstice. I just had a bad feeling all the time and I couldn't shake it. I was afraid of Jonah, so I left. It was the only time I didn't spend that celebration with the people I love.'

'But you came back.'

'Yes, I came back the following spring. Jonah wasn't here. I missed my life here and my friends. I was right though, Jonah must have killed Kern that night. I'm the only one that saw him come out of the woods. Now that Kern has been found there's nothing stopping Jonah coming back to keep me quiet.'

Chapter Eleven

Jerome looked around at the others that were sitting inside his yurt. Cosmo was jigging his legs as he chewed his nails, Iggy's face had a sheen and was creased with concern, and Jenny just looked sick. He'd suggested that they only talk as a group where they couldn't be seen. If they were always huddled together others would find it odd and mention it to the police.

'What now?' Iggy asked. 'Winter knows about Jonah. We didn't bank on Fern telling him everything.'

'We don't know exactly what she told him,' Jerome said. 'It couldn't be too much, or he would still be asking questions. We don't know how much she knows.'

'What does it matter now?' Jenny asked. 'We can't protect him anymore. He knows about the prison record.'

'That's all he knows,' Jerome said. 'That's bad enough but if he knew the whole truth about—'

'I don't want him to kn-know,' Cosmo cut in.

'It's OK,' Jenny said. 'He can't possibly find out. You just have to be careful what you say.'

'I don't want to say the wrong thing,' Cosmo said. 'I get... I get...' Cosmo hit his hand against his head.

'Confused?' Iggy asked.

'Yeah, that's it,' Cosmo said.

'Come on, matey, you can do this,' Iggy said. 'It will all blow over soon.'

'I'm not so sure,' Jerome said. 'Winter is not going to stop asking questions.'

'Then we just have to keep him distracted,' Jenny said. 'It's for his own good.'

'The police will carry out their investigation, they'll get nowhere and file it as an unsolved case. Happens all the time,' Jerome said. 'I don't want that for the boy, never having answers, but it's better this way.'

'What are we going to say about J-Jonah?' Cosmo asked.

'Nothing more than we have already,' Jerome said. 'Enough has been said to catch Winter's attention. He'll be concentrating on Jonah now.'

'That will only make things worse,' Cosmo said.

The conversation stopped when the yurt door opened.

'Mina,' Jerome said. 'I was getting worried about you. If you hadn't have shown up soon, I would have come to look for you.'

'I'm fine,' Mina said as she settled on a cushion next to Jenny. 'I just needed some time alone to think. You should all know that I told Winter about what I'd seen that night with Jonah.'

Jerome felt a twist in his stomach. It was like an icy fist squeezing him from the inside.

'We don't know for sure what you saw that night had anything to do with what happened to Kern,' Jenny said.

'Yes, we do. You wouldn't listen back then. I told you he was dangerous. Now look what's happened. Jonah could come back.'

'He's not going to come back,' Iggy said. 'Not now.' He rubbed his hand over his chin and sighed. 'This is all my fault.'

'No,' Jerome said. 'This isn't on you. Don't ever think that. You didn't know.'

'Didn't know what?' Mina asked.

'Iggy didn't know that Kern hadn't left. Didn't know it was him they found in the woods,' Jerome said.

'Well, who did you think it was?' Mina asked.

Jerome gave Mina a look. He didn't have to say anything.

'Oh, no,' she said.

Chapter Twelve

Meadows was emptying the washing machine when Rain came into the kitchen and yawned.

'How did you sleep?' Meadows asked.

'OK, thanks. I just feel a bit out of it,' Rain said.

Meadows looked at him. His long black curly hair resembled a crow's nest, and his usually sparkling green eyes were bloodshot. He was naked apart from a pair of boxer shorts.

'I'm not surprised you don't feel with it,' Meadows said. 'Two flights with hours of waiting in between, all after a day's work. You must be exhausted.'

'I'll take myself off and meditate in the garden, clear my head. That should help.'

'I don't think there's time for you to meditate.'

'I gotta align my chakras, then a quick shower, tea, and a smoke and I'll be good.'

Meadows laughed. 'Maybe not the smoke. I'm not sure Blackwell will be happy if you're stoned. Me being here isn't going to go down too well either, and on top of that he's working the weekend.'

'You worry too much,' Rain said. He grabbed a glass from the draining board and filled it from the tap. 'Where is everyone?'

'Mum's out the garden and Daisy has gone back to her place for the weekend.'

'About time the two of you moved in together.'

'Yeah, but her flat is close to her work and I like it here. It suits us to have our own space. To be honest I think she wanted to give us some time alone together.'

Rain nodded. 'Is Mum OK?'

'I think so, mixed emotions.'

'I know how she feels.' Rain drank down his water. 'I better get dressed before your friends arrive.'

Meadows was not sure he would refer to Blackwell and Valentine as friends, but he didn't say anything. He picked up the washing basket and carried it to the garden.

Fern was sitting under the shade. She smiled at Meadows, but he could see she was worried.

'How're you doing?' Meadows asked.

'Alright, I'll be glad to get this over with. Did he say anything to you on the journey home last night?'

'No, and I didn't want to ask. Let's see what he says to Blackwell. What I heard in the commune yesterday was encouraging. If Dad was seen at the summer solstice, then Rain was nowhere near at the time.'

Fern nodded but Meadows could tell she wasn't convinced. He knew she would be thinking the same as him. Those at the commune would protect Rain. They could've been signalling that they would provide him with an alibi. Even if this wasn't the case, he was sure they were hiding something.

'It will be OK once we hear Rain's version of events. You remember as a child he always told the truth, even if it meant getting in trouble.'

'That's what I'm afraid of,' Fern said.

'He doesn't seem stressed.'

Fern laughed. 'When have you ever seen Rain stressed?'

'Yeah, I think he was born chilled.'

By the time Blackwell and Valentine arrived, Rain was showered, dressed, and had his hair tied back in a ponytail. He sat cross-legged on the floor allowing the rest of them to take the chairs. Meadows watched as he exchanged pleasantries. Valentine's eyes sparkled and she gave Rain a warm smile. Even Blackwell was smiling. It amused Meadows to see his brother's good looks and charm weren't wasted on either of them.

The questions started off easily with Rain talking about the memories of his father, the commune, and the move to the cottage and attending mainstream school. Then they came to the night of the fight.

'So you came down the stairs and saw your father hit your brother then your mother. That must have been frightening for you,' Blackwell said. 'How old were you at the time?'

'Fourteen.'

'You're a tall man now,' Blackwell said. 'Is it fair to say you were probably taller than the average fourteen-year-old?'

Meadows could see where Blackwell's line of questioning was going. He was trying to establish if Rain was strong enough to overpower his father.

'I was tall, yes, but not muscular. I couldn't do anything to help back then. Dad was in such a rage; I'd never seen him like that. We had a wooden knife block on the counter. I took one out and threatened him.'

'You threatened to stab him?' Valentine asked.

'No, I just wanted him to stop. I didn't mean to hurt him. He came at me and I somehow managed to slash his forearm. He was as shocked as me. I dropped the knife and ran.'

Blackwell turned to Meadows. 'You saw this?'

'Yes, I saw him drop the knife.'

'Why didn't you tell me this when we spoke last?'

Good question, Meadows thought. 'I thought it was best you hear it from Rain. So you get the whole picture. All I can add is that I did see him drop the knife and run out. Dad ran after him, and Mum asked me to go after them. I did but I didn't catch up with them.'

Blackwell turned back to Rain. 'So what happened after that?'

'I ran, I kept running until I got to the woods at Rhos Farm. Then I climbed up a tree. Dad knew all my hiding places and came after me. I could hear him calling but it was dark, and he couldn't see me. He went away for a while but came back. I could see him below. He was shouting out that he was sorry, and he sat on the floor and cried. I still didn't go to him. Eventually he went and didn't come back.

'I waited for a while then climbed down and walked to the commune. It took a long time to get there, and I slept in a barn overnight. I stayed with Jerome. I didn't tell him what I had done. He said I could stay but he would have to call Mum as she would be worried. I said he could do that.'

'He did call me,' Fern said. 'I'd been up all night worried. Once I knew Rain was safe, I went to bed and slept.'

'Did your father find you at the commune?' Blackwell asked.

'No, he never came while I was there. I stayed for a few days, but Jonah kept on at me to talk about what had happened. He said I needed to reconcile with my father. In the end I told him what I had done. He said the only way to fix things was to talk with Dad face to face. I thought he would be at home, so I asked Jerome to take me. That's it. I never saw my father again.'

'I think Jonah is someone you need to talk to,' Meadows said. 'I saw Mina at the commune yesterday and—'

'You went to the commune?' Blackwell cut in.

'Yes.'

'You can't go there asking questions. You know you can't be part of this investigation,' Blackwell said.

'The commune was my home. Some of the people there are like my family,' Meadows said. 'They are holding a memorial service for my father, and I'll be going. It's not usual procedure to ask the family of a victim not to have contact with one another or to attend a memorial service.'

Blackwell's eyes narrowed. 'Please don't make things difficult.'

'I'm not,' Meadows said. 'I'm probably in the best position to get information which I will pass on to you.'

Blackwell huffed. 'Like you said, the people there are considered family. You have a conflict of interest.'

'I would if I was working on the case. My only interest is finding out what happened to my father.'

'Fine,' Blackwell said. 'I can't stop you going there and if I'm honest most of that lot at the commune refused to speak to me.'

Meadows tried his best not to smile. 'As I explained before, a lot of them, particularly the older generation, are wary of the police. When I spoke to Mina yesterday, I got the impression she was being honest. She said the last time she saw my father was the summer solstice 1999. It seems that's the last time anyone saw him. That night she saw Jonah coming out of the woods with blood on his clothes.'

'So where do I find this Jonah?'

'I don't know,' Meadows said. 'I've made some copies of a photo I have of him. Perhaps Chris Harley from tech can use a programme to age his features which you could show around some communes. It seems likely he would be part of one or set up his own. Other than that, I have no suggestions. Without a surname you can't check the electoral register. All I can tell you is my father was afraid of this man.'

'I don't mind showing the photo around and I'm sure Edris would like an opportunity to get out of the office,' Valentine said.

'Is there anything else that you haven't mentioned?' Blackwell asked.

'No,' Meadows said. 'Did you speak to the family of the crash victims?'

'Yes, I can't find anything to connect them to your father's death. We won't be following that line of enquiry.'

'But—'

'It's a dead end,' Blackwell said. 'You know I can't share information with you. You're going to have to trust me. There were never any threats made against your father. I'm sure a stranger would've been noticed in the commune, and the husband of the victim is dead. Checking alibis from 1999 would be a nightmare added to that we don't even have the exact date the crime took place.' He turned to Rain. 'I'm going to have to ask you to come to the station to give a formal statement and a DNA sample.'

'No problem,' Rain said.

'We'll grab a bite to eat then I'll bring him in,' Meadows said. He handed over the copies of the photo.

Blackwell stood and Valentine shut her notebook.

'Can I ask what lines of enquiry you are following?' Meadows asked.

Blackwell didn't answer immediately, and Meadows wondered if he was trying to decide how much information was permissible.

'Given the amount of time that has passed you can appreciate this is a difficult case. We have no crime scene or witnesses to work with. No trace of a murder weapon. People's memories are sketchy at the best of times. We will do all we can to find out what happened, but you have to consider the possibility that you may never know. I assure you that we are looking into the backgrounds of all those who were living at the commune at the time. It appears that it wasn't only your father that had a criminal record.' He glanced at Fern. 'Meanwhile we are looking at individuals that were in prison at the same time as your father. It may be that he had an altercation with someone, and they eventually tracked him down. All this is going to take some time. I will look into this Jonah character and see what we can find out.'

Meadows nodded. 'Thank you. If I get any more information, I'll pass it on to you.'

'It was nice to meet you, Rain,' Valentine said.

Meadows saw them out and felt the tension leave his body.

'You didn't think that I had anything to do with what happened to Dad, did you?' Rain asked.

Meadows smiled. 'I never doubted you for a minute.'

'Yeah, I know how your mind works,' Rain said.

'We were a bit worried,' Fern said. 'It was a long time ago.'

'And I was an angry teenager,' Rain said. 'Don't worry, I can see how it must've looked given that I had already used a knife on him.'

'The problem we have now is that you're going to be Blackwell's prime suspect,' Meadows said. 'You've already admitted to wounding with a knife. He's going to be looking into every aspect of your life.'

'Well, he won't find anything.'

'I know but while he's looking at you, he's not looking elsewhere for an explanation.'

'Then I guess it's up to us to find some answers,' Rain said.

'We'll go to the commune as soon as you've given the statement,' Meadows said. 'Are you coming with us, Mum?'

Fern shook her head. 'I'll go up soon but not just yet. Everyone will be sympathetic, and I'll feel like a fraud.'

'You're entitled to mourn,' Rain said. 'He was your husband.'

'I know. You boys go. I'll be fine. A little time on my own to reflect will do me good.'

Meadows had noticed an instant change in his mother when Blackwell had talked about others having criminal records. He wondered how much she knew and wasn't telling.

'I spoke to the olds about Jonah,' he said. 'They seemed reluctant to talk about him. What are they not telling me?'

'I'm not surprised they don't want to talk about him,' Fern said. 'Doing so would give away that part of them they want to keep hidden. I told you Jonah ran meditation classes, but it was more than that. There were therapy sessions, some of it involved sexual release.'

'You mean sexual assault or abuse?' Meadows asked.

'No, well, I didn't witness some of the things that went on in the big tent, but I heard things. All consensual and harmless. Each to their own, and some liked the freedom of expression. Sex wasn't seen as something to be hidden but a natural act. It wasn't that but the therapy sessions that were dangerous. Like I told you before, he was charming and persuasive. He could coax out your darkest secret. His theory was you had to confront your past, ask forgiveness from those you had hurt before you could move on.'

'You think that's what he asked Dad to do?' Rain asked.

'It makes sense now why Kern was afraid of him. I don't think he wanted to face up to what he had done. If he couldn't bring himself to tell me about his past, how could he ask the family of those he'd killed for forgiveness?' Fern said.

'Maybe that's what he did in the end. He could've contacted the family. Imagine coming face to face with the man that had killed your wife and child,' Meadows said.

'But didn't Edris say he was dead?' Fern said.

'Yes, he died in 2010, I still think it's worth following up. I'll contact the daughter and see if she is willing to meet with me. You can get a better sense if someone is lying face to face.'

'Do you really want to put yourself through that?' Rain asked. 'I imagine the daughter is going to be hostile. You'll be surrounded by negativity.'

Meadows laughed. 'I work in negativity most days. I'm immune. I need to do this. It's not like her father could be arrested. Her guard will be low. If he was involved in Dad's death, then at least we will have some answers. There will be tell-tale signs. A prepared alibi, things like that.'

Rain nodded. 'I'll go with you if you like.'

'No, if she does agree to see me then it's best I go alone. She may feel intimidated by the two of us.'

'I just hope Blackwell is going to look for Jonah, he seems more concerned with looking at anyone on the commune with a criminal record,' Rain said.

'He was talking about me,' Fern said. 'Your work colleagues know about it so it's not fair to keep you in the dark. I'm sorry, it's something I hoped you would never have to know.'

'It's OK, Mum, it doesn't matter what you did in the past,' Meadows said, although he was curious.

'Yeah,' Rain said. 'We all screw up at some point. Don't worry.'

'You boys have never screwed up,' Fern said. 'I can't make excuses but you both know I was brought up in care. It wasn't an easy life. At sixteen I found myself on the streets. I did what I had to, to survive. I needed money for food.' Fern sighed. 'I was charged with soliciting.'

'That's it?' Rain said. 'I thought you were going to tell us something worse than that. Come here.' He pulled his mother into a hug.

'I feel so ashamed,' Fern said.

'You've nothing to be ashamed about,' Meadows said. 'No one has the right to judge you if they haven't been in that position themselves. I've seen enough of it. Women forced into prostitution, on the streets with no protection. They get abused, assaulted, and in some cases murdered. They have no one to turn to.'

'Yeah, but I wasn't forced, it was my choice,' Fern said.

'No it wasn't,' Rain said. 'You felt like you had no other option. It's always the women who are stigmatised, isn't it? Not the men, but it's supply and demand, all you did was sell the only commodity you had to survive.'

Fern nodded and wiped away a tear. 'What about your work, Winny? They'll all know.'

'It doesn't bother me,' Meadows said. 'Blackwell could've said something, but he didn't. They're all fond of you and that's not going to change because of something you did over fifty years ago.'

'I hope so,' Fern said. 'Anyway Jonah started these therapy sessions, he persuaded me to join in and tell him about my life before I came to the commune. I was on my knees sobbing by the end of the session and still he pushed for more details. He said saying the intimate details out loud would cleanse me. I think now he probably got off on it. Jerome came into the tent. Told Jonah to stop. I don't know how much he heard but he had the decency not to mention it. The strange thing was I did feel better after getting it all out. Jonah still continued with his therapy and then something happened but it's not my story to tell. You can ask Jenny. After that we left.

'I knew something was eating away at your father,' she continued. 'Being away from the commune just made him worse. It was my idea that he go back and speak to Jonah, but he wouldn't. In the end I decided to tell him about my past, about how Jonah had helped me. When you boys were asleep I sat down with him and told him everything. He got up without saying a word and went to bed. The next day he went to work and came home drunk. He was in such a rage. That was the night he left us.'

Chapter Thirteen

It didn't take Meadows and Rain long to set up the tepee that they used when staying in the commune. Iggy, Jerome, and Cosmo had helped. By late afternoon thick mats had been rolled out for beds, supplies stored, and a steady stream of visitors bringing fresh fruit and vegetables, and various dried herbs for tea, made them feel at home.

'What now?' Rain asked as he sat on a cushion eating a bowl of raspberries.

'We'll go and talk to people. See what more we can find out about Jonah. It'd be good if we can catch Jenny when she's alone, she may be more willing to talk to us if no one is around. We'll just keep it casual.'

Rain laughed. 'Yeah, you don't want to go around acting like the police.' He finished the last of his fruit and got up. 'First I'd like to go and see where Dad was found.'

Meadows nodded. 'Come on then, I'll show you.'

As they walked towards the woods they saw Jenny sitting outside her tepee. She wore a wide-brimmed straw hat and a long, burnt-orange dress. In front of her was an easel and Meadows could see she was painting a winter landscape with a stag as the focal point.

'Wow that's impressive,' Rain commented.

'It makes me feel a little cooler painting frost on the ground; come winter I'll be painting arid landscapes.' She set down her brush and stood. 'It's lovely to see you,' she said as she put her arms around Rain.

'You haven't changed since the last time I saw you. Have you been drinking the blood of the immortals?' Rain teased.

Jenny laughed. 'And you're still a charmer.'

As they talked Meadows noticed a large clay pot with purple flowers placed at the side of the tepee. They were the same flowers he'd seen in the woods near the grave.

'They're pretty flowers,' Meadows said.

Jenny smiled. 'Sweet violets. That's where I keep Mag's ashes. They are supposed to bring peace in the afterlife.'

'Where did you get them?'

'From Cosmo. He grows all sorts of flowers and plants. He's set up polytunnels next to the orchard and sells them to the shops in the village. It's been great for growing herbs all year around. You should take a look. I'm sure he can give you a few for your garden.'

'You and Mags were together a long time,' Rain said. 'You must miss her.'

'Every day,' Jenny said. 'I have a lot of happy memories and pictures I keep here, and here.' She touched her head and heart. 'They can never be taken away. So she's not really gone. Make sure you only keep the good pictures of your father.'

'Sound advice,' Rain said.

'I think when we find out what happened to Dad we can throw away all the bad memories,' Meadows said. 'But for now without help we have no closure. Mina told me she suspected Jonah had something to do with Dad's murder and I get the feeling you've not told me everything. I know Jonah dug into peoples' pasts and if something happened with Jonah it may be painful to talk about.' He took her hand. 'You know I would never judge you. Right now I'm just Winter, not a detective. You watched me and Rain grow up. Please, if you know anything…'

Jenny nodded. 'I can only tell you what happened when I let Jonah into my life and the pain he caused me. I was married once. I guess you know that as you and my children played together.'

'Clover and Carl,' Rain said. 'Didn't you have a crush on Clover?'

Meadows smiled. 'Yeah, I did.'

'I wouldn't have minded you two getting together,' Jenny said. 'She's happy enough though. Marriage suits her. I never wanted to get married, well not to a man, but things were different back then. It was what was expected of me. I had studied hard, gained qualifications but it wasn't good enough for my parents. I was their only daughter and they found it odd that I didn't go out on dates. Everyone else my age was married and starting a family. Anyway I gave in to pressure. It wasn't a happy marriage, but I wouldn't change things because I wouldn't have had my children.

'Barry, my husband, was a nasty piece of work. No one used to interfere in what went on between husband and wife. Black eyes and broken bones were ignored. I had nowhere to go. Then I met Mags. She changed my life. She was a free spirit and didn't give a fuck.'

'I remember her well,' Meadows said.

'We fell in love, and I left Barry and moved in with Mags and her mum. We could never be ourselves in public and there was always the fear that Barry would find me. I rarely left the house. Then we met up with Kern at one of the festivals. He invited us to stay here. We could live our life as we wanted. No judgement. What a wonderful life we had together. Then Jonah came.

'His ideas made sense at the time. A way to put your past behind you and be peaceful. I carried a lot of guilt. I'd walked away from my parents, never spoke to them. I'd deprived my children of a father. I felt selfish. Only thinking of my own happiness. I did some therapy sessions with Jonah. We talked a lot about my past. I did feel better. It was like a cleansing. Then Jonah went away for a few days. When he came back, he called me into the big tent. Barry, my husband, was there. Jonah had tracked him down. He hadn't changed. Jonah just left me in there with him saying I would know what I had to do.'

Rain shook his head. 'What a bastard.'

'I tried to say sorry for walking out on him and taking the children, but I never got the chance to finish. He was in such a rage. It was as if years of hatred had built up in him and once he started hitting me he didn't stop. Cosmo heard me screaming and came into the tent. Poor Cosmo. He did his best to try and defend me, but he was no match for Barry. I managed to crawl out of the tent and shout for help. Jerome, Iggy, and Kern came running in. They dragged Barry out. Kern laid into Barry. I've never seen him so angry, nor did I see him lose his temper again after that day. Jonah just stood and watched. I'm sure I saw him smirk.'

Meadows noticed that Jenny's hands were trembling. 'It must have been a terrible experience for you,' he said.

'Physically it took a long time to heal, mentally even longer. Jerome and Iggy dragged Barry off the commune. I don't know what they said to him, but he never came back. Barry Jones is his name, if you want to check that they didn't harm him, although I hope the bugger is dead now. Poor Cosmo, he was in a state after that. He withdrew for a while. Kern was furious with Jonah. It wasn't long after that that he left with Fern and you boys. I stayed away from Jonah. I couldn't even look at the man let alone speak to him.'

'When was the last time you saw Jonah?' Meadows asked.

Jenny shrugged. 'He was just gone one day.'

'Thank you for telling us this. I know it can't have been easy,' Meadows said.

'I hope you find your answer,' Jenny said.

They left Jenny to her painting and walked towards the woods. Meadows' phone picked up a signal and rang. He looked at the screen and saw it was a voicemail. He stopped and listened to the message.

'That was Christine Williams. Anne Parry's daughter. She's agreed to see me in the morning.'

'That's good,' Rain said. 'Are you sure you don't want me to come with you?'

'No, I'll be fine. You, brother, can work your charm here. Try and coax out some more information on Jonah. If he managed to track down Jenny's husband, then who else did he bring here?'

'You're thinking he got Anne Parry's husband here to confront Dad.'

'Yeah, can you imagine what it would be like to come face to face with the man responsible for your wife and child's death? Ray Parry could have lashed out. He may have told his daughter what he did. He's dead now so if he did do something Christine has nothing to lose by telling me.'

'Yeah, and karma will get Jonah, unless it already has,' Rain said.

'It's beginning to sound like he got some sort of enjoyment out of people's pain; liked witnessing confrontation.'

In the woods they came to a small wooden hut and Meadows stopped.

'I think we should have a quick word with Haystack.'

'Are you mad?' Rain whispered. 'He's terrifying. I used to hide when he came out of the woods, and I never came this way as a kid.'

'He's OK,' Meadows said. He knocked at the door and tried not to laugh when Rain took a step back.

The door opened and a man stepped out. Despite Meadows being over six foot, he still felt dwarfed. Haystack was at least six inches taller and likely the brothers' weight combined. He had matted hair that hung on his shoulders, a bushy beard and thick eyebrows which gave him a wild look.

'What do you want?'

'I don't know if anyone has spoken to you but remains were found in the woods.'

'I don't need speaking to,' Haystack growled. 'The woods were crawling with outsiders. One of them came here. I saw him off.'

Meadows imagined that even Blackwell would have felt intimidated.

'I'm sorry that you've been disturbed,' Meadows said. 'The remains were my father's.'

'Kern, aye, I know.'

'I expect you know the woods well. Did you ever see anything odd?'

'I mind my own business,' Haystack said. 'This is my home, you don't shit on your own doorstep.'

'I understand,' Meadows said. 'I'm just trying to find out what happened. If you know anything.'

'I don't, or are you saying I do?' He took a step towards Meadows.

Meadows held up his hands. 'No, I'm not saying you know anything. I'm just asking for your help.'

'I've nothing to say.' He stepped back into the hut and shut the door.

'I told you,' Rain said. 'Bloody terrifying.'

Meadows smiled. 'Yeah, you were a lot of help. I'll leave him to Blackwell.'

'Good idea,' Rain said.

Meadows led the way to the place where Kern's remains had been found. There was still a cordon around the area but no police or forensics.

'So he was here all along,' Rain said. 'It's not a bad spot. He loved the commune.'

'I guess there are far worse places he could have been laid to rest,' Meadows said. 'Someone took care to bury him.' He knelt down and picked up one of the plants that had been disturbed. Its flowers had died in the sun. 'Sweet violets. The same as Jenny had in the pot with Mags' ashes. I saw these when I was first called out. They were blooming.'

'You think Jenny placed them here?' Rain asked.

'It's possible. Or Cosmo, as he grows plants. Then again it could have been anyone in the commune. Which means one of them definitely knows Dad was buried here.'

'Maybe Jonah,' Rain said.

'I think it would have been someone who cared for Dad. Doesn't sound like Jonah cared about anyone. We need to find him. Whatever he did, he's got away with it for long enough,' Meadows said.

* * *

The whole commune turned out to celebrate the life of Kern Meadows. A bonfire had been lit despite the warmth of the evening and as Meadows watched the dancing flames, he heard stories of his father in his younger days. A different picture emerged to that of the man Meadows last saw. Kern had been a natural at growing fruit and vegetables. Each year he would take it to the elderly in the village. Often having the door shut in his face. Then later he would take trips with Jerome where they would seek out the homeless, give them food and an offer of a place to stay on the commune. Tepees would be built, or wooden shacks made, to give shelter to those who took up their offer. Meadows laughed at a story of his father buying an old bus and driving it into one of the fields. It became home to a family for many years until it was eaten away by rust. Jenny and Mina spoke about how proud he was when his boys were born. There were tears and laughter then slowly the group returned to their dwellings until only Meadows and Rain remained with the olds.

'I didn't see Martin and his family this evening,' Meadows commented.

'His girls have come down with some sort of virus, either that or heatstroke,' Jenny said.

'I hope it's the latter or we'll all be sick,' Mina said. 'I'll make them some tonic and take it around in the morning.'

Meadows was relieved to hear that Martin wasn't avoiding him. He knew he'd been upset by Blackwell and Valentine asking questions.

Cosmo wandered off and returned with two bottles. 'My best b-brew.' He handed a bottle each to Rain and Meadows.

'Thanks,' Rain said. He took off the lid, took a gulp, and spluttered. 'That's some strong shit.'

Meadows laughed and handed his bottle to Iggy.

'Forgot you didn't drink,' Cosmo said.

'He'll have a smoke with me,' Jerome said and handed Meadows a joint.

Rain looked at the bottle. 'What is it?'

'Last year's p-pear wine,' Cosmo said. 'I've got a good s-stock so drink as much as you like.' He turned to Mina. 'Are you going to… to… sing for us?'

'No,' Mina said. 'I brought the guitar along for the boys to play.'

'I haven't played in years,' Meadows said.

'Hand it over,' Rain said.

As Rain strummed the guitar Meadows lit the joint and inhaled. It had been a long day and with each draw he felt his muscles relax. The guitar was passed around with each one singing a few songs until it came to his turn.

'What do you want me to sing?' Meadows asked.

'*Have You Ever Seen the Rain?* You boys always used to sing that,' Jenny said.

Meadows laughed. 'Oh yeah.'

He played a few bars then broke into song. Rain joined in but halfway through he appeared to have forgotten the lyrics. He mumbled some random words then stopped.

Meadows finished the song and set down the guitar. 'Are you OK, Rain?'

Rain was staring into the darkness. 'Someone's going into the woods.' His words came out in a slur.

Meadows followed Rain's gaze. 'There's no one there. Even if there was, you couldn't see them in the dark.'

'Naked,' Rain said. 'Dancing in the sea. They'll drown if they're not careful.'

'Alright, bro,' Meadows said. 'I think you've had a bit too much of Cosmo's brew. Come on.' He stood up and pulled Rain to his feet.

'Told you it was good stuff,' Cosmo said.

Rain staggered as Meadows helped him back to the tepee. All the while he mumbled. Most of it was nonsense and Meadows figured it was a combination of wine, the heat of the day, and jet lag.

'Into bed,' Meadows said. He just about managed to get him inside the tepee and onto the bed. He made him comfortable, put a bottle of water next to the bed, and covered him with a light throw.

When he got back to the bonfire, he found Jenny trying to hush Iggy who was leaping about trying to get her to dance.

'I'm going to take him to bed,' Jerome said.

'I'll do it,' Meadows said. 'If he falls you'll go down with him.'

'I'll come with you,' Jenny said.

'I can manage,' Meadows said. 'Stay and enjoy yourself.'

'I'm gonna call it a night,' Jenny said. 'I'll walk with you.'

'Come on, Iggy, time for bed,' Meadows said and took his arm. He led him away from the group. Iggy swayed as he walked. 'I think you've had a bit too much of Cosmo's brew as well.'

Iggy looked at Meadows. 'Kern, what are you doing here?'

'It's Winter, not Kern,' Jenny said. 'I guess you look like your father. Same dark hair and green eyes.'

'Winter, yes, so it is.' Iggy laughed. 'Sorry, kiddo. Poor Kern, it's the cry of winter that got him.'

Meadows stopped. 'What are you talking about?'

'He doesn't know what he's talking about,' Jenny said. 'It's summer, Iggy. Winter is a long way off.'

'I can hear the cry of winter. That's what Jonah said. It's all his fault,' Iggy said.

'What's the cry of winter?' Meadows asked.

'It a load of nonsense Jonah used to talk about. Midsummer, he would say, you can hear winter's cry as summer waned. Then midwinter you'd hear the cry again when winter was at its strongest. Jonah said the veil between this life and the next was at its thinnest on those nights.'

'Mina thinks Jonah is responsible for Dad's death. That it happened on midsummer. Did you see something, Iggy?'

'He's always in her tent,' Iggy said.

'Who? Jonah?' Meadows asked.

'Yeah, with Mina. They were together. He told her things.'

'What things?'

'Prison, he–' Iggy tripped over his own feet and nearly took Meadows down with him.

Meadows, with the help of Jenny, pulled Iggy upright. They put him in between the two of them. Each with a grasp under his arm. They moved forward slowly.

'What were you saying about Jonah and prison?' Meadows asked.

Iggy stopped and put his finger to his lips. 'Shush, we don't talk about Jonah.'

'Yeah, I figured that one out,' Meadows said.

'He upset us all, didn't he, Ig,' Jenny said. 'Come on, we're nearly there.'

'Is it true that Mina and Jonah had a thing?' Meadows asked.

'Yes, for a while,' Jenny said.

'Then she'll probably know more about him than anyone.'

'She doesn't know any more than the rest of us,' Jenny said. 'All you're going to do is dig up the past. People bury their crap for a reason. It stinks.'

'We'll look after you, kiddo,' Iggy said.

Meadows smiled. 'Right now I think we need to look after you.'

It took a long time to get Iggy into bed. Several times he called Meadows Kern and Jenny had to correct him. They pulled off his shoes and covered him with a blanket, but it wasn't until three of his cats settled on the bed that he became quiet.

'My head hurts,' Iggy said as he stroked a cat.

'Well, what do you expect?' Jenny said. 'It's going to hurt a lot worse in the morning.'

'He doesn't look well,' Meadows said.

'He'll be fine, you go and check on Rain. I'll sit here until he goes to sleep.'

Meadows got the impression that Jenny didn't want him left alone with Iggy. Is she worried about what he might say to me? he thought. He figured whatever Iggy said now wasn't going to be of much use anyway, so he returned to the tepee. He passed Mina on the way.

'Is he OK?' Mina asked.

'Yeah, just drunk,' Meadows said. 'Jenny is with him.'

'Oh, I'll go and see if she wants me to sit with him. She said she was tired.'

Meadows nodded. 'I'll see you in the morning.'

Inside the tepee he stripped off and lay on the bed but he couldn't sleep. Iggy had been trying to tell him something. He needed to find out what happened on the summer solstice. It was clear that all of the olds knew more than they were willing to tell. But why? What were they afraid of?

Chapter Fourteen

Meadows awoke to the sound of Rain grumbling.

'Are you OK?' Meadows asked.

'No, I feel like shit,' Rain said. 'My head is thumping, my skin is on fire, and my tongue feels like sandpaper.'

Meadows laughed. 'I think you better stay away from Cosmo's brew and maybe stay out of the sun.'

Rain twisted off the top of a bottle of water and glugged it down without pausing. He got up, rummaged in his bag and pulled out a pair of sunglasses and put them on.

'Hell, I didn't drink that much last night, and I spent the last ten years in heat worse than this.'

'If it's any consolation Iggy is probably feeling as bad as you this morning. I had to put him to bed last night. Why don't you go down to the stream to cool off? Take the day to relax. You haven't stopped since you arrived.'

'Yeah, I might just do that.'

'I'll come with you. A cold wash will do me good,' Meadows said.

Despite the heat of the morning the water was icy cold. Meadows washed his hair then dunked his head in the stream before fully submerging himself. He sat for a few moments watching the foam drift away before getting out and rubbing himself dry.

'I'll see you later,' he said to Rain.

On the walk back he stuck his head into Iggy's caravan to see how he was doing.

'Shut the door, you're letting the light in,' Iggy moaned.

'Sorry, I'll let you go back to sleep.' He stepped out and closed the door quietly.

'Morning.'

Meadows turned and saw Mina holding a jug of liquid.

'Thought Iggy could do with this,' she said.

'I think he needs some paracetamol,' Meadows said.

'Doesn't want that rubbish.' She held up the jug. 'Mint, ginger, and a bit of turmeric. He'll be right after a few glasses of this.'

Meadows nodded. 'I'm glad I ran into you. I wanted to ask you something. Iggy mentioned last night that you and Jonah were together for a while.'

'Yes, we were. Not something that I'm proud of.'

'You must have got to know him pretty well.'

'Not really, he had a knack of getting information out of you without giving much away. He wanted me to talk about my life before the commune.'

'Let me guess, he interfered and brought someone here from your past.'

'No, not exactly. When I was sixteen, I was supposed to go back to Pakistan to get married. It had all been arranged. I was terrified of the thought of meeting my husband for the first time on my wedding day. I ran away and ended up sleeping rough before I came here. Jonah wanted details of my family, but I wouldn't give them to him. I hadn't seen my parents or brothers in years. He kept on at me and that's why we broke up. I couldn't be doing with the stress. He did tell me one thing though. I think he thought I would give him my parents' address in return. He told me he had been in prison.'

'What for?'

'He didn't say.'

'OK. Thanks, Mina.'

On the way to meet Christine, Meadows called Blackwell and gave him this information. He wasn't met with much enthusiasm even when he suggested that Jonah may have been in prison at the same time as his father and it may be a way to trace him. He guessed he would just have to trust Blackwell was doing his job.

* * *

The traffic was light on the M4, but it still took him nearly two hours to reach Cardiff. He headed for Roath Park where Christine had agreed to meet him. The park was busy with families enjoying a hot Sunday morning. Babies were pushed in prams, toddlers ran around, and retired couples strolled along the paths. As Meadows walked along admiring the lake a gaggle of geese waddled towards him looking for food. A young boy ran down the path with a handful of bread and the geese turned their attention to him.

Christine was waiting near a bench which Meadows was pleased to see was under a large tree.

'You must be Winter,' she said.

'Yes.' He sat down. 'Thank you for agreeing to meet me.'

She looked at him for a moment. Pale blue eyes scrutinised his face. She didn't look angry which was a relief. She had ash-blond hair which hung in a bob around a heart-shaped face. He guessed her to be in her sixties although she had a youthful look.

'I was curious,' she said. 'To meet the son of the man who killed my mother and sister.'

'I am sorry for your loss,' Meadows said. 'I understand the hatred you must feel towards my father.'

'Do you? I guess you think what happened was a tragic accident. Accidents are things that are unavoidable. Your father knew what he was doing. He knew how dangerous

106

it was to drive at that speed and he did it for fun. I don't feel sorry for myself, if that's what you think. I'm not full of bitterness but neither can I forgive him. He took too much from me.'

Meadows nodded. 'I'm not here to make excuses.'

'You said on the phone that you are a detective.'

'Yes, that's right.'

'Interesting career, given your father's background. You could have used that fact to talk to me. I wouldn't have known the difference.'

'I suppose but that would've been dishonest. Not a good way to start up a conversation with you.'

Christine smiled. 'It was partly because you were honest that I agreed to meet you. So you're investigating your father's death?'

'Unofficially, yes,' Meadows said. 'My father wasn't around for almost half of my life. It's only a few days ago that I found out why. It was also when I found out he had a prison record.'

'That must've come as a shock.'

Meadows smiled. 'Yes, it was.'

'You seem decent enough,' Christine said. 'Not what I was expecting. Then again, I don't know what I expected or what you want from me. I already talked to the police.'

'Yes, I know. I wanted to ask if your father ever met up with Kern Meadows. I know before my father was murdered he was trying to make amends for the past.'

Christine shook her head. 'I never met him and I'm sure Dad would've said something to me or Steven if he did. The three of us were very close.'

'Steven is your brother?'

'Yes, he was in the car. I don't know how much know about the crash.'

'I've only read the initial reports into the incident.'

'Then you don't know much, certainly not the impact it had on my family. We'd been to visit my grandparents. Grandad had been ill. It was a long journey, so we were travelling back late. Mum was driving, Donna was sitting behind her, Steven in the middle and I was behind the passenger seat. We were all tired. Mum said we didn't have far left to drive and she would take the backroads to save time. It was dark on the road, lots of high hedges and overhanging trees. Steven was making up ghost stories. Then there were headlights, and I don't remember anything else until I woke up in hospital.

'I found out later that the driver side had taken the worst of the impact,' she continued. 'Mum was killed instantly along with Donna. Steven had head injuries but was conscious. He was trapped in the car with a dead mother and sister. He didn't know that I was still alive. He was only seven at the time. No mobile phones in those days so he was stuck in the car for hours. He was still screaming when the ambulance came.'

'That's horrendous,' Meadows said. 'I imagine it's difficult to recover from an experience like that.'

'It was and poor Dad lost his wife and child. Steven and I were in a bad way. Dad didn't have time to grieve, he had to take care of us. Then we had to move.' She tapped the arms of her wheelchair. 'The house wasn't suitable for me. There were a lot of expenses and no insurance payout. We stuck together no matter what, now it's just me. If you're thinking that my father had any involvement in Kern Meadows' death then you're wrong. He'd never risk putting Steven and me through losing him as well.'

'Can I ask what happened to Steven?'

'I honestly don't know. He suffered with his mental health. Sometimes he would take off for months. Go on a drinking binge. He started to use drugs and would sleep rough. Dad would go looking for him, bring him home and clean him up. He'd be OK for a while then something would trigger him and off he'd go. The last time I saw him he seemed to be doing well. He'd cleaned up and had a job. He said he'd been having some therapy and it had helped. He did seem better, even excited, like he had something to look forward to. I never saw him again. I did look for him and even went to the police. They weren't interested. He wasn't considered at risk. He was an adult who had disappeared for long periods of time in the past. They said he would probably just turn up when he was ready.'

'Can you remember the date you last saw him?' Meadows asked.

Christine thought for a moment. 'It was my daughter's birthday. She was ten, yeah, I'm sure, because he wasn't around for the millennium celebrations. So May 1999.'

'Are you sure it was 1999?' Meadows asked.

'Yes, because we visited Mum and Donna. It was the last time we went to the graveyard together. I remember Steven commenting it had been thirty years since the crash.'

'One more thing. Does the name Jonah mean anything to you?'

Christine shook her head.

Meadows stood. 'Thank you for talking to me.'

'Not sure I've been any help.'

Meadows smiled. More than you think, he thought.

* * *

Rain was sitting outside the tepee when Meadows got back to the commune.

'You're looking much better,' Meadows said as he sat down.

'Yeah, Mina brought me a tonic. How did you get on?'

Meadows filled him in on the conversation with Christine.

'So you think now that Steven Parry killed Dad?' Rain asked.

'It's possible. The dates fit. He was living on the streets and getting therapy. Sounds like he could have run into Jonah. Blackwell probably discounted the Parry children but by the time Dad was killed they were grown up and it sounds like Steven had PTSD. Imagine what would happen if Jonah invited Steven to the commune.'

'He meets Dad and loses it,' Rain said. 'I guess it makes sense but where is he?'

Meadows shrugged. 'Could be anywhere. I'm going to have to tell Blackwell.'

'Is that Daisy?' Rain asked.

Meadows looked and saw Daisy walking towards them. He stood up and went to her.

'Well, this is a lovely surprise,' Meadows said. He kissed her and pulled her into his arms.

'I had to come,' she said. 'We don't have much time to talk. Blackwell will be on his way. The remains we found were not your father's.'

Chapter Fifteen

Daisy sat down on a cushion inside the tepee and Meadows poured her a glass of lemonade.

'Thanks,' she said, taking a sip.

'Are you sure about this?' Rain asked.

'Yes. After you read out your father's file, I started thinking about the injuries that the other passengers had sustained. I thought it would be a miracle if he walked away unscathed. I didn't want to say anything to you until I had checked. I chased your father's medical records up this morning. He sustained a compact fracture to the right fibula, some broken ribs, as well as other injuries. He had a plate fitted.'

'OK,' Rain said.

'The bones were intact,' Meadows said.

'Yes,' Daisy said. 'The remains that were found definitely do not match Kern Meadows' medical records.'

'If it's not Dad then who is it?' Rain asked.

Daisy shrugged.

'This is a real head spin,' Rain said. 'First we thought he had left us, then he's murdered, and now he's alive again.'

'We don't know he is alive,' Meadows said. 'I sent out emails to all the communes that had a website. That was before we thought the remains were his. So far no one has seen him. I don't think we can check them all.'

'Are there that many?' Daisy asked.

'You'd be surprised by the number of intentional communities,' Rain said. 'There's shared housing, ecovillages, and spiritual communes, to name a few. Some are well known. You must've heard of the Bruderhof.'

Daisy shook her head.

'It's one of the largest communities in the UK. Then there are some so remote they don't have internet access or advertise their existence.'

'There's always the possibility he is living in a cosy house somewhere,' Meadows said.

'Yeah, I can't see that,' Rain said. 'He struggled when he left here. If he wanted to make a fresh start, he's more likely to have gone somewhere where he wouldn't easily be found. Somewhere he felt comfortable. I better call Mum and tell her the news. I'll take a walk, let you two have some time together.'

'I should go before Blackwell gets here,' Daisy said. 'I had to send him my findings. If he catches me here, he will know I've told you.'

'I think he'll guess you'd give me the information whether you're here or not,' Meadows said. 'Stay a while.'

'OK, but not for the night. I like my creature comforts.'

Meadows laughed. 'Yeah, and you wouldn't want to be sharing with the two of us. Rain snores.'

Daisy leaned up against him. 'Are you OK? All this must be playing havoc with your emotions. If it was my father, well, I'd have been in pieces.'

'I'm good. I just need to gather my thoughts.'

He didn't want to tell her about the guilt he felt for thinking the worst of his father. The grief for the man he had loved growing up, the shame he felt for the suspicion he had of those who had only showed him love. Now this had all been turned on its head and he felt a kind of hollowness in his stomach.

'What about the DNA, is Blackwell looking for a match?'

'We haven't got a sample yet. There's a backlog with people being on holiday. I'm afraid this wasn't seen as a priority. I have chased it up.'

'It is a priority now if we are going to make an identification.'

'Will you be back on the case now?' Daisy asked.

'I doubt it. I'm too involved.'

Other thoughts were going through Meadows' mind, but he didn't want to voice them. Not yet. Once Blackwell came things would change. Rain and his mother would not have realised the significance of the discovery yet. Right now he just wanted time so he could digest the facts and be there for them.

'Come on,' he said. 'Let's take a walk.'

They strolled through the commune and paddled in the stream while splashing each other with the cold water. They returned with their clothes drying in the late afternoon sun and the scent of sweet peas from the pagoda lingering in the air. For a short time Meadows had shut out the turmoil, then he saw Blackwell and Valentine waiting outside the tepee.

'I take it you've already heard the news.' Blackwell shot Daisy a look, then held up his hand. 'Don't bother with denials or explanations. Let's not waste each other's time.'

Meadows noticed that Blackwell was red in the face and his hair wet with sweat. Next to him Valentine pulled a face to indicate that Blackwell was in a bad mood.

'Fair enough,' Meadows said. 'Let's go inside, it's cooler.'

Blackwell followed Meadows and Daisy inside where Rain was sitting on the bed.

'Have a seat,' Meadows said.

Blackwell looked around, seemingly unsure what to do. Meadows sat on one of the cushions, Daisy took a seat next to him and Valentine plonked down next to Rain.

Blackwell grunted and lowered himself to the floor looking uncomfortable.

'This is nice,' Valentine said. 'Cosy.'

'Can I get anyone a drink?' Rain asked.

'Yes, please,' Valentine said. 'The walk up here is a killer.'

Rain poured out the lemonade and handed it around.

Blackwell took a sip and set down the cup. 'As the remains are not that of Kern Meadows, we now have no idea who the victim is. What we do know is your father's bracelet and ring were found along with the remains. A bracelet your mother said he never took off. I think that it's safe to say that he had some involvement in the burial of the victim.'

'You don't know that,' Rain said.

'It's nothing that I haven't already thought of,' Meadows said. 'As for the victim, I think it may be Steven Parry.'

'Why would you think that?' Blackwell asked.

'Steven Parry hasn't been seen since 1999. He was seven at the time of the accident. It would make him ten years younger than the estimate of the victim's age, but–'

'You've talked to the family?' Blackwell asked.

'Yes,' Meadows said.

'You've no bloody right to do that. Where did you even get the information and the names of the victims?'

Meadows could see a pulse throbbing in Blackwell's temple.

'If I find out someone has been leaking confidential information I'll–'

'Chill man,' Rain cut in. 'You're going to give yourself a heart attack.'

It had only been a couple of years ago that Blackwell had a stent fitted because of a blockage to the heart. Meadows wondered if it was this that caused Blackwell to pause for a moment.

'You told me the year of the car crash yourself. Information isn't hard to come by if you know where to look. Yes, I spoke to Christine Williams but not in an official capacity. She told me Steven had therapy sessions. It's possible they were with Jonah. He could have invited Steven to the commune.'

'So you think your father killed Steven Parry?' Valentine asked.

'It's a possibility,' Meadows said. 'All it would take is a DNA sample from Christine to see if she is a match.'

'If it is a match then I'll be issuing a warrant for Kern Meadows' arrest. If you know where he is I suggest you tell me now,' Blackwell said.

'I honestly don't know. Up until a few hours ago I thought he was dead.' Meadows didn't know what was worse, a murdered father or a father that was a murderer.

Rain shook his head. 'Man, this just keeps getting worse.'

'I'm going to talk to these so-called olds,' Blackwell said. 'If I have to, I'll take the lot to the station and interview them under caution. One of them or all of them know whose body was buried in the woods.'

'If you're going to go charging at them like a bull you're not going to get anywhere,' Meadows said. 'You need to find Jonah, he's involved in this, I'm sure. He's been inside, maybe he was in prison at the same time as Kern Meadows. You need to check it out.'

Blackwell's eyes narrowed. 'Are you trying to tell me how to do my job?'

'I'm just making a suggestion. I'm trying to help.'

'Help? You're interfering. You need to stay out of it. If you're not careful, you'll find yourself the subject of an IPC investigation.' Blackwell stood up.

'Is that a threat?' Meadows felt a spike of anger. He got up from the floor and glared at Blackwell.

'Look at how you're behaving. Questioning victims, hanging out with a bunch of criminals and–'

'What's that supposed to mean?' Meadows asked.

'I told you that there are people here with criminal records. You even drag Daisy into it.' He turned to look at her. 'You gave out confidential information. If you act again in such an unprofessional manner, then I'll report you.'

'Get out,' Meadows said.

'You can't–'

'Out!'

Blackwell's nostrils flared. 'Fine.' He turned and stormed out of the tepee.

Valentine gave them an apologetic look and followed.

A silence followed. Meadows sighed and felt the anger drain away. 'I shouldn't have lost my temper,' he said.

'He was being a dick,' Rain said. 'Don't worry about it.'

'He'll calm down.' Daisy laughed. 'I thought he was going to burst a blood vessel.'

'It's not funny. He was right. I have dragged you into this,' Meadows said.

'I came here of my own free will,' Daisy said. 'Blackwell can bugger off.'

'You don't think that Jerome and the others would let us think that Dad was dead, rather than tell us who was really buried there, do you?' Rain asked.

'No, I don't believe they would,' Meadows said. He sat on a cushion and sighed.

'So what do we do now? Look for Dad?'

'What's the point?' Meadows said. 'We find him, then what? Ask him if he killed Steven Parry, buried him in the woods, then ran away? Persuade him to turn himself in or drag him to the police station?'

'No,' Rain said. 'What if there is some other explanation? He could have witnessed the murder. Or it could have been self-defence. The least we can do is give him the chance to explain before Blackwell gets to him.'

'His bracelet was found along with his ring. It doesn't look good,' Meadows said.

'Why don't you wait until the DNA results are in?' Daisy said. 'You don't know yet that it is Steven Parry.'

'Could it be Jonah?' Rain asked.

'No, I don't think so,' Meadows said. 'Jonah was still around after Dad left the commune for good. Besides, Mina said she saw Jonah coming out of the woods covered in blood the night of the summer solstice.'

'Then it has to be Steven Parry. If not, then who the hell is it?' Rain asked.

* * *

Daisy stayed until dark, and Meadows was glad of the distraction. He walked her to her car and hugged her tight. 'I kinda wish I was coming with you,' he said.

'This will pass,' Daisy said. 'At the moment you are trying to solve a case without any resources. You care about all the people that are involved. You thought your father was dead, now he isn't, and now you're worried he might have killed someone. I'm amazed you haven't had a meltdown.'

'I threw out Blackwell.'

Daisy laughed. 'That's your idea of a meltdown? I should tell you to step back and leave the investigation to Blackwell, but I know you wouldn't be able to do that. Just promise me that you will be careful.'

Meadows could see that Daisy was worried. 'Nothing is going to happen to me. I'm safe here.' He kissed her. 'Drive safely. I'll see you soon.'

As he walked back up the track, he saw a figure coming towards him carrying a flashlight. It wasn't until they were close that Meadows recognised Cosmo.

'Everything alright?' Meadows asked.

'Yeah, I came to check on you. Didn't want you to… to… you know, be on the floor.'

'Trip? Fall?'

'Yeah, that's it.'

'I'm fine, I've got a torch on my phone if I need it. Besides, I know my way, even in the dark. Come on, let's walk back.'

'I'm glad Kern's not… Well, it wasn't him. It's been like a bad dream all this time.'

Almost a week, Meadows thought, but to Cosmo it probably feels like months.

'And there we were celebrating his life and giving him a good send-off with your brew,' Meadows said.

'Now we have to cel-celebrate someone else.'

'The question is who?'

Cosmo didn't say anything.

'Do you have any idea who it might be?'

Cosmo shook his head. 'Kern didn't do it.'

'Why do you say that?'

'Because… erm… Kern wouldn't h-hurt anyone,' Cosmo said.

'But you think Jonah would,' Meadows said.

'I don't want to t-talk about Jonah.'

'I know what happened with Jenny. I know her ex-husband beat her and you. Mina told me that Jonah had blood on his clothes the night of the summer solstice and no one saw Dad after that night.'

Cosmo stopped. 'I said I don't w-want to talk about it.'

Even in the darkness Meadows could see the anger on Cosmo's face. It was clear that Jonah had caused Cosmo a lot of anxiety but was it more than what had happened with Jenny and her husband?

'I understand,' Meadows said. 'We don't have to talk about him. I just thought if I could find him, he might know where Kern is.'

'Don't go looking for him,' Cosmo said. 'I don't want him coming b-back, ever.'

'He's been gone for a long time. I don't think he's coming back,' Meadows said.

'Don't be too sure,' Cosmo said.

Meadows decided it was best to drop the subject. He didn't want to agitate Cosmo. Instead he talked about Cosmo's plants and what he'd been growing and by the time they reached the pagoda Cosmo was calm.

Jenny, Iggy, and Jerome were sitting with Rain, all looked serious.

'Are you going to join us?' Jerome asked.

'Yeah,' Meadows said. 'I'm just going to grab a cup of tea first. Anyone want one?'

'I've got more wine,' Cosmo said.

'Wine!' Iggy said. 'That stuff was radioactive. I don't remember getting to bed last night. I still don't feel right.'

'Me neither, I'll stick to tea,' Rain said. 'Or better still, Mina left a few bottles of dandelion water. I'll drink that.'

'Bunch of p-pussies,' Cosmo said. 'I drank it, and I was fine.'

Iggy laughed. 'You're probably immune to the stuff.'

Meadows went to the tepee and chose the camomile tea. He walked back to the pagoda and handed a bottle to Rain.

'Tough day for you, my boy,' Jerome said.

'It was a surprise turn of events,' Meadows said

'How did your mum take the news?' Jenny asked.

'She was OK,' Rain said. 'A bit emotional.'

'The whole thing doesn't make much sense,' Meadows said. 'I can understand Dad's bracelet coming off if he was involved but his wedding ring? It's not something that would fall off easily.'

'That's because he didn't d-do anything,' Cosmo said.

'I think Cosmo's right,' Jenny said. 'I can't see Kern doing something like that.'

'The police will be looking for Dad now,' Rain said. 'The only thing we can do is find him before they do. Give him a chance to explain. Do any of you know where he might have gone?'

They all shook their heads.

'You thought that he might have gone off with some people from another commune. The ones that were here that midsummer,' Meadows said.

'I can't remember that far back,' Jerome said. 'They came from all over the place. Jonah invited a lot of them. He moved around a lot before he came to stay here. Kern could have gone anywhere.'

'You know, someone could have stolen his bracelet and wedding ring,' Iggy said.

'No one here would steal,' Jerome said.

'He never took them off,' Rain said. 'They wouldn't have been left lying around.'

Meadows nodded. 'I'm sure Mum would've noticed if he wasn't wearing his wedding ring before he left us. Whatever happened in the woods must've taken place when he came back here after the fight with Mum. He took off suddenly after the solstice celebrations. Mina saw Jonah with blood on his clothes. It has to be that night. So who else went missing at that time?' He looked at each of his companions in turn.

'No one I can think of,' Jerome said.

Cosmo and Jenny shook their heads.

'Where's Mina?' Meadows asked.

'She was tired, said she was going to have an early night,' Iggy said.

'I hope she's not going down with this virus. There's a few got it now,' Jenny said.

'She's just upset by everything that's been going on,' Iggy said.

'That's understandable,' Meadows said. 'I did talk to her about Jonah this morning. She said he had been in prison. Did he tell any of you about that?'

Another shake of heads.

'What about the night Mina saw Jonah come out of the woods with blood on his clothes? Did any of you see him?'

'She did mention something at the time,' Jerome said. 'I didn't think anything of it, I had no reason to believe

Jonah had hurt someone, but now I guess he could've done. It was a long time ago. We're talking over twenty years. Jonah was here for a while. I can't say with certainty that it was midsummer when she saw this. It could have been any number of celebrations we had over the years.'

'But she remembers Dad being here, coming back after he had left us, so it had to be that midsummer,' Meadows said.

Jerome shrugged. 'Her memory is better than mine.'

'What about the other communes Jonah lived in? He must've mentioned them. You said the visitors that came that midsummer were his friends. If Dad went with them it's likely to a place known to Jonah,' Rain said.

'Jonah talked about one somewhere in Kent,' Jerome said.

'Well, that's a start,' Meadows said.

'He also travelled abroad,' Jenny said.

'Great,' Rain said. 'We're going to have to take a hell of a road trip if we're going to find Dad.'

'Even if you did find him would you want him to come back?' Jenny asked.

'At the moment it's not looking good for him,' Meadows said. 'Someone is murdered and his bracelet and ring are found with the remains. Then he takes off. Doesn't look like the actions of an innocent man. He needs to explain what happened and yeah, I guess face the consequences.'

'He might have witnessed something,' Iggy said. 'Think about it. If Jonah knew about your father's past he could have threatened to tell Fern and you boys if he didn't keep quiet and help him bury the body. I imagine he was so ashamed of his past that he never wanted his family to find out.'

'He was always on at us to be truthful and do the right thing,' Rain said. 'He'd be worried we'd see him as a hypocrite.'

Meadows nodded. 'He'd never allow any display of anger. He drilled into us to think before acting. He also taught us to be tolerant and never judge.'

'It's because he wanted the best for you boys,' Jerome said. 'He'd made a huge mistake in his life, and he didn't want the same for you.'

'He wasn't himself the last few months he was with us,' Rain said. 'That wasn't him.'

'No,' Meadows agreed. He'd finished his tea, but he still felt thirsty and now his head was pounding. He was getting nowhere with his questions, and everything seemed muddled in his mind. 'I think I'll call it a night,' he said. 'I want an early start in the morning to check out the other communes. See what I can find out. Dad never had a passport so at least we know he didn't leave the country.'

'Think I should get off to bed as well,' Rain said. 'I still need to sleep off the hangover from Cosmo's brew.'

They all laughed but Meadows thought it sounded forced.

'I'll come with you tomorrow,' Rain said as they walked back to their tepee. 'With two of us we'll get around quicker.'

'Yeah, OK. I'm not sure what I'm going to say to Dad when we find him.'

'Something like, "Hi, Dad, remember us? Just want to know if you killed someone and buried them in the woods at the commune."'

Meadows laughed. 'Yeah, I think we better come up with something better than that.'

Inside the tepee Meadows got undressed, placed a bottle of water by the side of the bed and lay down. He was asleep in minutes, but it wasn't restful. He was dreaming he was in the woods looking into an empty grave so deep he could barely see the bottom. Then he felt a thud on the back, and he pitched forward. His arms flailed in the air as he fell deeper and deeper. He landed on his back. He looked up and saw the olds peering down at him.

Among them was his father. He tried calling for help but no sound came from his mouth. His father lifted a shovel in the air and the others did the same. Then they began to chant as they shovelled earth on top of him. He cried out but his mouth was filled with earth.

He awoke with a start, gasping for air. His mouth was so dry he couldn't swallow, and his skin felt like it was on fire. He sat up, reached for the bottle of water, and glugged it down. Movement in the tepee caught his attention. He blinked but the shadowy figure was still there. It moved towards the entrance of the tepee, drew the canvas aside and disappeared outside.

'Hey,' Meadows shouted as he jumped up from the bed.

Rain mumbled something as Meadows tried to pull on his shorts and fell over. He cursed as he pulled them up and slipped his feet into his sandals. He grabbed a torch and ran outside waving it about. All was still and quiet apart from his heart which thudded in his chest.

He spun around scanning his surroundings and just caught a glimpse of the figure heading in the direction of the forest. Meadows took off running past the yurts and tepees. The figure stayed ahead, just out of range of the torch beam. Meadows called out, his voice cutting through the darkness, but the figure didn't stop. Near to the forest the grass was longer and it caught between his toes and his sandals. He stumbled but kept going. Once he reached the edge of the forest he paused briefly. Whoever it was could have a weapon, he thought. He didn't have his phone, and no one would hear him shout for help. Was this how it had been for the poor soul that died here? Maybe he chased someone in. He shook these thoughts away and pushed forward.

There was no sign of the figure now and the shapes of the trees and branches made it difficult to pick out someone hiding. The darkness pressed against his back, and he was sure he could hear whispering. He moved quickly, going deeper in. Each snap of a twig and rustling of leaves seemed magnified in the dark. He swung his torch back and forth.

What was Iggy saying about the veil between this world and the next? He looked wildly around. His imagination was taking him to places he didn't want to go. He couldn't think clearly. I'm just tired, he told himself.

He heard another noise and stopped. It wasn't part of the forest. It was a kind of scraping noise followed by a thud, it repeated in a rhythm. It took him a moment to recognise the sound. Someone was digging.

He moved quickly towards the noise until he saw the figure crouching in a small clearing ahead. He sprang forward and felt a low branch whip across his face. He kept moving. He was almost to the figure when his toe caught a tree root and he crashed to the ground. The torch flew from his hand and went out.

He lay still and listened. Whoever was in the woods would have the advantage. They weren't using a torch and his eyes hadn't adjusted to the darkness. The powdery smell of violets tickled his nose. Slowly he pulled himself to his feet. He turned around and saw a light, and behind it, two figures.

Chapter Sixteen

Cosmo had got up to relieve himself and was returning to his yurt when he saw Meadows burst out of his tepee and take off across the field. Must be desperate for a pee, he thought. He turned to go back to his bed, but an uneasy feeling crept over him. He looked again. The light from the torch was flitting back and forth as Meadows got further away. He wouldn't be able to go back to sleep now. What if something was wrong? He wouldn't be running that far when he could easily use Jerome's toilet, he thought.

He walked to Meadows' tepee and peeked inside. Rain was lying on his back emitting a steady stream of snores. Cosmo let the canvas drop back and hurried to Jerome's yurt. Inside he found him sleeping naked on top of the bed covers.

'Oi! Oi!'

Jerome stirred.

'Wake up,' Cosmo said.

Jerome groaned and sat up. 'Cosmo. What the hell are you doing?'

'I just saw Winter running across the field with a torch.'

'And?'

'He was heading towards the woods. It's the… the… halfway…' Cosmo clenched his fist in frustration. 'It's not morning. What's he doing?' What if he's in t-trouble? What if… if the same thing happens again?'

'OK, clam down. Nothing is going to happen to the boy. There's no reason. You're getting yourself worked up over nothing.'

'What if Jonah… if he…'

'Jonah is an old man like the rest of us. Let me get some clothes on and we'll take a look.'

Cosmo hopped from foot to foot. He felt all the fear from the past come rushing at him.

'Right, let's go,' Jerome said as he grabbed a torch.

'Should we go and w-wake the others?' Cosmo asked.

'There's no point. What if he just got caught short? How's he going to feel if we all turn up and he's taking a crap in the woods?'

'I thought of that,' Cosmo said. 'He could have used your loo or the communal ones by the pagoda.'

'Yeah, I suppose. What about Rain?'

'Sleeping,' Cosmo said.

'OK.'

Jerome was walking fast, and Cosmo struggled to keep pace. He could tell that Jerome was worried and this made him even more anxious. Jerome was the sensible one, the one that kept calm in any situation. The one that always had a solution.

They reached the edge of the woods and Cosmo stopped.

'I don't w-want to go in there.' Memories of Jonah came back, the shouting, the blood.

'Get a grip of yourself, mate,' Jerome said. 'There's nothing in here to be afraid of.' He stepped forward.

Cosmo didn't want to be left alone in the dark and he didn't want Jerome to go in on his own, so he followed.

'Kern–'

'Don't,' Jerome cut in.

'Sorry, it's just—'

'You have to be careful,' Jerome whispered. 'Think before you speak. You know what you're like when you get flustered. Winter could be close by and hear you.'

'I'm sorry.' Cosmo hated how he blurted things out. It was like a thought came to his mind and was out of his mouth before he could stop it. Then when he wanted to say something, some words seemed to get jammed. Lethologica is what Jerome called it. Iggy said it was not enough gigabytes to store his data. Cosmo preferred Iggy's explanation. He didn't know what he would do without Jerome, and Iggy. While everyone thought this was about protecting Winter and Rain, for him it was about protecting himself, Jerome, and Jenny. Out of all of them Jerome meant the most. He had given Cosmo his life, saved him. This was the only thing that drove him further into the woods. He would not leave Jerome alone in this place.

A cry echoed around the woods making them both jump.

Cosmo grabbed Jerome's arm. 'It's happening again.'

'No,' Jerome hissed. 'You have to forget about what happened before. Do you understand?'

'Yeah,' Cosmo said. 'I'm trying but it's all I can think about since they found his bones.'

'Come on. The sound came from that direction.' Jerome pointed the beam of the torch.

They moved forward. Cosmo's heart was racing. He looked around wildly as he kept pace with Jerome. They were deep into the woods when he caught sight of a figure on the ground.

'What's that?' Cosmo whispered.

Jerome stopped and they both watched as the figure got up and turned towards them.

Cosmo heard Jerome let go of his breath. 'It's just Winter.'

Cosmo felt relief wash over his body.

'What are you doing out here?' Jerome asked when they got closer.

'There was someone out here,' Meadows said. 'They came in my tepee then ran off. I followed them. They were digging.'

'There is no one here but us,' Jerome said.

'You must have had a b-bad dream,' Cosmo said. 'Let's go back. This place gives me the… the…'

'Creeps?' Jerome asked then laughed.

'I wasn't dreaming. I saw someone,' Meadows said.

'Well, it's no good looking now,' Jerome said. 'They'll be well gone. We can come and check it out first thing in the morning.'

Cosmo watched Meadows look around. He was afraid he was going to insist they stay but in the end he nodded. As they walked back they met with Haystack.

'Jerome.' Haystack gave a nod in greeting.

'Have you seen anyone digging out here?' Meadows asked.

Haystack looked at Cosmo who felt his heart quicken. He stepped a little closer to Jerome.

'You should get out of here. It's dangerous walking around the woods in the dark.' Haystack started to walk away.

'Wait,' Meadows said. 'There was someone digging. Was it you? What are you doing wandering around in the middle of the night?'

Cosmo wished he would shut up. Haystack wasn't the type of man you wanted to make angry. He was relieved when he ignored the questions and kept walking.

'Let's go,' Jerome said. 'You can talk to Haystack in the morning if you want.'

'OK,' Meadows said.

The three of them walked back into the commune and Jerome took Meadows into his tepee. Cosmo waited outside. He heard them talking for a few moments then Jerome came out.

'Do you think he's alright?' Cosmo asked.

'Yeah, he'll go back to sleep and in the morning he'll realise that he was imagining things.'

'What if he wasn't?' Cosmo asked. 'I think he suspects something. He's going to find out about Phillip then we'll–'

'Don't ever mention that name,' Jerome said.

Even in the dark Cosmo could see Jerome was angry.

'I'm sorry, it just popped into my head,' Cosmo said.

'Then you have to erase it. If you can't you're going to have to go away until this is over.'

Cosmo felt sick at the thought. 'I can't, please.'

'Alright.' Jerome patted Cosmo on the shoulder. 'Remember what we talked about?'

Cosmo nodded. 'Winter must never know.'

Chapter Seventeen

Meadows awoke feeling disorientated. He sat up and felt pain shoot through his head like a bolt of lightning. He reached for the bottle of water beside his bed, but it was empty. He got up to look for another then felt his stomach heave. He just managed to get a bowl before he was sick.

'Are you OK?' Rain asked.

'No, I feel like hell,' Meadows said.

'Don't feel much better myself,' Rain said. 'I told you it wasn't Cosmo's brew. We've probably picked up the virus that's going around.' He sat up.

Meadows located a bottle of water, swilled his mouth then sat down on the bed. 'I was having some weird dreams last night.' He looked down at his feet and saw they were covered in dirt.

'What have you done to your face?' Rain asked.

Meadows put his hand to his cheek and felt a deep scratch. He remembered running through the woods. The figure in the tepee.

'I wasn't dreaming,' Meadows said. 'Someone came in here last night.'

'Who was in here?' Rain asked.

'I don't know, I chased them into the woods. They were digging. Then Jerome and Cosmo came.'

'Dude, you sure you weren't tripping?'

'No, I'm going to take a look.' He stood up and swayed.

'I think you need to get back into bed,' Rain said.

Meadows shook his head. 'We need to go and find Dad, and Jonah.'

'You're not driving anywhere today,' Rain said. 'It can wait until you feel better.'

'Yeah, I guess you're right.'

Meadows lay back on the bed. He was just drifting into sleep when Jerome came in followed by Jenny.

'We've come to see how you are feeling,' Jerome said. 'You had me worried, my boy.'

'I'm OK,' Meadows said.

'You don't look it,' Jenny said. 'Mina sent you something to make you feel better.' She held up a jug.

Meadows looked at the black murky liquid and felt his stomach churn. 'I don't think so.'

'Nonsense,' Jenny said. She filled two glasses and handed one to Meadows and one to Rain. 'Drink it down. It will help. Tom, Kai, and Willow are also sick. It's a nasty bug. You two better stay in bed.'

Meadows drank it down in one go and set the glass down. He looked at Jerome. 'What were you and Cosmo doing in the woods last night?'

'Looking for you,' Jerome said. 'Cosmo saw you running across the field, so we came to see if you were OK.'

'Did you see anyone else?'

'No, it was just you, and then Haystack. I think he just came to see what we were doing. You must've been running a temperature. You weren't making much sense.'

'Someone was digging,' Meadows said.

'No one was digging. You were alone.'

'How far in was I?'

'You were near the old sycamore,' Jerome said.

'The mistletoe tree?'

'Yeah,' Jerome said.

'I need to check it out.' Meadows stood up.

'I'll go with you later. First you need to rest and have something to eat.'

The last thing Meadows wanted was food, but he agreed to go back to sleep.

'I'll come back in a couple of hours,' Jerome said. 'If you're feeling better, we'll take a walk.'

'You need to get some rest,' Jenny said. 'You've both had a shock, it's no wonder you don't feel well.'

Meadows nodded and settled back on the bed. When he woke next he did feel a little better and after a quick wash he joined Jerome and Rain in the woods.

'You were about here,' Jerome said.

'Are you sure? There were violets, I remember smelling them when I fell,' Meadows said.

Jerome shrugged. 'They grow all over the place.'

'I've only seen them near where we found the remains,' Meadows said.

'And with Mags' ashes in a pot,' Rain added.

Meadows looked around. He could see the old sycamore next to some smaller siblings.

'Plenty of mistletoe,' Meadows said.

'Yeah, we still come and pick it for the winter solstice,' Jerome said.

'Have you always been a pagan?' Rain asked as they walked further past the old tree.

Jerome laughed. 'I wouldn't call myself a pagan. I just like a peaceful life. Mutual respect for people and the earth. All that stuff is down to Iggy. He started it off and the rest of us just followed. It's more out of habit. It marks the passing of the year, and it gives us all a chance to get together and celebrate. We don't much bother with birthdays. I also say my prayers before I go to sleep. I wouldn't want to die without ever having spoken to God. Can't just turn up at the pearly gates. That would be rude.'

'I guess that's one way of looking at it,' Meadows said. He stopped walking. 'Look over there.' He pointed to a clump of purple flowers on the forest floor.

'You think someone else is buried here?' Rain asked.

'They're just flowers,' Jerome said. 'I think you're reading too much into it.'

'These ones have been trampled.' Meadows knelt down.

'Yeah, probably by you last night,' Jerome said.

Meadows examined the earth near the flowers. 'Someone has been digging here. Look, the earth's been disturbed.'

'Maybe a little,' Jerome said. 'But it looks like some animal has been scrambling around. Probably one of Iggy's cats. They bury their business. I would get up if I were you. Think of the amount of people that have taken a pee around here. You don't know what you're putting your hands in.' Jerome laughed.

'Why would the flowers be here and near the remains?' Meadows asked as he stood up. 'If it was a case that they seeded themselves the whole place would be covered. Someone must have planted them.'

'I'll ask around,' Jerome said. 'If Jenny has them for Mags, then someone else could have planted them here as it was a special place for a loved one, even a pet.'

'Or ashes,' Rain said.

Meadows wasn't convinced but he let it go. His head was still sore.

'How about I make you boys a veggie curry tonight,' Jerome said. 'Spices are good for you in this weather.'

'Sounds great,' Rain said.

'Come on then, let's go back. You two can relax by the stream.' He patted Meadows on the shoulder. 'You still don't look well, my boy.'

Once they were out of the cover of the trees Rain's mobile phone trilled. He took it out of his pocket and looked at the screen.

'It's a text from Mum. Blackwell wants to see her, and he suggested that the two of us be present.'

Meadows looked at his own phone and saw the same message. 'That doesn't sound good,' he said. 'I'm surprised Blackwell didn't contact me.'

'I guess he's still pissed off with you,' Rain said.

'We better get going, he'll be there in an hour,' Meadows said.

'Hope everything is OK,' Jerome said. 'I'll have food ready for you when you get back.'

Meadows let Rain drive. He put the seat back and turned the air con on full and still he felt too hot. The winding roads made him feel nauseous and the sun glaring through the windscreen hurt his eyes. They reached the top of the mountain and Rain pulled over into the car park.

'What are you doing?' Meadows asked.

'Ice lolly,' Rain said.

He jumped out of the car and went to the ice cream van. Meadows watched an elderly couple sitting on a bench and thought it could easily have been his parents if circumstances had been different.

Rain got back in the car and handed Meadows an ice lolly, then peeled the wrapper off his.

'Mmm, that's good,' Meadows said as the ice hit his tongue.

They drove down the other side of the mountain and passed through the villages in the valley and arrived in Dan y Coed, five minutes past Blackwell's given time. Fern was waiting outside the door. Meadows could see Blackwell's car already parked.

'Are you OK?' Meadows asked as he hugged his mum.

'Yeah, Stefan's already here with Reena. What do you think he wants?' she whispered. 'Do you think he's arrested your father?'

'I don't know,' Meadows said. 'I guess it could well be that. Whatever it is, we'll deal with it.'

'Well, it can't be anything worse than we've heard the last few days,' Rain said.

Meadows hoped he was right. 'Let's go and find out.'

Blackwell stood up as soon as Meadows entered the room.

'Sorry we kept you,' Meadows said. 'Before we start, I want to apologise for yesterday.'

Blackwell held up his hand. 'There's no need. I was out of order. I guess we were both hot and bothered. I do appreciate this is a difficult and unusual situation for you. Let's say no more about it.'

Meadows smiled and nodded before taking a seat on the sofa. Now he was concerned. Blackwell didn't usually back down easily which meant that this wasn't going to be good news. Fern sat next to him and Rain on the other side.

'Now you're all here I need to tell you about a development we had in the case,' Blackwell said. 'You know that we requested a DNA sample to be taken from the remains and tested against your sample. That's come back now and it's a positive result.'

It took a moment for this information to set in. 'I don't understand,' Meadows said. 'The medical records were not a match. Was there some error?'

'No,' Blackwell said. 'The medical records were not a match for Kern Meadows.'

'We ran the DNA sample again, this time using the sample Rain provided,' Valentine said. 'The results were the same.'

Blackwell looked at Fern. 'Can you shed any light on this?'

Meadows knew what Blackwell was driving at.

'Are you saying the medical records were not Kern's?' Fern asked.

'He's asking if, erm… He's asking if our father was not Kern Meadows,' Meadows said.

'Don't be ridiculous,' Fern said. 'Of course he is, or was, your father. Is he dead, or isn't he?'

Blackwell shook his head. 'There isn't a straight answer to that. The remains that we found are those of the father of your sons, so yes, he is deceased. However, they are not the remains of Kern Meadows. They are not the same person. The only conclusion that we can draw from that is that your husband was not who he said he was.'

'Do you have a marriage certificate?' Valentine asked. 'Or better still, Kern Meadows' birth certificate?'

'I don't have his birth certificate,' Fern said, 'but my marriage certificate is somewhere in a drawer upstairs. Would you like me to get it for you?'

'That would be very helpful, thank you,' Valentine said.

Fern left the room and there was silence for a moment.

'Is it possible that there is more than one Kern Meadows?' Rain asked. 'I'm sure if you searched your own name you would find more than one Stefan Blackwell.'

'We've checked the registry of birth and deaths,' Blackwell said. 'There is no other Kern Meadows within the date range. There is only one, but he'd be too young to be your father.'

'So my father is definitely dead, but you don't know who he is. Is that about right?' Rain asked.

Blackwell nodded.

'This is seriously messed up,' Rain said.

'I've brought a copy of the DNA results for you,' Valentine said. She handed the paper to Meadows.

Meadows looked at it and handed it to Rain. He didn't know what to say.

'I think it's best we leave you to have a talk with your mother,' Blackwell said. 'I understand it may be uncomfortable for her to talk freely in front of us.'

'If our father was someone other than the one we called Dad she would have told us,' Meadows said. He tried to think of an explanation or someone who could shed light on the situation. Kern Meadows' parents are dead, and his brother died in the crash, he thought. Then he remembered the report he had read. 'What about Lee Morris?'

'What about him?' Blackwell asked.

'Well he survived the crash. He was obviously friends with Kern Meadows so he would know what happened to him. Maybe he stayed in touch.'

'We'll look into it,' Blackwell said.

'What about Jonah?'

'We're still looking. Without a surname it's not easy.'

'So where does that leave the investigation?' Meadows asked.

'We're still looking for any trace of Kern Meadows,' Valentine said. 'Talking to anyone he shared a cell with, and where he went when he was released. If your father took his identity, then the likelihood is that he knew him at some stage. It could be that Kern Meadows is our killer.'

'As for identifying the remains, I'm afraid there is not a lot we can do. If I'm honest I was hoping your mother would have an explanation,' Blackwell said.

'You can see that she is as confused as the rest of us,' Rain said.

Blackwell nodded.

'There is something I wanted to talk to you about,' Meadows said. 'I think there is a chance that other remains are buried in the woods.' He told them about his experience in the woods during the night and the flowers.

'Someone wandering around at night and some flowers is not enough to authorise a team of forensic officers to spend days digging up the woods. It's not as if we have a missing person who we suspect is buried there,' Blackwell said.

'Kern Meadows is missing,' Rain said.

'We don't know that,' Blackwell said. 'Unless you're thinking that your father killed Kern Meadows and stole his identity, then someone killed him,' Blackwell said.

'No,' Meadows said. 'That's highly unlikely. What about Steven Parry? He's missing.'

'Steven Parry was known to go off of his own accord. There is no connection between him and the commune and as far as we know Kern Meadows was never there.'

'Steven Parry didn't know that,' Meadows said. 'As far as he was concerned my father was Kern Meadows.'

'If that was the case we would be looking for him in connection to a murder. Not looking for his remains. What you're saying doesn't make sense. Don't make it more complicated than it already is.'

What he's saying is right, Meadows thought. What he couldn't explain was the feeling he had while he was in the woods.

'Here it is.' Fern came back into the room with a certificate. 'See, Kern Meadows.' She handed it to Blackwell.

Blackwell looked closely at the certificate. 'It looks genuine.'

'It is,' Fern said. 'We also provided identification. So no matter what you say, my husband was Kern Meadows.'

Blackwell handed the certificate back. 'Thank you for showing us. I'll be in touch if we have any more news. We'll see ourselves out.'

'I'll be glad when you're back,' Valentine whispered before she followed Blackwell out.

'Well, that was a load of crap,' Fern said. 'I don't think they know what they're doing.'

'You do know that Blackwell is going to think that our real father turned up and Kern killed him,' Meadows said. 'I know how his mind works.'

'Kern was your real father,' Fern said.

'This is like a bad trip,' Rain said. 'I need a smoke.' He pulled his tin from his pocket.

'I promise you that Kern, well, the man who called himself Kern, was your father,' Fern said.

'I know,' Meadows said. 'The question is, why steal the identity of a man who has a criminal record?'

'Maybe he just chose the name randomly and didn't know,' Rain said.

'He must have used a birth certificate for identity. To do that he would have had to have known the real Kern Meadows' date of birth,' Meadows said.

'He could have read about the car crash and the court case in the paper,' Fern said. 'That way he would know the real Kern was stuck behind bars. All he would need to do is apply for a copy of the birth certificate. I don't think it was that difficult back then.'

'I think it's more likely he knew him, and well enough to have details of his life,' Meadows said. 'Then there's the question of why. What was he running from?'

'Or what did he do?' Rain asked.

'Well, it wasn't something good,' Fern said. 'I don't think I want to know.'

Meadows sighed. 'If anyone knows, it will be Jerome. He was Dad's oldest friend. I'm going back to the commune. See if we can get some answers.'

Fern turned to Rain. 'Go with your brother, and don't let each other out of your sight. Someone killed your father, and they are not going to want you to find out the truth.'

* * *

Jenny and Cosmo were the first people they met when they got back to the commune.

'Where's Jerome?' Meadows asked.

'He's sitting with Iggy under the pagoda. Is everything alright?' Jenny asked.

'Not really,' Meadows said. 'Maybe the two of you should come with us. I'll explain when you're all together.'

'OK,' Jenny said.

They walked together silently. Meadows didn't feel like talking and he only wanted to explain once. He also wanted to watch everyone's reactions.

When they reached the pagoda they found Jerome, Iggy, and Mina drinking from mugs.

'Oh good, you're back,' Jerome said. 'Food is nearly ready.'

'And I've left you a jug of tonic in your tepee. I hope you don't mind me going in,' Mina said.

'Thanks,' Rain said. 'I think it's working wonders.'

'I need to speak to you all,' Meadows said. He quickly explained the latest developments.

Cosmo was the first to speak. 'Dead, a-again. No, I thought it would be... that it wasn't... that he.'

'It's OK, Cosmo,' Jenny said. She put her hand on Cosmo's arm.

'It's not bloody OK.' He shrugged off Jenny's hand and stood up. 'I c-can't do this anymore.' He hurried away.

'Let him be,' Jerome said. 'He'll be alright.'

'So what are you going to do now?' Iggy asked.

'I don't know,' Meadows said. 'If there's anything you know about Kern's past you need to tell us, it doesn't matter how bad it is.'

He looked around the group. No one spoke.

'Did any of you know that Kern wasn't his real name?'

They all shook their heads.

It was clear to Meadows that he wasn't going to get any answers. He felt his best option was to speak to Jerome alone later.

'Tomorrow morning Rain and me are going to start digging in the woods.' That got a reaction, he thought.

Jenny stiffened, Iggy shot Jerome a look and Meadows was sure he'd seen a hint of a smile on Mina's face.

'What's the point of that?' Jenny asked.

'Because I think someone else is buried there,' Meadows said.

'Are the police coming to help?' Iggy asked.

'No, why?' Meadows asked.

'Well it's a big area, you'll be digging for years.'

'No, I have an idea where to look,' Meadows said.

'I think the food will be about ready,' Jerome said.

'I'll just go and find Cosmo,' Jenny said.

'I'll give you a hand with the food,' Mina said.

'I'll fetch some plates, shall I?' Iggy said.

They all scuttled away leaving Meadows and Rain.

'Like that wasn't odd,' Rain said.

'Yeah, I think the only way to get any answers is to get them alone.'

'Yeah, preferably stoned or drunk,' Rain said.

Meadows laughed. 'That's not usually the tactics I employ to get answers.'

Jerome, Iggy, and Mina returned with the food and Cosmo came back with Jenny. Meadows decided not to ask any more awkward questions and although they were quieter than usual it was a pleasant evening, and everyone seemed to relax.

'Right, I'm off to bed,' Jerome said. 'I need an early night if I'm going to help you two treasure hunt in the woods in the morning.'

The comment took Meadows by surprise. 'Oh, there's no need for you to come,' he said. 'We'll manage.'

'It's not a problem,' Jerome said. 'Iggy and Cosmo will help as well.'

'Yeah, OK,' Cosmo said.

'You'll need a bit of weight behind those shovels,' Iggy said and patted his stomach.

'Great,' Rain said.

'We'll walk back with you,' Meadows said. 'An early night will do us good.'

They all stood up and Meadows was disappointed that it wasn't just Jerome walking with them. They chatted as they walked and when they were close to Jerome's yurt Meadows stopped.

'Actually there was something I wanted to show you, Jerome. Do you mind coming back to our place for a few minutes? I'll make you some camomile tea, it will help you sleep.'

'I don't think he needs any help sleeping,' Jenny said. 'At our age we need help staying awake.'

Meadows smiled. 'He can share some of Mina's tonic then.'

'Now that I won't say no to,' Jerome said. 'You're lucky, Mina doesn't give it to anyone. Can't remember the last time I had a jug.'

'That's because you're hardly ever ill,' Mina said.

'What about my arthritis?'

'I give you medicine for that.'

'So you do, and it works wonders.' Jerome blew Mina a kiss.

'See you all in the morning,' Meadows said.

The group moved on and Jerome followed Meadows and Rain into the tepee.

'Tea?' Meadows asked.

'I wasn't joking about the tonic,' Jerome said.

Rain picked up the jug. 'Looks better than the one we had this morning. It looked like black sludge.'

'Probably charcoal,' Jerome said. 'Great for an upset stomach.' He took the glass from Meadows and held it out for Rain to pour. 'What was it you wanted to show me?'

'Nothing,' Meadows said. 'I wanted to speak with you alone.'

Jerome raised his eyebrows. 'Why do I get the feeling I'm not going to like this?'

Meadows smiled. 'It's nothing bad, I just need information.'

'OK,' Jerome said and sat down.

'Can you tell me about the first time you met my father?' Meadows asked.

Jerome took a sip of his drink. 'That's not a secret, you could have asked in front of the others. I'm sure I already told you I was doing some volunteer work with the homeless.'

'Dad was homeless?' Rain asked.

'No, a volunteer like me.'

'Where was this?' Meadows asked.

'In Cardiff.'

'That's a long way to travel from here?' Rain said.

'I didn't always live here,' Jerome said. 'I moved around a lot as a youngster. I lived for a while in Grangetown before coming here.'

'What did you do there, I mean other than volunteer work?' Meadows asked.

'What's this about?'

'I'm just interested,' Meadows said.

'You two have known me all your life. Am I a suspect in your eyes?'

'It's the job, he can't help it,' Rain said. 'You were the one to encourage him.'

'Oh yeah,' Meadows said. 'I would never have had the courage to go to university and join the force without your encouragement. Look I don't suspect you of anything. I just need a little help and starting at the beginning seems like a good place. You probably knew Dad the best. I'm trying to understand who my father was.'

'He was Kern Meadows. That hasn't changed,' Jerome said. 'You know who he was. Just because he changed his name didn't change him as a person.'

'But why would he do that?' Rain asked.

Jerome shrugged. 'People run away for all sorts of reasons. Who knew what he was trying to escape from? Not everyone has a loving family.'

'Did you?' Meadows asked.

'I did once but we drifted apart.' Jerome glugged down his drink and held out his glass for a refill.

'When Dad left us, someone paid off the mortgage on the cottage. Anonymously,' Meadows said.

'You think he did that?' Jerome asked.

'No, I don't think it was him,' Meadows said. 'We never had much growing up. When we moved to the cottage, I know Mum and Dad were struggling financially. Dad worked long hours labouring on the farm. If he had money, I don't think he would have kept it secret.'

'No I don't suppose he would have,' Jerome said. 'I never saw him splash out on anything.'

'Then that leaves someone here,' Meadows said.

Jerome laughed. 'Well it wasn't me. My grandfather left me a little bit of money with the land but just enough to set up here. I don't think there's anyone here that could afford to pay off a mortgage and besides why would they?'

'Guilt, maybe,' Meadows said. 'I guess we'll never know. What we do know is Dad had a life and a family before he came here. If we can learn more about that we may be able to find out his identity.'

'What if you don't like what you find out?' Jerome asked.

'Better than not knowing,' Rain said. 'Otherwise all we're left with is our imagination. I don't even want to talk about what's been going through my mind.'

'Fair enough,' Jerome said. 'If I could help you, I would.'

'If Dad was volunteering with you, he must've also had some other form of income,' Meadows said.

'Yeah, I'm sure he did a lot of labouring. Casual work. You could walk from one job to the other in those days.'

'What about accommodation? Did he live with his parents? Have his own place?'

'Boarding.'

'Do you remember where?'

'You're asking something there. Near the docks maybe. I never went to his place. There was no reason to.'

'Mina thought he may have been inside. Would make sense if he was Kern Meadows but maybe that's where he met the real Kern.'

'He was a private man back then. Didn't talk much about his life.'

'Was he friendly with anyone else?'

'He kept to himself. He was quiet. He wasn't one to go off to the pub drinking, well not back then. We hit it off. I asked him if he would come here and help me sort the place out. It was a mess. He came and he never left. That's all I can tell you. All this talk of prison and stolen identities means nothing to me. He was my friend. I loved him like a brother. That's how I will remember him. I don't want to know anything else. I promise you this, neither I nor anyone here hurt your father.' Jerome stood up and swayed. He put his hand to his head.

Meadows jumped to his feet. 'Are you OK?'

'I got up too quickly. I need to go to bed, I'm an old man and if you insist on digging in the woods I'll help you, but I need my sleep.'

'Take the rest of the tonic with you,' Rain said. 'I'm sure Mina will bring us more in the morning.'

'Thanks.' He hugged Meadows tightly. 'I love you. Both of you.'

'We love you too,' Meadows said.

Jerome hugged Rain before taking the jug and leaving.

'What did you make of that?' Rain asked.

Meadows shrugged. 'I think he's holding something back.'

'He seemed genuine to me. We have to assume he is telling us the truth and he doesn't know anything about Dad's identity.'

'The first rule of investigation is ABC: Assume nothing, Believe nothing, and Challenge everything,' Meadows said.

Rain laughed. 'So your starting point is everyone is lying. They all seemed happy to help us dig the woods.'

'Yeah, but maybe they are too keen. Maybe they want to keep an eye on us to make sure we are not digging in the right spot. Someone led me into the woods and wanted me to find what's there. I also think the flowers were more widespread when I first saw them. Like they are where we found Dad's remains. Someone has removed some of those flowers.'

'Why not take them all?' Rain asked.

'Either they didn't have time, or they want us to dig in a spot they know won't yield anything.'

'You think we are being managed?'

'That's exactly what I think.' Meadows took a notebook from his backpack.

'What are you doing?'

'Writing up notes. I've kept a record of everyone we've talked to and what's been said. Easier to keep track of inconsistencies.'

'You should try and unwind. All this stress is not good for you,' Rain said. He took up the liberation pose. 'I need to cleanse my mind.'

'I'll be quiet,' Meadows said.

'No need, I can zone you out.'

Meadows wrote up his notes and got into bed. Not long after, Rain turned the lamp off and Meadows heard his brother's breathing change rhythm. It felt like he had only closed his eyes when he was awoken by a rustling in the yurt.

'What are you doing?' Meadows asked.

Rain grunted in his sleep. Meadows sat up and saw a figure near the entrance of the tepee.

'Oi!' he shouted. He jumped up from the bed as the figure made its escape. Meadows swayed and the ground seem to move under him. 'Rain! Rain!'

'What?'

'Someone was in here.'

Meadows slipped on his sandals and dashed out of the tepee. He looked around and just caught sight of something moving towards the second field. He heard Rain come out of the tepee as he took off. This time the figure moved down the field in the opposite direction of the woods. Meadows gave chase, through the orchard, the raised beds, and into the polytunnel. It was stifling inside, and the heady scent of the various plants filled the air.

'What do you want?' he called out.

There was silence. Tables ran the length of both sides of the tunnel. Meadows moved along slowly looking under each one. A noise behind him made him jump, he spun around but it was only Rain holding a torch and panting.

'There's someone in here,' Meadows said.

'OK, I'll stay here at the entrance, and you take the torch,' Rain said.

Meadows searched under all the tables but there was no one hiding.

'Are you sure they came in here?' Rain asked.

'Yeah.'

'There must be another way out,' Rain said. 'Probably lifted the plastic and crawled underneath.'

Meadows nodded. He could feel sweat trickling down his back, his heart was racing, and he felt like there wasn't enough oxygen in the air. He tried to draw in breath, he felt like he was suffocating. He needed to get out. He moved forward but lost his balance. He crashed into one of the tables knocking the plants to the floor.

'Win.' Rain grabbed him under the arm. 'Let's get you out of here.'

Meadows shone the torch on the floor. 'The plants.'

'Never mind about the bloody plants,' Rain said.

'No, look, they're sweet violets. Cosmo's growing more of them.'

Chapter Eighteen

It was another hot morning and Iggy was fed up. The heat was making him irritable, and he had to fight hard against snapping at people. It wasn't who he was. He was known for being the cheerful one, always optimistic, but ever since the remains were found a week ago, he felt like a darkness was hovering over him. The world seemed off balance. He just wanted things to go back to normal. He'd built this simple, peaceful life for himself. The outside world with all its problems wasn't supposed to come here, he thought. The last thing he wanted to do today was to go digging in the woods, but it would look odd if he didn't join in. He didn't want to give them any cause to suspect him of having a hand in Kern Meadows' death. Well not Kern Meadows. What a tangle, he thought, shaking his head.

'What's up with you?'

Iggy looked up and saw Mina. 'What are you doing creeping up on people?'

'I'm not creeping,' Mina said. 'I wanted to catch you before you go into the woods with the others.'

'I'm hoping they will forget about me. Digging is not my thing.'

Mina laughed. 'Physical exercise of any sort has never been your thing.' She moved a cat from the deckchair and plonked herself down.

'He was sleeping,' Iggy complained. 'How would you like it if someone dumped you on the floor when you were asleep?' He reached down and stroked the cat.

Mina rolled her eyes. 'You've got more to worry about than an upset cat.'

'What do you mean?'

'Jerome and Cosmo. You know how close those two are. They are going to look after themselves.'

'No, I don't think so,' Iggy said. 'We all look out for each other, like we've always done.'

'Like the way we looked out for Kern? You need to talk to Winter, you told me that—'

'Shush,' Iggy cut in. 'You don't know who is listening.'

'There's no one around,' Mina said.

'I told you those things when I was drunk. It was just a load of nonsense. Besides, we all agreed we need to protect the boys.'

'They are not boys anymore and what are we protecting them from? They already know about their father.'

'They know about Kern Meadows,' Iggy said. 'Jerome said—'

'Yeah Jerome,' Mina huffed. 'That's what I'm talking about. The only person he's interested in protecting is himself.'

'What's that supposed to mean?'

'Jonah told me things,' Mina said.

'What?'

'It doesn't matter but Kern Meadows wasn't the only one hiding things. Jerome isn't going to protect you.'

Iggy thought about what she was saying. Would Jerome side with Cosmo? I can't go back to prison, he thought. The idea made his skin crawl.

'What do you suggest we do?' Iggy asked.

'We stick together,' Mina said. 'We'll say we were together the night of the summer solstice.'

She has no idea how much I would like that to be true, Iggy thought.

'You already told Winter you saw Jonah coming out of the woods.'

'Yes, and I told him I'd just gone for a pee. I left you, saw Jonah, then came straight back. Right?'

'So, what am I going to say to Winter?'

'That's up to you.'

'I think I'd rather not say anything. What if it was Jonah that Winter saw in the woods two nights ago?'

'Then you're all screwed,' Mina said. 'Jerome said he found Winter by the old sycamore tree. Why would Jonah lead him there? If it was Jonah.'

'I don't know but Jerome says we should go with Winter. Make sure he stays there digging. Once he sees there is nothing there, he'll stop asking questions.'

'He's never going to stop,' Mina said. 'I wish things would just go back to the way they were before.'

'Well, things can never be the same now,' Iggy said.

'I guess not.' Mina stood up. 'Just think about what I said.'

Iggy watched Mina walk away. He didn't want to believe that Jerome could be that selfish. Mina was up to something, he was sure of it. When Jerome and Cosmo had been searching the woods for Winter, he'd seen a light on in the distilling shed. Only Mina used that place. It's where she made her oils and tonics. What was she doing there in the middle of the night? he wondered. Clearly it wasn't only Jerome that had something to hide. Now he didn't know who he could trust.

Chapter Nineteen

Bright sunlight streaming into the tepee awoke Meadows. Pain seemed to go through his eyes and into the depth of his head.

'Shut the door,' he said.

'What time do you call this to wake up?'

'Edris?' Meadows sat up and the pounding in his head increased. 'What are you doing here?'

'Come to see you. Are you OK? You look… well… rough.'

'Yeah.' Meadows ran his hands over his face. He could no longer feel stubble, now it was a prickly beard. 'Caught a virus.'

'That's why I never go camping. Too many germs,' Edris said.

'We're not camping,' Rain grumbled from his bed.

'What time is it?' Meadows asked.

'Ten-thirty,' Edris said.

'Oh hell. I wanted to get up early.'

'Doesn't matter,' Edris said. 'You're on holiday.'

'I've tried telling him that. It doesn't work.' Rain sat up in bed, looked at Edris and ran his hand through his hair. 'I don't think we've met.'

'Tristan Edris.' Edris held out his hand. 'You can just call me Edris. Everyone else does. You must be Rain. You look just like your brother.'

'Yeah, just better-looking,' Rain said.

'So is this a social visit?' Meadows asked.

'Erm, officially I'm on duty. Blackwell has me checking out all the communes looking for this Jonah guy. I'm on my way to North Wales. Unofficially I'm just visiting a friend.'

Meadows smiled. 'Meaning you have some information for me.'

'I'll give you a chance to get yourself together then we can have a chat,' Edris said. 'I've brought a towel, so I'll go and dip my feet in the stream.'

'Go ahead, we'll be right behind you,' Meadows said.

'He's hot,' Rain said.

Meadows rolled his eyes. 'Behave yourself.'

'What? I'm just saying. No harm in admiring, and perhaps a little flirting.'

Meadows laughed. 'Flirt all you want. You won't get anywhere.'

'Damn shame,' Rain said. 'Still, just as well if I look as bad as I feel. I think I'm going to have enough problems getting out of bed let alone digging in the woods.'

'I'd like to say the mind is willing, but the body is weak, but not even the mind is willing,' Meadows said. 'I don't think we're the only ones not wanting to dig given that no one has bothered to wake us up.'

'So much for Mina's tonic,' Rain said.

'I've still got some paracetamol somewhere.' Meadows rummaged around and found a packet in his backpack. He popped two and handed the rest to Rain. 'Stay in bed if you like. I'll go and talk to Edris.'

'Nah, I'll come with you. A dip in the cold water will do me good.'

Meadows pulled on a pair of shorts and a T-shirt and grabbed his sunglasses and a bottle of water. There was the usual activity in the commune. Children running around, repairs being made to the shower cubicles, and water being carried. People seemed to be talking too loudly and it echoed around Meadows' head.

'I hope it's quiet by the stream,' Rain said. 'I can't stand the noise today.'

Edris had chosen a place downstream where he sat alone with his feet dangling in the water.

'Enjoying that, are you?' Meadows asked.

'Yeah, I could stay here all day, but I haven't got long.'

'I appreciate you coming to see us.' Meadows sat down next to Edris.

Rain jumped into the water and sat down so it ran over his back and around his waist.

'How are things going with the investigation?' Meadows asked. He didn't want to put Edris on the spot by asking specific questions.

'Honestly, not great. I can't wait until you can come back to work. Blackwell is driving me mad. Paskin has only been back a couple of days and she already looks like she needs another holiday.'

Meadows laughed. 'He's not that bad.'

Edris raised his eyebrows. 'Anyway, the truth is we are not getting anywhere. We've been searching for Kern Meadows, the real one that is. We've checked his prison records. Looks like he kept his head down. Stayed out of trouble and served his time. He was moved around a lot. Only one visitor the whole time he was inside. Lee Morris.'

'The one in the car crash with him?' Rain asked.

'Yeah,' Edris said. 'We thought that would be a good lead, but it turns out that he's also dropped off the grid. No social media accounts, not on the electoral roll. There's something odd going on here.'

'What about Steven Parry?' Meadows asked.

'That's what I mean by odd. Same thing. Not a trace. There was an assault charge against him in the early nineties. He didn't serve time, but did community service.

He was squatting at the time. A charge for possession, then nothing, no trace.'

'And I expect you'll find it's the same for Jonah,' Meadows said.

'That's worse because we don't even have a starting point. No surname. All we've got is the old photograph you gave us to show around. Chris from tech has the original. He's using some sort of programme to see if he can get a match to anyone on the PNC and Paskin is looking at everyone that served time with Kern Meadows.'

'Has Blackwell said anything about searching the woods?' Meadows asked.

'He doesn't think it's worth it,' Edris said.

'Well, we do,' Rain said.

'There was someone in our tepee again last night,' Meadows said. 'We followed them down to the polytunnel, but we didn't catch up with them. I'm sure they are trying to tell us something.'

'Then why not just talk to you or leave a note?' Edris asked.

'I guess they want to remain anonymous,' Meadows said.

'I walked around the commune after, there was no sign of anyone going back to their homes. I think it's an outsider,' Rain said.

'You better tell Blackwell,' Edris said. 'There's one more thing. Jerome Gwyn.'

'Don't tell me, he has a record,' Meadows said.

'No. Well, yes. It's complicated. We had a hit on his name, but we couldn't access the file. Then Blackwell gets called in by Lester. He was asked why we are looking at Jerome and if he was a suspect in the case. So Blackwell explains we are looking at everyone connected to the commune but there is nothing to tie Jerome to the murder. He's told to leave it alone. The order coming from higher up. That's all we know.'

'What does that mean?' Rain asked.

'Possibly a new identity,' Meadows said. 'Either witness protection or because his crime was so serious that he would be at high risk of a revenge attack. Not many are granted an anonymity order.'

'So Jerome and the fake Kern Meadows have either done something so heinous they had to have new identities, or they witnessed something,' Rain said.

'I don't know about the fake Kern Meadows,' Edris said. 'If it was a new identity the name would've been checked carefully to make sure there were no ties to criminal activity.'

'Yeah, I think you're right,' Meadows said. 'Still I think our father must have done something serious to be concealing his identity.'

'Well whatever Jerome has done we're not going to find out unless…' Edris looked at Meadows.

'I ask him,' Meadows said.

Meadows thought for a moment. 'So if Jonah interfered and brought Steven Parry to the commune to confront Kern, he would've been forced to confess his true identity. So he… oh, I don't know. You'd think his first instinct would be to run.'

'Or kill Steven Parry,' Edris said.

'And bury him in the woods,' Meadows said.

'If there is another body in the woods,' Edris said.

'We don't know that Steven Parry is dead. What we need to be asking is who killed the fake Kern?' Rain said.

'Jerome,' Edris said.

Meadows shook his head. 'Why would Jerome kill Kern? They were best friends.'

'Exactly,' Edris said. 'We don't know who Jerome really is or what he did in the past. I'm betting fake Kern knew. It's too much of a coincidence that both men have hidden identities. They have to be connected by more than friendship. A crime perhaps, but only Jerome was granted anonymity. Fake Kern's identity being revealed could have blown Jerome's cover. They both kill Steven Parry, then Jerome kills fake Kern as he became a liability.'

'Good theory but I can't see either of them killing a man,' Meadows said. 'Then again my father did keep his identity secret all these years and Jerome is hiding something. The thing is, I have never seen Jerome violent; I don't think I've heard him raise his voice. We've known him all our lives.'

'He could have just snapped,' Edris said.

'What about Jonah?' Meadows asked. 'He would know if Steven Parry came to the commune and if he didn't leave alive. He may know who killed our father and is hiding.'

'So it could be him creeping around our tepee and the woods,' Rain said. 'He hears about the discovery in the woods and wants to point you in the right direction.'

'It's possible. It was dark, so whoever it was could've attacked me,' Meadows said. 'That clearly wasn't their intention. I'm still sure there is something in the woods. There are only a few of the violets left in that place in the woods now. It's like they are marking the spot. Then we were led to more violets last night. They must be leading us to something.'

'Or someone is playing a sick game,' Rain said. 'Trying to distract you.'

'So what are you going to do?' Edris asked.

'Speak to Jerome then we start digging,' Meadows said.

'I better get going,' Edris said. He pulled his feet from the water.

'We'll walk back with you,' Meadows said.

The three of them walked to the bottom of the track where they waved off Edris.

'I bet you wish you were going with him,' Rain said.

'Yeah, it feels odd being on the outside of the investigation. At least we are not completely in the dark.'

'Yeah, it was good of him to come and give us the info.'

'And risky,' Meadows said. 'We may as well start digging. There's not much else we can do.'

Rain groaned. 'If we must.'

'Even if we don't find anything it will satisfy my curiosity,' Meadows said. 'We'll go and find Jerome first. See if he will speak to us about his past.'

'I doubt it,' Rain said. 'You're better off speaking to him alone. You're his favourite.'

'I'm not,' Meadows said.

'I don't mind, you've spent the most time with him.'

'That's what makes all of this harder.'

They reached the pagoda and found Jenny setting up for lessons. 'I thought you two were going to play around in the woods this morning,' she said.

'We got delayed,' Rain said.

'Maybe it's a sign,' Jenny said. 'It's too hot for manual labour and you've both been ill.'

'I'm used to working in the heat,' Rain said.

'You may be, but Jerome, Iggy, and Cosmo are too old for all that.'

She's right, Meadows thought. 'We don't expect them to dig,' he said. 'They'll probably stand around telling us how we should be doing the job. Have you seen them this morning?'

'Iggy was sitting outside his caravan, I saw Cosmo going off to water his plants, and I haven't seen Jerome.'

'Maybe he's hiding indoors to get out of the trip to the woods,' Meadows said. 'I'll give him a shout.'

Jenny turned to Rain. 'While he's doing that can you give me a hand? I need to get some jugs of water and glasses for the children.'

'I remember you teaching me,' Rain said as they walked along. 'You used to scare the shit out of me.'

'Good. You were a little sod, couldn't stay still for a minute.'

'Now it's a job to get him moving he's so laid back,' Meadows said.

They reached Jerome's yurt and Meadows stopped. 'I'll see you back by the pagoda. Jerome!' he called out. There was no answer. 'Jerome, are you still sleeping?' He pulled open the door.

The first thing that hit him was the acrid smell of vomit, then he saw Jerome. He was lying naked just inside the door. His eyes wide and mouth gaping. One arm was stretched out as if he had been trying to reach the door.

'No!' Meadows cried out. He reached down to touch Jerome but stopped himself. He didn't need to feel for a pulse. He'd seen enough death to know. He backed out of the yurt and crashed into Jenny.

'What's happened? I heard you shout.'

Meadows turned around and did his best to block Jenny's view. Rain was standing behind her. 'I'm so sorry,' Meadows said.

'No!' Jenny tried to push past him.

'You can't go in there,' Meadows said.

'You don't tell me what I can do,' Jenny shouted.

'Please,' Meadows said. 'We need to call the police. He'll have to be examined so the fewer people that go inside the better.'

'Who would do this?' Jenny asked.

Meadows shook his head. 'He may have been unwell and just died in the night.' He didn't believe his own words, but he needed to calm Jenny. 'You'll get a chance to see him but not now.'

'Come on.' Rain put his hands on Jenny's shoulders. 'I'll take you to Iggy. Let Winter deal with this.'

Jenny shrugged away Rain's hand. 'This is your fault,' she said. 'You couldn't leave things alone. I'll never forgive you.' She stormed away.

Chapter Twenty

The peace of the commune had been shattered. There were police everywhere, their faces red and patience short in the heat. They asked questions and scribbled in notebooks. Forensic officers were in Jerome's yurt and, all around, members of the commune stood in groups crying.

The mercury had broken Wales' heat record and Jenny felt like her heart had shattered into a thousand pieces and would never be whole again. It didn't seem right to her that the sun beat down from a cloudless sky whilst strangers examined Jerome's body. It should be raining, she thought. The wind howling and the cold stinging your face. That's what she wanted, to be soaked to the skin and freezing to numb the pain. This wasn't supposed to happen. Jerome was the one that held them all together. She felt the heavy ball of grief just below her ribs. She knew what it was as she had felt it when her son died, and then with the loss of Mags. It will spread and consume me, she thought. It was Jerome that brought her back to life those times, now he wasn't here to help. It was all coming back, the smoky darkness that swilled around her mind and seemed to be in the air she breathed, always present.

Iggy sat down next to her, his face was red and his eyes puffy from the tears.

'Did you find Cosmo?' she asked.

'No,' Iggy said. 'He'll come back.'

'He was in such a state,' Jenny said. 'He can't deal with it.'

'Yes, he can.' Iggy covered her hand with his own and gave it a gentle squeeze. 'He'll deal with it in his own way.'

'I don't know. He was throwing things around and shouting before he ran off.'

'It's just his way of expressing his feelings. Better he lets out the grief.'

'What are we going to do?' Jenny asked.

'I don't know. Jerome left a letter with me to give to Winter when he died. I just didn't expect it so soon.'

'Don't give it to him,' Jenny said.

'I promised.'

'When was this?'

'A while ago,' Iggy said.

'Where is it?'

'It's safe with my solicitor.'

'You have a solicitor?'

'Well, yes, there is no one to carry out my wishes when I go. I have his details in my caravan so whoever has to sort through my stuff will find them. Do you think I should tell Winter about the letter?'

'Not yet. We don't know what's in it. Maybe he wanted a clean conscience when he died.'

'Do you think that's what happened?' Iggy asked. 'That would mean…'

'Yeah, you, me, Cosmo, or Mina,' Jenny said.

'I would never hurt Jerome or any of you,' Iggy said.

'That's what you would say,' Jenny said. 'I can't be certain that I can trust you or the others.'

'I could say the same about you,' Iggy said. 'You're the one that knew Jerome the best. You're the one he confided in.'

'Do you see my point, Ig?' Jenny looked at him and saw uncertainty in his eyes.

'Mina has been acting strange. I saw… oh, never mind.'

'What did you see?'

'Nothing, it doesn't matter,' Iggy said.

'Do you want to be next?' Jenny asked. 'You can't just blurt things out without explaining. Now it sounds like you know something.'

'Well I don't,' Iggy said. 'We don't know that someone is responsible for Jerome's death. He could have just died in his sleep.'

Jenny wished she hadn't put ideas of mistrust into Iggy's mind. Now she would never find out what Mina was up to. Mina was the only one she couldn't be sure of. She wished she didn't have to play this game.

'I'm sorry, Iggy,' she said. 'I don't know where my mind is.'

'It's OK. You've had a shock. We all have. I still can't believe it. Look, the boys are coming. This must be awful for them, first their father and now this.'

Jenny looked up and saw Rain and Meadows walking towards them. 'They're not boys anymore,' Jenny said. She didn't feel like talking to them, but it would look odd if she took off now.

'How are you two holding up?' Meadows asked.

'To be honest I feel dazed,' Iggy said.

'The police will want to talk to the two of you,' Meadows said. 'If there is anything you know, please tell them.'

Jenny didn't say anything. She looked at Iggy who shook his head.

'If you don't want to talk to the police you can talk to me,' Meadows said.

'It's the same thing,' Jenny said then instantly regretted it. 'We don't know anything.'

'Do you think that someone killed him?' Iggy asked.

'We won't know until after the post-mortem,' Meadows said. 'If it's any consolation I didn't see any marks on him, so I don't think he was attacked.'

'He went back with you last night,' Iggy said. 'Did he say he was feeling unwell?'

'No,' Rain said. 'He stayed for a while, had a drink with us then went off. He just said he was tired.'

'Earlier you said it was my fault Jerome had died. Why did you say that?' Meadows asked.

Jenny could see the hurt in his eyes. 'It was just the shock. I'm sorry, I didn't mean it.' But it is your fault, she thought. Both of them had caused Jerome's death, they just didn't know it.

Chapter Twenty-one

Meadows watched the activity around Jerome's yurt. Blackwell was giving out orders to Valentine, and Edris who had been called back. Uniform were walking around collecting information and Daisy was inside examining Jerome.

It felt odd being on the outside watching his team at work. He wanted to be part of the investigation, the one asking the questions. There was a gnawing pain just below his ribs, he tried to ignore it, block out the pain of what had happened, but all he could think of was Jerome lying on the floor. He wondered if he had cried out for help during the night and no one came. This felt so much worse than when he had discovered his father's death. There hadn't been a relationship for so long. With Jerome it was different. He'd been a constant in his life, always there. Meadows couldn't imagine life without him, the commune wouldn't be the same.

Blackwell hadn't said much when he arrived, he just glanced his way now and again. Mike from forensics had offered his condolences on the death of his father and his friend and talked for a few moments. Everyone else on the scene had acknowledged him but said very little. He guessed it must be as awkward for them as it was for him. He'd spoken briefly to Iggy and Jenny. Cosmo had run off somewhere and he suspected that Mina was in her yurt, hiding with her grief. All he could do now was sit and look at the scorched grass and hope he heard some snippet of information.

Finally Blackwell approached him. 'Can we talk?'

'Yeah, of course,' Meadows said.

'I am sorry about Jerome,' Blackwell said. 'I know you were fond of him.'

'Thank you.'

'Where is Rain? I will need to speak to him.'

'He took a group of children to the stream. Thought it best to keep them out of the way.'

'Probably a good idea,' Blackwell said. 'So you were the one to find the body.'

It felt odd to refer to Jerome as "the body" it was like he was already being depersonalized. Meadows nodded.

'I shouldn't have to ask you if you touched anything.'

'No I didn't but I've been inside his yurt on numerous occasions. As you'll find so have most of us.'

'When was the last time you saw him?'

'Last night. He came to my place for a chat before going to bed.'

'Just you and him?'

'No, Rain was with us.'

'What time was this?'

'About ten.'

'What did you talk about?' Blackwell asked.

'Just about everything that's been going on and how he met my father.'

'Did he tell you anything of interest?'

'No, not really. They met volunteering for a homeless project. Dad came to help him work here and stayed. Before you ask, no he didn't know him by any other name.'

'Did you get the impression he was lying?'

Meadows thought for a moment. 'I think he knew more than he was telling me, I would say more evasive than lying.'

'Did he seem worried? Depressed? Say anything that in hindsight may have been a warning sign?'

'No, nothing like that. He was just tired. I thought he didn't look well but none have us have been feeling that good. There's a few people gone down with a virus in the commune, including me and Rain. I thought Jerome was going down with it or it was just the heat.'

'Did you see or hear anything out of the ordinary last night?'

Meadows told him about the intruder and the polytunnel.

'Did you get a good look? Was it male or female?'

'It was dark,' Meadows said, 'and I had just woken up. It was not a small person. That's the second time someone has been creeping around.'

'And it's this Cosmo character who grows these plants you say are used to mark graves?'

'Well they're not only for graves. People have them in their gardens. Still, you can't ignore the fact that some believe they bring peace in the afterlife.'

'So maybe he was growing them ready for Jerome.'

'No, I don't see it. Cosmo and Jerome are very close. He reacted badly when he heard the news. Besides, Cosmo is small. I'm fairly certain it wasn't him.'

'OK, but this person could've been in Jerome's yurt,' Blackwell said.

'I guess so, before they came to me, but not after. Rain checked all around the commune. I stayed outside watching. No one came back. I should've checked on Jerome and the others,' Meadows said.

'You weren't to know,' Blackwell said.

'So what's the initial impression? Natural causes? He was in his seventies. Or do you suspect foul play?'

Blackwell was thoughtful for a moment and Meadows thought he wasn't going to answer.

'I'm not sure,' Blackwell said. 'As you saw, he wasn't in bed, he'd been violently sick and looked like he was trying to get help. We'll have to wait for the post-mortem but given the recent discovery of the remains and other information that I can't share, I will be treating his death as suspicious.'

'Maybe now would be a good time to search the woods,' Meadows said.

'And what exactly would I be looking for?' Blackwell asked.

'Steven Parry, Kern Meadows, Lee Morris, and Jonah are all missing. I think there's more going on than just the remains that were found.'

'Who says all these men are missing?' Blackwell asked.

'Well, you haven't found them,' Meadows said.

'And you think they are all buried in the woods.' Blackwell shook his head. 'I think the heat is getting to you.'

'I didn't say they are all in the woods, but I think there's something to be found there.'

'Yes, because of the flowers.'

Meadows didn't like the sarcasm in Blackwell's voice. 'The same flowers that were found with my father's remains and the fact that someone led me to that particular spot in the woods. The flowers are nowhere else that I've seen. That and the fact that none of these men have been seen for years. You must admit that something isn't right.'

'Yeah, remains found in the woods and now a suspicious death, but that's not a good enough reason to search the woods. I can't waste valuable resources because of some bloody flowers,' Blackwell said. 'Unless of course there is something you're not telling me.'

'No, I've told you everything I know but one of the missing men might have information.'

'I think there are people here that know what happened,' Blackwell said. 'I'll be starting with them.'

Meadows noticed that Valentine and Iggy were walking towards them. Iggy was mopping his brow with a handkerchief, in the other hand he carried a mobile phone. It was the first time Meadows had ever seen Iggy with a phone. Most people on the commune had them but as the signal was sporadic, few carried them.

'You found him, good,' Blackwell said. 'Take him to the station, I'll be there as soon as I can. Take Edris with you.'

'Why are you taking in Iggy?' Meadows asked.

'It's OK,' Iggy said. 'I've got nothing to hide. Look after the others, especially Cosmo, he's taking it badly. Oh and if I'm gone a while, feed my cats.' He turned to Valentine. 'Come on then, lovely, let's go and find this lad and get on our way.'

Meadows watched them walk away then turned to Blackwell. 'Why Iggy? He wouldn't hurt anyone.'

'Are you sure about that?' Blackwell asked. 'Did he tell you about his past? Or his name? Tobias Ignatius Sealy.'

'No.'

'Clearly you don't know these people at all,' Blackwell said and walked away.

Meadows could feel anger mixing with his grief. The feelings of frustration of not knowing the facts and being unable to help those he cared for made him want to throw something. Jenny was right, he thought. Jerome's death was his fault. Someone had been wandering around the commune. If he'd been at home and someone was in his house then the police would have been called, forensics would have been checking for traces of the intruder. Why should it be any different here? Someone had come into his home. Twice. He should have acted.

Meadows walked back to his tepee, took the notebook and pen from his backpack and started writing. When Rain came back from the stream, papers were laid over the floor.

'What's all this?' Rain asked.

'I'm trying to make sense of everything and in the absence of an incident board this is the best I can do.' He pointed to the paper in the centre where he had written "Dad?"'. 'Steven Parry, Lee Morris, and Kern Meadows are all linked.' He pointed to their names listed down one side. On the other side were the names of the olds. 'We know Kern Meadows and Jerome Gwyn had been in prison, now it seems that Iggy also served time.'

'Iggy? What did he do?'

'I don't know, Blackwell wouldn't tell me. We can conclude from the block on Jerome's file that he was given a new identity. Our father also used a false name.'

'Let's just call him fake Kern,' Rain said.

'OK, so they both hide away here. Then along comes Jonah. We know he likes to play games. He gets a kick out of stirring up people's pasts. He went out of his way to track down Jenny's ex-husband. We know that Steven Parry hasn't been seen since 1999, around the same time that fake Kern was murdered. There is a strong possibility that Jonah tracked down Steven and brought him to the commune to confront fake Kern. This could have forced fake Kern to reveal his true identity.'

'Makes sense so far,' Rain said.

'Mina said she saw Jonah coming out of the woods with blood on his clothes. She remembers it well because it was the summer solstice celebrations. Whose blood?'

'It has to be fake Kern's as he was buried in the woods and that evening was the last time he was seen,' Rain said.

'So if Jonah killed fake Kern what happened to Steven Parry?'

'Maybe he was never here,' Rain said.

'OK but we're still down to Jonah being our prime suspect. So what's his motive? Unless Steven killed fake Kern and ran off. Jonah tries to cover it up by burying the body.' Meadows thought for a moment. 'No, I can't see that. Jonah would likely have enjoyed the drama of the police being called. Why would he cover it up if he hadn't killed fake Kern himself? Maybe we should be asking why Jonah took pleasure in uncovering people's pasts.'

'Could be he was looking for someone,' Rain said. 'He wants revenge for something that happened to him or someone close. He plays these games so he can delve into people's histories. Maybe he gets some release for his anger. He pushes the people in the commune because he guesses they are not who they say they are.'

'My thoughts exactly,' Meadows said.

'Yeah, so Jonah brings Steven Parry to the commune and fake Kern reveals his true identity. Jonah kills him because he's the person he's been looking for.'

'That's a good theory,' Meadows said. 'You could've made a good detective.'

'The other possibility is that Steven Parry and Jonah are one and the same. He bides his time and kills fake Kern thinking he is the real Kern Meadows.'

'It's not how Steven's sister, Christine, described him. He was a drug addict, suffered with his mental health. Jonah was a fit confident man from what I remember. No signs of drug abuse. Mina would have noticed if he was an addict. She also said that Jonah had served time. Steven Parry has never been to prison.'

'OK, so Jonah killed fake Kern,' Rain said.

'Seems logical but why did the other olds discount Mina's concerns? Kern was missing the morning after she saw Jonah with blood on his clothes. Why is it that no one has seen or heard from Jonah? Mina said Jonah left the commune the day fake Kern went missing, then he came back. Why would he come back if he had killed Kern?'

'Oh, too many questions, man, my head is starting to spin,' Rain said. 'OK so if you were in charge of this investigation what would you do?'

'I'd be actively searching for Lee Morris, Kern Meadows, Jonah, and Steven Parry. Then there is an intruder in the commune. The witness, namely me, says they were led into the woods where there are the same flowers that were also found with the remains of one unknown male.'

'So you would search the woods on this information.'

'Given the meaning some of the members of the commune place on the plants, yes I would.'

'So why haven't you?' Rain asked.

'Because there's always something stopping us.'

'Something or someone?' Rain asked. 'So, let's go now.'

* * *

They dug in the woods until dark, starting beneath the patch of violets and working their way out in a circle. Then at first light the next morning they started again. They didn't see Cosmo, Iggy, or Jenny but Mina brought them something to eat and topped up their water bottle. She didn't talk much. Meadows could see she was weighed down by grief, her eyes were dull, and she appeared to have aged years since the discovery of Jerome's body.

They had been digging for a few hours and Meadows was beginning to wonder if their efforts were in vain when he spotted discoloration in the soil.

'Hold on,' he said. He knelt down and gently moved the earth with a gloved hand.

'What is it?' Rain asked.

'A bone.'

Chapter Twenty-two

Meadows and Rain watched from behind the cordon as forensics continued the excavation of the bones. Blackwell stood watching the proceedings. Valentine broke away from the group and walked over to Meadows.

'I guess you are tempted to say I told you so,' she said.

Meadows shook his head. 'Blackwell didn't have enough to justify a search. He wants to look like he is doing a good job in my absence. It would have been a huge risk to use resources on my hunch and some flowers. Can you imagine if he had, and the search didn't yield anything?'

'You're too nice,' Valentine said. 'If you hadn't taken the initiative those remains may never have been found.'

'Well someone wanted them found,' Rain said.

'Your tent creeper,' Valentine said.

'Don't call them that,' Rain said. 'I'll never sleep tonight.'

Meadows laughed. 'If they were going to harm you, they would have done it by now. Plenty of opportunity. It's a bit late to be worrying.' He turned to Valentine. 'I take it you let Iggy go. I heard he's back, but I haven't seen him.'

Valentine checked over her shoulder to make sure Blackwell was still occupied. 'We haven't charged him, and we had no reason to hold him. That's all I can tell you, but he does have a connection to the real Kern Meadows. Things might change depending on what we find here. Do you think he could be involved?'

'I don't think so but who knows?' Meadows said.

Blackwell strolled over to the cordon. 'The two of you may as well come and take a look. I owe you that much as you were the ones to find the remains.'

Meadows ducked under the tape and followed Blackwell with Rain and Valentine. The makeshift grave wasn't more than four feet deep, even so Meadows thought it would take a lot of effort to dig it alone. He crouched to look at the bones which were all intact, the victim laying prone. His eyes travelled from the skull downwards.

'Oh,' he said.

'Yeah, that was my thought,' Blackwell said.

'What?' Rain asked.

'No visible plate in the right femur,' Meadows said. He looked at Mike who was collecting samples. 'I take it the plate would've been securely fitted?'

Mike nodded. 'Even if it wasn't, you would see some damage to the bone.'

'So not Kern Meadows, well, the real one,' Blackwell said. 'That's who I would have expected.'

'Steven Parry?' Meadows suggested.

'We collected a DNA sample from Christine Parry when we were trying to identify the first remains that were found. I thought at the time it might have been Parry given what you told me. As soon as we can extract a DNA sample, we'll compare the sample along with dental and medical records.'

'Will you now consider searching the rest of the woods?' Meadows asked.

Blackwell frowned. 'You think there are more bodies buried here?'

'You have four missing men, Jonah, Lee Morris, Steven Parry, and Kern Meadows. Unless you have found one of them.'

'No,' Blackwell said. 'No trace of any of them.'

'One is probably this poor soul. Still leaves three missing,' Meadows said.

'Then there's our father,' Rain said. 'We still don't have a name for him. Could he have been Lee Morris?'

'That would make sense,' Meadows said. 'He would have known Kern Meadows.'

'I guess that's possible. We'll need to get medical records and track down a family member for DNA,' Blackwell said. 'In the meantime we have two unidentified sets of remains and Jerome Gwyn lying in the morgue. What the hell do you think is going on here? I thought this was supposed to be some loved-up hippy camp. Peace Valley, my arse. It looks like a bunch of ex-cons killing each other off, or one of this lot' – he threw is arm in the direction of the commune – 'is a serial killer.'

Meadows didn't know what to say. It wasn't the place he thought it to be. The place he grew up surrounded by love, where people respected each other.

'I don't have any answers for you,' he said. 'It does look like this has something to do with the car crash, or maybe something more sinister they were all involved with.' He expected Blackwell to say something about Jerome, but he made no comment. If he brought up the subject he would risk getting Edris into trouble. 'I don't have any good reason to believe there's more to be found here but unless we look, we can't be sure.'

'We? Oh I don't think so,' Blackwell said. 'You've already done enough. I'll take what I have to Lester, it will be up to him to authorize a thorough search.'

'I don't suppose you have Jerome's post-mortem results?' Meadows asked.

'I am expecting the results soon, but you know I can't discuss the details with you.'

'I understand that,' Meadows said. 'At the very least I would like to know if it was natural causes or foul play.'

Blackwell nodded. 'We are trying to trace his next of kin.'

'I can't help you with that. He mentioned a family but said they were estranged.'

'I bet he did.'

'What do you mean by that?' Rain asked.

'Jerome Gwyn isn't who you thought he was. That's all I can tell you. I think it's best the two of you go home now and let us do our job. And I would appreciate it if you stayed out of the woods.'

'OK,' Meadows said. He knew he wouldn't get any more information from Blackwell. He was grateful that he had been allowed to see the uncovered remains.

'What now?' Rain asked as they walked out of the woods.

'I don't know. It's clear Jerome must have done something bad in the past but we're not likely to find out anytime soon.'

'Yeah, but I can't see Jerome killing two people,' Rain said. 'I never saw him lose his temper or even raise his voice.'

'No,' Meadows agreed, 'and if Jerome is the killer, then who killed him? That's if someone did. The danger is that without another explanation Jerome could well end up taking the blame whether he is innocent or not. He's not here to defend himself. He'll be judged on his past deeds.'

'Well being given a new identity means he must've done something serious,' Rain said. 'Then there's Blackwell's talk of a serial killer.'

'I can't see Jerome as a cold-blooded killer, but maybe my judgement is clouded,' Meadows said.

'Don't be so hard on yourself,' Rain said. 'Let's go back to your makeshift incident board. Smoke a few joints, which will help you think, and I'm sure you'll come up with something.'

Meadows laughed. 'If only getting stoned would solve everything.'

'Maybe not but it will make you feel better.'

'I want to find Cosmo first, ask him about the plants in the polytunnel. Then I think we should talk to Iggy. He's been avoiding us.' Meadows' phone trilled. He took it out of his pocket and looked at the screen. 'Edris,' he said before answering.

'Can you talk?' Edris asked.

'Yeah, it's just me and Rain.'

'Good,' Edris said. 'Can you meet me somewhere? I don't want to come to you and risk running into Blackwell.'

'I could meet you at my cottage or I could come to your place,' Meadows said.

'Your place is probably best. I'll get Daisy to meet us there.'

'Daisy? Is everything alright?'

'Yeah, yeah, I just don't want to do this over the phone and Daisy has some info for you. I'll explain when you get there. See you in about an hour.' Edris hung up.

'That didn't sound good,' Rain said.

'No, if Daisy is involved then I'm guessing it's the post-mortem result.'

'Wouldn't she have called you herself?'

'I did tell her not to share information, I don't want to get her into trouble. Edris could've given the news to me on his own. Unless Jerome was poisoned in which case we are going to fall under suspicion as we were the last ones to see him or – actually I don't have an "or".'

* * *

They had only been in the cottage for a few minutes when Edris turned up.

'You look a bit better today,' Edris said.

175

'Yeah, I feel a lot better,' Meadows said. 'While I'm here I'm going to take a shower and get this beard off.' He noticed Edris had two files in his hand. 'You got something for me?'

'Yeah, shall we wait for Daisy?'

'I'm sure you can explain,' Meadows said.

'She's just good with the details,' Edris said.

Meadows thought that Edris looked uncomfortable. 'Let's go into the sitting room. It's cooler there. Something to be said about old stone walls.'

Edris sat in the armchair and Meadows on the sofa. Rain handed Edris a drink then sat cross-legged on the floor.

'So what have you got for us?' Meadows asked.

'As much as I can. Blackwell's beady eyes are watching everything I do. Lucky for us he's occupied in the woods. As you already know we found Iggy's identity and he has a prison record. Tobias Ignatius Sealy. The guy is minted and titled.'

'Really?' Rain asked. 'I know he has a posh accent, but he carves out bits of wood to sell for a living. Not to mention that battered caravan he lives in.'

'He's the son of Lord Robert Sealy,' Edris said. 'Sole beneficiary to his father's estate. Added to that he already had a trust fund left by his grandfather which matured when he was twenty-five. Part of the reason we held him so long yesterday was that we had to wait for his lawyer, or I should say a team of lawyers, to turn up. As you can imagine he grew up privileged. Went to boarding school then on to Cambridge University studying physics. Clever bugger. During his time there he got involved with a group of animal rights activists.'

'I can see that of Iggy,' Meadows said.

'He attended a lot of protests and had some minor charges for criminal damage. He got off. No doubt daddy paid to keep him out of prison. Then the group took things a bit further. They started targeting laboratories,

176

letting animals out, smashing up things. Then one night they blew one up. A security guard was caught in the explosion and died. Iggy was charged with manslaughter and served five and a half years.'

'Shit,' Rain said. 'I can't imagine Iggy in prison.'

'We've looked at his prison records. He didn't have an easy time. He was a target I suppose. Because of that he ended up moving around a lot. At some point he would have been inside at the same time and same prison as Kern Meadows and Jerome Gwyn. We're not certain that they were placed on the same wing. We're still looking into it.'

'So he could well have known the real Kern Meadows and the identity of Jerome Gwyn.'

Edris nodded. 'What we do know is that they were all released around about the same time, within months of each other, and stayed at the same halfway house.'

'So what did he have to say about that?' Rain asked.

'Not a lot. He said he didn't mix with the other residents, and we have no proof. We challenged him on the fact that he ended up in the same commune as Jerome Gwyn. That's where his lawyers stepped in. They weren't messing about. We had nothing on him. So we were told that he had answered our questions and any more should be addressed to them in the future. I thought Blackwell was going to burst a blood vessel.'

'Even if Iggy did know Jerome's true identity and the real Kern Meadows he would have no reason to harm them,' Meadows said. 'It would be the other way around.'

'Why not tell us that our father wasn't Kern Meadows?' Rain asked. 'It would have saved us a lot of stress and the police a lot of time.'

'Maybe he didn't want us to know his part in the lie,' Meadows said. 'In his own way he may have thought he was protecting us.'

'Yeah, but from what?' Rain asked.

Edris shifted in his seat. 'This is where it gets complicated. You remember I told you that information on Jerome Gwyn was blocked? Well now he's dead we've been granted access to the file. His real name is Phillip Carew. He was convicted at the age of eleven for murdering eight-year-old Craig Wilson.'

Rain shook his head. 'Jerome? I don't believe it. He was such a gentle soul.'

The name Craig Wilson stirred something in Meadows' memory, but he couldn't grasp it. Before he had a chance to ask any questions the door opened, and Daisy walked in.

'Sorry I'm late,' she said. 'Bloody traffic with everyone either coming from or going to the beach.' She looked at Edris. 'Have you—'

'Not yet,' Edris cut in.

'What?' Meadows asked.

'I've completed the post-mortem on Jerome Gwyn, and he's not, well, he's not Jerome Gwyn, or who Jerome Gwyn is supposed to be.'

Chapter Twenty-three

Iggy crept out of the caravan and looked in both directions. There was no one about. He wanted to get to Mina's yurt without being seen. So far he had managed to avoid everyone on the commune so there had been no questions. He knew they would come. Everyone had seen him being taken away by the police. Now shame covered his body like a prickly heat rash.

Mina's yurt was further down the field, and he moved quickly, keeping his eyes fixed ahead. He made it without seeing anyone and called out.

'Come in,' Mina called back.

Iggy opened the door and found Mina sitting with Cosmo and Jenny. 'Oh,' he squeaked and backed away.

'Don't be silly, Iggy,' Jenny said. 'Come in and sit down.'

Iggy closed the door and sat on a cushion next to Mina.

'You OK, Ig?' Mina asked.

'No, everyone is talking about me. They'll think I killed Kern.'

'No one th-thinks that,' Cosmo said.

'What did the police say?' Jenny asked.

'Just asked a lot of questions about Kern and Jerome,' Iggy said.

'Why did they want to talk to you?' Jenny asked. 'Why not one of us?'

Iggy looked at Mina. 'What does it matter now? Everyone is going to find out. It's because I did time.'

'Yes, but a long time ago surely,' Mina said. 'You've been here as long as me.'

Iggy was relieved that she didn't look angry or disappointed. The truth was that he always liked Mina. He would have liked it if they were more than friends, but she was too good for him, he thought.

'What were you in f-for?' Cosmo asked.

'What does it matter?' Jenny said. 'It's none of our business. What's important is what we do now.'

'What is there to do?' Iggy asked. 'The police know about Kern and if they don't know now about Jerome they soon will.'

'They're going to come for me,' Cosmo said and jumped up. 'I have to… to… go. Leave.'

'Calm down,' Jenny said. 'They're not going to come for you. Even if they do, it will only be to ask questions.'

'They'll know.'

'How can they possibly know?' Jenny said.

'Know what?' Mina asked.

Cosmo looked from Mina to Jenny.

'Nothing,' Jenny said. 'We've all run from something in the past.'

'Enough of this,' Iggy said. 'Mina knows.'

Cosmo turned to Iggy. 'What! Why the f-fuck would you tell her? It's none… not… argh…' He hit his head with his fist.

'Alright, matey, there's no need to get angry,' Iggy said. 'I had a few to drink and I had to talk to someone. After the remains were dug up, I didn't know what to do. Jerome, well, I didn't bloody know. He said it was all sorted. I never thought…'

'None of us did,' Jenny said. 'You just have to keep calm, Cosmo. Everything will be alright.'

'Will it?' Mina asked. 'What I want to know is who they've dug up by the old sycamore tree.'

'What?' Iggy couldn't believe what he had just heard.

'If you hadn't been hiding out in your caravan you would've heard,' Jenny said. 'Winter and Rain found... well, bones. Early this morning.'

'So Winter was right. Someone was leading him to the woods to show him.' Iggy looked at each of them in turn.

'Well, it wasn't me,' Cosmo said. 'I was with Jerome.'

'Don't look at me,' Jenny said.

'It has to be one of you,' Mina said. 'Which means you also put the body in the ground in the first place.'

An uncomfortable silence fell. Iggy had a good idea of who was found. What he couldn't understand was what he was doing in that part of the woods.

Chapter Twenty-four

'You mean Jerome is Phillip Carew,' Rain said. 'Edris just told us that.'

'That's not what I mean,' Daisy said. She sat down on the arm of Meadows' chair and took his hand in hers. 'Jerome had a plate fitted in his right femur, that and the other injuries–'

'Show that he's Kern Meadows,' Meadows finished for her.

'Well that's a turn up,' Rain said.

'I had already requested Jerome's medical and dental records or rather Phillip Carew's,' Daisy said. 'I checked them against the remains that were discovered, those of your father. They are the same.'

Meadows saw the same look of shock on Rain's face that he knew must be showing on his own. Death by reckless driving was one thing but a child killer, a child that had murdered another child...

'I'm sorry,' Daisy said. 'There's no doubt. It must be an awful shock for the two of you.'

'This is why I didn't want to do this over the phone,' Edris said.

'Does Blackwell know?' Meadows asked.

'No, not yet,' Daisy said. 'I tried to call him with the results, but his phone went straight to voicemail.'

'He wouldn't have reception in the woods,' Rain said.

'I called Edris,' Daisy said.

'I couldn't leave you in the dark,' Edris said. 'I spoke to Lester and told him the situation. He agreed that I should be the one to tell you about Phillip Carew.'

'Blackwell is not going to like you going over his head,' Meadows said.

'Screw Blackwell,' Edris said. 'Actually, at first Lester wanted to speak to you himself, but I thought, well, as we're partners... I hope you don't mind. I expect he will contact you.'

Meadows nodded. 'Thank you.'

'Why did Kern and Jerome swap identities?' Rain asked.

'Good question,' Meadows said. 'We also have to ask ourselves what else Jerome lied about.'

'We're talking about the fake Jerome now?' Edris asked. 'I can't get my head around it.'

'Tell me about it,' Rain said.

'Let's just call them by the names they were using,' Meadows said, 'or we'll all get confused.'

'Maybe that's why they swapped identities,' Edris said. 'To cause confusion.'

'Yeah, but who did they want to deceive?' Meadows asked. 'When I think about it, they did look similar. Both dark hair, tall, and trim. I guess it wouldn't have been difficult to step into each other's shoes.'

'There's more I need to tell you,' Daisy said. 'Without overcomplicating things, it appears that Jerome was poisoned.'

'With what?' Meadows asked.

Daisy shrugged. 'I ran the initial tox screen. It came back negative for alcohol and the usual drugs. Now we have to look at rarer poisons. Despite his age he was in good health. Whatever he took stopped his heart. There are other markers to indicate poisoning. What I am certain of is that he didn't die of natural causes.'

'He could have taken something voluntarily, if he killed Kern Meadows, the fake one, and this other unidentified individual,' Edris said.

Meadows shook his head. 'There was nothing in his behaviour that would suggest that he intended to take his own life. Besides, he would've left a confession. I take it no note was found?'

Edris shook his head. 'There was nothing found at the scene. No empty bottles of pills or liquid. Everything taken will be tested for traces of substances.'

'There's also the way I found him. He was near the entrance of the yurt, stretched out. It was like he was trying to get help.'

Daisy squeezed his hand.

'We better go and see Mum,' Rain said.

'Yeah, I better get back before Blackwell picks up his messages,' Edris said. 'These are copies of the files on Iggy and Phillip Carew.' He handed them to Meadows. 'I gathered all the information I could on Phillip. Court transcripts, newspaper articles, all the statements, even contacts for Phillip's remaining family. Chris from tech and Paskin helped put it together. We thought you would want to know, well, all the details.'

'Thank you,' Meadows said. 'Thank the others for me, I appreciate everything you've done.'

'I'll come with you to see Fern,' Daisy said. 'I'm not in a hurry to get back to work.'

* * *

Fern Meadows sat on the sofa looking from Meadows to Rain and back again.

'I'm so sorry for the two of you,' she said. 'You must be devastated. All I can say is he was eleven years old at the time. I know that is no excuse but there has to be more to it. I knew your father, maybe not by his given name, but you don't share a bed for over seventeen years without getting a sense of a person. I just don't see him as a cold-blooded killer. You have to ask what sort of upbringing he had to have caused him to kill another child at such a young age.'

'I haven't read the file yet,' Meadows said. 'I thought you should see it first.'

Fern shook her head. 'I don't think I want to read through the details. You read it and just tell me the bare facts. I'll go and make us all something to eat. The two of you look like you've lost weight since this all started.'

'I'll give you a hand,' Daisy said.

Rain sat down next to Meadows who opened the file and took out a newspaper article. The headline was large and bold.

Devil's Spawn

The trial continues today in the case of murdered schoolboy Craig Wilson. Craig was just eight years old when he was tortured and murdered by eleven-year-old Phillip Carew. Testimonies were heard from Craig's older brother, Gareth, and friend, Alan Penny. The two boys along with Craig had been out playing with Carew on that fateful day. Both boys told how that day Carew had been angry that Craig had to tag along with them. Carew then persuaded the boys to go to Gregson's Quarry to swim in the lake. The quarry is well known to locals, with the lake having dangerous undercurrents and freezing water fed from underground. Surrounding the lake are rugged cliff faces with a dangerous path leading down. The area is fenced off with warning signs. Local children are forbidden to go near the quarry.

It appears that Carew goaded the other boys to go with him, claiming he had swum in the lake many times. During the long walk to the quarry Carew became increasingly agitated with Craig and tormented him, going as far as throwing him to the ground at one point. The little boy had cried, begging Carew to let him go home to his mother. Carew had then dragged Craig to the cliff face. The

*other two boys were too frightened to stand up to Carew.
Carew, a tall boy for his age, is a known bully at school.
Once they reached the cliff, Carew then threw Craig from
the top.*

*Gareth Wilson wept as he told how he had seen his brother
go over the edge and hit a ledge before falling into the water.
He then scrambled down the path and pulled Craig's
lifeless body from the water. Carew threatened to kill the
boys if they didn't help bury Craig and keep it a secret.
The boys were terrified and went along with the story
Carew had concocted, that Craig had wandered off alone
and they couldn't find him. A large-scale search was
launched to find Craig.*

*It was two days later that Gareth, after being questioned
by the police, broke down and told them what had
happened to his brother.*

*During the trial Carew showed no remorse for his actions
and has been seen grinning during the proceedings. Carew's
parents have not been present at the trial and it is believed
they have fled from the area. A verdict is expected later this
week.*

Below the article was a large picture of Craig Wilson.
The baby-faced boy smiling at the camera. Two of his
front teeth were missing and long lashes framed innocent
eyes. Meadows handed the article to Rain.

'I thought they were not allowed to name minors in the
press,' Rain said.

'It was 1966,' Meadows said. 'Things were different
back then. That's why he would've been granted lifelong
anonymity. He wouldn't have stood a chance of a normal
life after he was released.'

Meadows took out more articles and looked through
them. They were all similar and used the words "Evil" and
"Monster" to make an impact. One even had a photo of
Phillip Carew. The dark-haired boy was unsmiling with sad
eyes. Meadows studied the photo to see if he could see any
resemblance to his father or to himself. He set them aside
and read through the rest of the file. The last thing he saw

were the photos from the post-mortem. The sight of the small body on the gurney made Meadows feel nauseous. All he could think about was the fear the child must have felt in his last moments.

'It's no wonder he never spoke of what he had done,' he said.

'I can't look at those,' Rain said and shoved the photos back in the file. 'I don't know how you deal with this shit every day.'

'It gets to me sometimes but at least I'm out there trying to get justice for the victim. This' – he pointed to the file – 'is different. I'm looking at a crime my father committed. He did this, there was no doubt. There's no looking for the perpetrator, no bringing closure for the family so they can try and rebuild their lives. This time the guilt and shame is on our family. I don't know who I am anymore.'

'Yes you do,' Rain put his hand on Meadows' shoulder. 'You are Winter Meadows, my brother, someone who has dedicated their life to putting balance back in the world. Making sure those who do wrong pay. This is not your legacy.'

'It's bad, isn't it?' Fern came back into the room. 'I can see by the look on your faces.'

'Well, it's not good,' Meadows said. 'The newspapers always sensationalize a story to sell so we can discard anything they report. He did do it, although in his statement he said it was an accident. It differs from the story that the other boys who were there that day told. It sounds like he was a troubled child.'

'Well I guess we'll never know the why, it's not like he is here to ask him,' Fern said.

'I guess we have to ask ourselves what sort of upbringing he had,' Meadows said.

Fern nodded. 'Children aren't born evil.'

'It looks like his parents just up and left him to deal with it,' Rain said.

'I guess they were ashamed,' Meadows said.

'I would never leave you, no matter what you did,' Fern said. 'The parents should've taken some responsibility.'

'But when does that stop?' Rain asked. 'He's not the only child that has committed murder. When does a child become responsible for their own actions?'

'Ten years old, according to the law,' Daisy said as she came into the room.

'There were others there that day,' Meadows said. 'Craig Wilson's brother, Gareth, and a friend, Alan Penny. Craig's mother is still alive. There are contact details.'

'You're not thinking of talking to them, are you?' Daisy asked.

'I just want to know more, to try and understand. It would be also interesting to know if he tried to contact them, or if Jonah did.'

'You may not like what you hear,' Fern said.

'It can't be worse than this.' Meadows pointed to the file. 'Anyway the family may not want to see me, especially if they are involved in Dad's murder. The fact that Dad could never be his true self makes me think that he was ashamed and still haunted by what he had done.' He glanced at the file. 'I remember where I've seen Craig Wilson's name. It was on a headstone in the graveyard you found when you followed Dad.'

'It shows he never forgot what he did,' Fern said.

Meadows nodded. 'According to the others at the commune he was talking to Jonah those last months. What if he did make contact with Craig's family?'

'Even if that was the case, they would be unlikely to tell you,' Rain said.

'He's right,' Daisy said. 'Why put yourself through that?'

'I just want to know,' Meadows said. 'If he did make contact with them, then he would've had to reveal his identity. After that he wouldn't have to hide. He may have wanted to take back his own name. Maybe Jerome didn't want people knowing who he really was, what *he* had done.'

'No,' Fern said. 'Jerome would never have hurt your father.'

'Doesn't Jerome own the land?' Daisy asked. 'That belongs to Phillip Carew, and now you. Maybe he didn't want to lose it.'

'Good point,' Rain said. 'We didn't have any money back then. What if Dad wanted to sell the land so he could pay off the mortgage?'

'Then who killed Jerome and why?' Meadows asked. 'It's probable that Jerome was murdered to stop him revealing the killer. Iggy knew them both. Was in the same prison and halfway house as them. He must've known about the swap. I think it's time for him to give us some straight answers.'

'I don't think you should go back there,' Daisy said. 'Jerome's been poisoned. It's not safe for you. You already said someone's been creeping around your tepee while you're sleeping.'

'I'm with Daisy,' Fern said. 'I couldn't bear it if anything happened to either of you.'

'Whoever was creeping around has had plenty of opportunity to hurt us. I don't think it's their intention. I'll be fine. I won't eat or drink anything I haven't prepared myself,' Meadows said.

'We,' Rain said. 'I'm coming with you.'

Fern shook her head. 'Well I guess I can't stop you and at least the two of you will be together. Come on, let's eat.'

After the meal was finished Meadows walked out into the garden with Daisy.

'I'll be home soon,' Meadows said.

'Just promise me you'll be careful.' Daisy put her arms around him and rested her head against his chest. 'I worry about you.'

'No need, Rain and me have each other's backs. Nothing is going to happen to us.'

Chapter Twenty-five

Meadows woke up feeling better than he had in days. He got up and dressed before stepping outside the tepee. Rain was sitting cross-legged on the grass reading a book.

'You're up early,' Meadows said.

'Yeah, I'm feeling good this morning. There's a nice breeze. I think the heatwave is on the way out.'

'I think you may be right,' Meadows said. 'I better get going. Sure you're going to be OK here?'

'Yeah, I'm going to sit here or by the pagoda and watch out for Iggy. He can't stay away much longer.'

'I wouldn't be too sure. Jenny says he went with Cosmo to some other communes to spread the word about Jerome. They want to hold a memorial here for him. I guess a lot of people will come.'

'Well, they've already been gone a night. I doubt Iggy will stay away from his cats much longer.'

Meadows smiled. 'Yeah, you're right.'

'Don't worry. I'll work my charm on him and get the information you need. I've got tea, water, and plenty of the bottles of dandelion water Mina gave us. You going to be alright seeing Craig's family? I can't see it will be an easy conversation.'

'I'll be fine. It's just his brother and his mother, Dorothy, who is in her nineties.'

'I'll see you when you get back. I'll have food ready, and I'll make sure no one even sniffs it.'

* * *

It took over two hours for Meadows to reach the retirement home in Gloucester by which time he was feeling nervous. The gated complex was surrounded by trees and after he was granted access he was shown into the gardens, which were a rainbow of colour with filled wide borders and pots that laced pathways to seating areas. In the centre was a large fountain, which looked enticing. He followed a warden to the corner of the garden who then pointed out a man sitting with an elderly lady under the shade of a tree.

The man looked to be in his mid to late sixties, stocky with thinning grey hair. As Meadows drew closer, he could see the lady's eyes were cloudy and her face a map of wrinkles. Her skin was so translucent he could see her veins.

'Gareth Wilson?' Meadows asked.

'Yes.' The man didn't offer a smile. 'You must be Winter Meadows. This is my mother, Dorothy.'

'Thank you both for agreeing to meet me,' Meadows said.

'You can thank my mother,' Gareth said.

'What an unusual name you have,' Dorothy said.

'It does raise some eyebrows,' Meadows said

'Come and sit down,' Dorothy said. 'I'm afraid I can't see you very well. My eyesight is not what it used to be. Tell me a little about yourself,' she said as he took a seat at the table.

Meadows gave a brief outline of his family and life.

'A detective,' Dorothy said. 'It sounds like you have an interesting life. You've done well for yourself, and your brother sounds like a character. Your parents brought you up well. I'm glad to hear that Phillip's life changed after he left prison, and he had a family of his own.'

'Which is more than Craig had,' Gareth said.

'There's no need for that, Gareth,' Dorothy said. 'Imagine if the shoe was on your foot. It is not his fault. I didn't raise you to be unkind.'

Meadows smiled to himself. A child was never too old to be told off. Even at his age Gareth looked suitably chastised.

'I'm sorry,' Gareth said. 'It's just that it stirs up a lot of bad memories, but I guess this can't be easy for you.'

'I understand,' Meadows said. 'The last thing I want to do is cause you both any upset.'

'So what is it you would like to talk to us about?' Dorothy asked.

'As I explained on the phone to Gareth I only found out about my father's past after he was murdered.'

'Must have been quite a shock for you,' Dorothy said.

Meadows nodded. 'Yes, it was. I've read the case files and what he did was inexcusable. I did find out that he regularly visited your son's grave which leads me to believe that he did feel remorse for what he did. I was wondering if he ever tried to contact you.'

'Yes, he did,' Dorothy said.

'What?' Gareth looked genuinely surprised. 'You never said.'

'It was a long time ago. He didn't contact me directly. It was a friend of his. I don't recall his name.'

'Jonah?' Meadows asked.

Dorothy thought for a moment. 'That sounds familiar, it could have been. Anyway we were told of Phillip's release but not his knew identity. Part of his release was that he would have no contact with the family. I expect that's why the friend came to see me. Arrangements were made for him to come and see me, but he never showed up. I guess he couldn't face me in the end.'

'Can you remember roughly when this was?'

'No, I'm sorry. Like I said, it was a long time ago. It was years after his release because Gareth had grown up and left home. Is it important?'

'I don't know,' Meadows said. 'What about your husband? Did he agree to meet with Phillip?'

'Not that I know of. Mark and I were no longer together. Once Gareth had left home there was nothing left holding us together. I can't say whether Phillip tried to contact him, he never said, and well, he's long gone now.'

'I think Phillip did intend to come and see you, but he was murdered before he got the chance.'

'I hope you're not suggesting that we had anything to do with it,' Gareth said.

Meadows didn't want to bring up the fact that Dorothy, her ex-husband, and Gareth all had a good motive for murdering his father. There would be many who wouldn't blame them, he thought.

'I think he was mistaken for someone else,' he said.

'Oh dear,' Dorothy said. 'Well, if it's any consolation to you, if we had met, and he had asked my forgiveness, I would've given it to him. I forgave him a long time ago. I had to for my own peace of mind. Hatred is a double-edged sword. It not only damages the one you hold a grudge against, but it also pierces your own heart. Phillip was just a child.'

'That's no excuse for what he did,' Gareth said.

'No, but you knew the sort of life he lived. His father was a horrible man. He used to beat Phillip and I'm sorry to say his mother was no better. He was unloved and uncared for. He took my Craig from us. I hated what he did but it's not so easy to hate a child. Especially one that suffered years of neglect and abuse.'

Meadows felt his throat constrict with emotion. All he had felt was shame for what his father had done. Throughout his career he had always tried to find the good in people. Even those who had committed murder, he had found were often driven by the horrors in their own past.

He had shown understanding and sometimes compassion. Yet he had condemned his own father.

'That's very gracious of you,' Meadows said.

'Well, I hope you got what you came for,' Dorothy said. 'Take some advice from an old woman. Don't let what happened in the past taint your life. In your case it is not your shame to carry. Once you find out what happened to your father, lay it to rest. Time passes so quickly you need to fill your life with as much happiness as you can. Now Gareth will see you out. I'm sure he can enlighten you more on your father's childhood.'

'I don't see how,' Gareth said.

'I think you do,' Dorothy said. 'I don't need to hear it, but I know a lot of things were never said and a lot of questions went unanswered. You were just a child yourself when you witnessed the death of your brother. I know something from that day weighed heavy on you. Even after all these years. Perhaps it's time you talked about it.'

Gareth nodded. 'I'll walk you to your car.'

'Thank you for talking to me,' Meadows said.

They walked silently back through the gardens. Meadows didn't want to push Gareth to talk, and he could sense his unease. 'Your mother is a remarkable woman,' he said when they reached the car.

'Yes,' Gareth said. 'I guess I've been lucky. She's right, there are things about that day I never talked about. I'm ashamed to say I wasn't truthful about what happened. I don't think it would've made a difference to Phillip's sentence, but it may help you.

'It was a hot summer day, the weather much like the heatwave we're having. Phillip, another friend, Alan, and me had planned to go to the quarry to swim. It was forbidden to go there, and we all knew we would be in trouble if anyone found out. It was never just Phillip's idea. You know what kids are like. You don't see the danger. Anyway we told our parents we were going for a picnic. Mum packed plenty of food and drinks and as I was leaving Craig started to whine. He wanted to go with me. I wasn't happy about it. Whenever he tagged along he was a pain in the arse, bless him. I tried to get out of taking him saying it would be a long walk, but Mum was having none of it, so he came along. We met up with Alan first, then Phillip. Mum was right when she said he wasn't cared for. He had no food or drink with him that day. I didn't realise at the time but looking back, the dirty clothes, the bruises, and him being always hungry should've been a warning sign. Something would have been done about it now but back then no one interfered.

'Anyway it was a long walk to the quarry. We stopped about halfway to have our picnic. Phillip must have been hungry, but I think the thirst would have been worse. Craig teased him. He had some of his drink left and offered it to Phillip. When Phillip reached out to take the drink Craig pulled his hand back and tipped the rest of it on the ground. It was a cruel thing to do.'

'Kids can be cruel,' Meadows said. 'They do things without thinking.'

Gareth nodded. 'Craig thought it was funny and was laughing. If I'm honest Craig was a little spoilt being the youngest and he used to give me a hard time. Alan and me were no better, we could've offered to share our drinks and food, but we didn't. Phillip got angry and shoved Craig. He fell but I don't think he was hurt. He started crying and wanted to go home. The only way we got him to carry on to the quarry was by Phillip giving him a piggyback. Phillip struggled. He tripped once or twice and dropped Craig who yelled some more.

'When we got to the quarry I think we were all a little frightened. The cliffs were steep, and it looked impossible to get down to the water. There was a narrow path cut into the side, but it wouldn't have taken much for one of us to lose our balance and fall in. As we stood peering over the top into the water Craig started off again. He wanted to go home and threatened to tell our parents where we had been if we didn't take him straight away. Phillip just wanted to swim. We were all hot and tired but Phillip more so after carrying Craig without anything to drink. He just snapped. He pushed Craig and he went over the edge. He hit a ledge on the way down before landing in the water.

'We all scrambled down the path, but it was too late by the time we got to the water. I think he was probably dead from the fall. Have you read all the statements given at the time?'

'Yes, and all the newspaper coverage.'

'Then you'll know I said Phillip threatened me. He didn't. I was scared that my parents would find out I had taken Craig to the quarry. We all agreed to bury him and say he had wandered off. The days after were horrendous. My parents kept hoping Craig would be found while all along I knew he was dead. I couldn't keep quiet anymore. Alan and me came up with the story that we were afraid of Phillip and that he had threatened to kill us if we told. Like I said, I don't think it would have made much of a difference. He did kill him, but maybe public opinion would have been different. They called him a monster.'

'I'm not sure the truth would have made a difference to the public. The newspapers still would have painted a grim picture. It's what sells. You were just a boy who had witnessed your brother's death. You shouldn't have any regrets about what you said back then.'

Gareth nodded. 'That's all I can tell you.'

'Thank you for your honesty,' Meadows said. 'It has helped to know a bit about Phillip's past.'

* * *

As Meadows drove back to the commune he played over the conversation he had with Dorothy, and Gareth, in his mind. He hadn't got a sense of hatred towards his father from either of them. Both claimed they didn't know his new identity. Or so they say, he thought. Then there was the ex-husband, Mark Wilson; it was possible that Jonah had contacted him. He could have taken revenge for his son. The trouble was that Dorothy couldn't give a time frame of the visit and even if any of them were involved, he would have no proof. They certainly weren't the ones creeping around the commune, he thought. Added to that there was no motive for killing Jerome. Jerome had to have been murdered because he knew too much. All these thoughts swirled around with no conclusion. He phoned his mother and filled her in. Then he listened to music for the rest of the journey. He only hoped that Rain had had more luck with Iggy.

When he arrived at the commune he walked the track and stopped to talk to a few people on the way to his tepee. Rain wasn't sat in the pagoda so he guessed he must be indoors.

'You in, Rain?' he called out as he pulled the canvas back.

The sight that met his eyes caught his breath and time seemed to freeze. Rain was lying on the floor next to a pool of vomit. Next to him Mina knelt, one hand cradling his head, the other trying to force a black substance into his mouth. Meadows pitched forward and pushed Mina's hand away.

'What have you done?' he shouted.

'Nothing,' Mina said. 'I found him like this. I'm trying to help him.'

'Rain,' Meadows said, as he put his face close to his brother's.

Rain groaned.

Meadows turned to Mina. 'Go and call for an ambulance. Now!' He turned his attention back to Rain. 'Hold on, help is coming. You're going to be OK.'

Rain's eyes were open, but he didn't seem to be able to focus. 'Make them go,' he said.

'Who?' Meadows asked.

'Stick men.'

'OK,' Meadows said. 'I'll make them go away.'

'No, they're outside. Don't go out, they're everywhere. They're gonna get us.'

Meadows could see the terror on Rain's face. Whatever he was seeing was very real to him. 'I won't let anything get us. I'll make sure nothing comes in here.'

Rain nodded and closed his eyes.

'Stay awake,' Meadows said. 'Come on, open your eyes. Talk to me.'

Rain opened his eyes for a moment then they rolled back and he started to convulse.

'Help us!' Meadows cried out as he cradled his brother.

Chapter Twenty-six

Meadows paced the hospital corridor as he waited for news on Rain. He had still been breathing when the ambulance brought him in, but his pulse was weak. He heard footsteps approaching and turned around. Fern and Daisy were running towards him.

'Where is he?' Fern asked.

'The doctors are with him, they are doing everything they can.' Meadows put his arms around his mother. 'I'm so sorry.'

'Don't,' Fern said. 'This is not your fault.'

Daisy put one arm around Meadows and the other around Fern.

'How did this happen?' Fern asked.

'I don't know,' Meadows said.

'We still haven't had a result from Jerome's toxicology. I've called to chase it up,' Daisy said.

'Thank you,' Meadows said. 'Come and sit down, Mum.' He led Fern to a seat and then sat next to her holding her hand while Daisy held his other hand. They sat in silence until Blackwell and Valentine arrived.

'What happened?' Blackwell asked.

Meadows stood and moved away from Fern and Daisy to speak to Blackwell. 'I don't know. I found him in the tepee barely conscious. He wasn't making any sense. He wouldn't have eaten or drank anything that was given to him. He was fine when I left this morning.'

'Then someone must have spiked his food or drink,' Blackwell said. 'Valentine, get on to forensics, I want a team up there to go over the tepee.' He turned to Meadows. 'Whoever has been in there will have left some trace.'

'Problem is most of the commune at some time have been in there,' Meadows said.

'Then at least I'll have reason to get them all in for questioning,' Blackwell said.

Meadows nodded.

A doctor approached and Fern jumped up from her seat. 'How is he?'

'We are doing all we can,' the doctor said. 'Until we know what he's ingested the best we can do is flush his system. We've given him something to help with his blood pressure and we are trying activated charcoal. It may bind the poison and stop it being further absorbed into his bloodstream.'

Meadows thought of the black substance Mina was trying to get Rain to drink. Maybe she was trying to help, he thought.

'That's the best we can do for now,' the doctor continued. 'Until we know what we are dealing with, we can't administer an antidote.'

'Can we see him?' Fern asked.

'Of course,' the doctor said.

'I'll head up to the commune,' Blackwell said. 'If I have to tip that place upside down, I'm going to get some answers.'

Meadows didn't doubt Blackwell would come down heavy on those in the commune. At this point he didn't care, if it meant getting answers.

'Keep us updated,' Valentine said. She touched Meadows' arm before following Blackwell down the corridor.

Meadows walked into Rain's room behind his mother. The sight of Rain lying with monitors attached to his chest, a drip in his arm and an oxygen mask tightened Meadows' throat.

Fern took a seat next to the bed and held Rain's hand. 'You fight this. The doctor has just got to find the right stuff to give you and you'll be fine. I know you can hear me. I'm staying right here until you wake up.'

Meadows felt helpless as he took his brother's other hand. Daisy went to fetch drinks and silent tears fell down Fern's face. Time ticked away with the bleeping of the monitors. A nurse came periodically to check Rain's vitals. Then a doctor. Plastic cups of tea were drunk and they talked any nonsense to fill the silence until Meadows could stand it no longer.

'I'm going to the commune,' he said.

Daisy shook her head. 'It's too dangerous.'

'Let him go, love,' Fern said. 'He needs to do this for Rain. Standing here watching isn't helping.'

Daisy nodded. 'I'll stay with your mum, promise you'll call to let me know you're OK.'

'I'll call every hour to check in on Rain.'

'I'll keep pestering the lab,' Daisy said.

Meadows leaned down and kissed Rain on the forehead before hugging his mother. He squeezed Daisy's hand. 'Look after them for me.'

* * *

It was chaos at the commune. Most were gathered near the pagoda where uniformed officers were trying to take statements. It was clear the people there didn't like the invasion of privacy. They were close up to the police officers and shouting.

One of the group, Martin, rushed over to Meadows.

'How is he?'

'Not good,' Meadows said.

'I'm sorry, honestly, but this isn't right. They want to search our homes.'

'There looking for whatever was used to poison Rain and Jerome.'

'You're saying someone poisoned them?' Martin shook his head. 'There's no one here that would do that. Are you going to stand by and let this happen? For fuck's sake, these are your people. We're your family.'

'Rain is my brother, and I will do what it takes to save his life,' Meadows said. 'There is no doubt that someone here tried to kill him. If you truly think yourself as my family then you'll help. The sooner they find what they are looking for the quicker they'll go.'

'Fine,' Martin said. 'Oi! Oi!' he shouted.

A hush came over the crowd and they looked towards Martin.

'We know we have nothing to hide. Answer their questions and let them search. I know you're not happy about it but do it for Rain. He needs our help.'

There was a general murmuring and slowly the crowd backed down.

'Thank you,' Meadows said. 'Did you see Rain today?'

'Yeah, he was sitting under the pagoda reading. I stopped for a chat.'

'Did you see him eat or drink anything?'

'He had that water bottle he usually carries with him. He looked fine.'

'Anyone else come to talk to him when you were there?'

'No.'

'OK,' Meadows said. 'I'll leave you to take control here and make sure there aren't any problems. The last thing we need is for someone to be arrested. Any distractions will only damage the police's efforts to help Rain.'

Meadows left Martin and walked to his tepee where Blackwell was talking to Mike from forensics.

'What are you doing here?' Blackwell asked.

'Looking for answers,' Meadows said. 'I can't stand around watching my brother fight for his life and do nothing.'

Blackwell nodded. 'We haven't found anything of interest so far.'

'It doesn't help that someone cleaned up before we got here,' Mike said.

'Who?' Meadows asked.

'Mina,' Blackwell said. 'Claimed she didn't want you coming back to the mess.'

'She was with Rain when I found him, trying to get him to drink something. Charcoal, I think. She claims she was trying to help him.'

'Do you believe her?' Blackwell asked.

'I can't think of any reason why she would want to hurt him but just now I don't trust anyone. She hadn't called for help, and she would've had to run back to her yurt or the distillery to get the charcoal. There was no one else around.'

'Sounds like a good enough reason to take her to the station for questioning,' Blackwell said. 'Anything else?'

'No, she has no motive that I can think of for killing Jerome or my father. She does have knowledge of plants and herbs. She makes all sorts of tonics, oils, and lotions. The distillery, which is basically a wooden cabin, is mainly for her use.'

'Right, I'll go and find her and take her to the station. Mike, you might want to check out this cabin, see what you can find.'

'Yeah, I'm not going to get any more from here.'

'What did you find?' Meadows asked.

'Not a lot. We've bagged up a cup that was used along with a stainless-steel water bottle which was on the floor.

There's a half-drunk bottle of something or other.' Mike pointed to the evidence crate.

'Dandelion water,' Meadows said. 'He's been drinking it for days.'

'I guess someone could've dropped something into it when he wasn't looking,' Mike said. 'We'll get it all tested. If there's a trace of any unusual substance we'll find it, even if we have to stay up all night.'

'Thank you,' Meadows said. 'Come on, I'll show you the distillery.'

'You can suit up if you're going inside,' Mike said with a smile. 'It could be a crime scene so technically I shouldn't be letting you in.'

Meadows slipped on protective clothing and led Mike to the wooden cabin. He didn't know what he hoped to achieve going in but at least he felt like he was doing something. He opened the door and stepped inside.

'Is it usually kept locked?' Mike asked.

'No,' Meadows said. 'Nothing is locked here. We work on trust.'

In the first section of the cabin there were rows of herbs drying on racks. Meadows examined them. Mint, thyme, and rosemary he recognised along with some other common herbs. Above them lavender hung in bunches and shelves held bottles and containers ready to be filled. Below, a long table of demijohns, filled with amber liquid, bubbled away. Meadows moved forward and opened the door to the partition. In this section there was a copper kettle sitting above a burner. Piping was attached to the spout and ran across to a metal cylinder. There were various chopping knives and grinders on the bench along with dried roots and leaves.

'Recognise any of these?' Mike asked.

'No, well that looks like ginger root. The others I'm not sure.'

'OK we'll bag the lot and take them to the lab. See what we can identify. Maybe we'll get lucky.'

'I'll leave you to it,' Meadows said.

Outside he peeled off the protective clothing and made a call to Daisy. There was no change in Rain's condition. The only upside was that he hadn't deteriorated further. He promised to call again then hung up as he heard a commotion. He hurried towards the noise where he found Blackwell with Mina, and Iggy protesting.

'You've no reason to take her,' Iggy said.

'If you're going to be obstructive then I'll have you arrested,' Blackwell said.

'I'll be fine,' Mina said.

Meadows thought she looked anything but fine. He could see her hands trembling and tears pooled in her eyes.

Iggy turned on Meadows. 'Are you going to just stand there and let him take her?'

It was a rare sight to see Iggy angry. He was red in the face and his fists were clenched into balls. Jenny and Cosmo came hurrying up to them.

'What's going on?' Jenny asked.

'This buffoon is taking Mina to the police station,' Iggy said, 'and he's not doing anything about it.'

'I couldn't stop him even if I wanted to,' Meadows said.

'What's that supposed t-to mean?' Cosmo stepped closer to Meadows.

Jenny grabbed hold of Cosmo's arm and pulled him back. 'Let's just all calm down,' she said.

'You're supposed to be… to be… on… one of us,' Cosmo said. 'Not taking s-sides with them.'

'I'm not taking anyone's side,' Meadows said. 'Rain is seriously ill. All I'm interested in is helping him.'

'That's all we want to do,' Jenny said.

'Then you all better start talking. Let Mina go with Blackwell so he can do his job.'

'Fine,' Iggy said. 'Just give me a few minutes.' He took off before Blackwell had a chance to protest.

'What's he up to?' Blackwell asked.

Meadows shrugged. 'Just give him a moment.'

'I would never hurt Rain,' Mina said. 'You have to believe me.'

'I don't know what to believe anymore,' Meadows said. 'I don't think any of you have told me the whole truth. If you want to help, then answer Blackwell's questions. We need to find out what poison was given to Rain.'

'I don't know,' Mina said.

'What were you giving him when I found you?'

'Charcoal, I mixed it with water to try and get him to drink it. I thought it might help him.'

'Why didn't you just call for an ambulance?' Blackwell asked.

'There wasn't time,' Mina said.

'But you went to get charcoal. You could've called out for help,' Meadows said.

'I had the charcoal with me. I was afraid after what happened to Jerome. I thought if the same happened to me I could take the charcoal and get help.'

'How did you know that Jerome had been poisoned? I've only just found out myself.'

'I overheard the forensic officers talking about it.'

It's a reasonable explanation, Meadows thought. Although she could be covering her tracks.

'I'm sorry, Mina, you still need to go to the station.'

'It's fine,' Mina said. 'I don't trust anyone either.'

Iggy came back panting heavily. He handed a card to Mina. 'That's the details of my solicitor. I'll call him to tell him to come and help you. Wait for him.'

'I can't afford–'

'It will all be taken care of,' Iggy said.

'Thank you.'

'Right, let's go,' Blackwell said.

Meadows turned to the others. 'We need to talk now.'

'I have to call the solicitor,' Iggy said.

'I want to make sure the police don't make a mess in my yurt,' Jenny said. 'They are making their way towards me.'

'OK fine,' Meadows said. 'I'll meet you all by the pagoda in an hour.'

'I need a drink,' Cosmo said. 'I'll bring some of my brew.'

Meadows shook his head. 'I suggest we all bring our own drinks until we know what's going on.'

'I can't believe you think that one of us would be responsible,' Jenny said.

'Are you going to tell me who is then?' Meadows said.

Jenny bristled. 'I don't bloody know.'

'You all know more than you think you do, or more than you are willing to tell. There's been enough death. I think it's about time you were all honest with me.'

'You're right,' Iggy said. 'We'll meet you in an hour.'

Chapter Twenty-seven

Meadows spent the next hour sterilizing the remaining mugs, glasses, and bottles. Then using the water he brought with him, he brewed mixtures of tea and filled the glass bottles. He had a feeling it was going to be a long night and the cold ginger and mint tea would give him some energy. He didn't want to leave the bottles unattended, so he put them in his backpack and then walked to higher ground to make a call to Daisy. Rain's condition remained the same. It was not what he wanted to hear. The more time that passes the more damage the poison will do to his body, Meadows thought. I need answers, fast.

He checked the time then walked to the pagoda where Iggy, Cosmo, and Jenny were sitting quietly. Meadows sat on one of the cushions, cross-legged, and took a bottle of cooled ginger tea from his bag. He took a sip then placed it safely between his legs. The light was fading and dotted around the pagoda were jars of candles with flickering flames. The air was warm and scented with honeysuckle that twisted around the posts and mixed with sweet peas. The atmosphere should have been serene, but it was charged with anxiety which seemed to fill the air like static.

Cosmo was twitchy, Iggy's face creased with concern, and Jenny looked ill.

'Are you OK, Jenny?' Meadows asked.

'I'm perfectly fine,' Jenny said. 'Other than being ordered to come here on top of having police go through my things.'

'I'm sorry,' Meadows said, 'but it was necessary. You do want to help Rain?'

'Of course I do. We all do, but I don't see how.'

'You'd be surprised how often people hold valuable information without realising it,' Meadows said. 'Just now I would be happy if you went to the hospital to get checked out. Given what's happened to Rain. You don't look well, and I'm worried about you. I can arrange to have someone take you and bring you back while I talk to Iggy and Cosmo.'

'I told you I'm alright,' Jenny snapped. 'I don't feel ill. I'm just tired, so can we get on with it?'

'OK,' Meadows said. 'I know you all knew about the swap.'

'What s-swap?' Cosmo asked, his legs jigging.

'Enough of the bloody lies,' Meadows said. He took a deep breath. I sound like Blackwell, he thought. He took a drink from his bottle. 'I'm sorry, I'm just worried about Rain. I don't mean to take it out on all of you.'

'That's understandable,' Iggy said.

Meadows nodded. 'The swap I'm talking about is the one Kern and Jerome made. Kern was Jerome and Jerome was Kern, but Kern was also Phillip Carew.'

'What?' Cosmo said. 'You're n-not making any… any…'

'Sense,' Iggy said. 'They don't know. They came along after me, Kern, and Jerome moved here.'

'But you knew,' Meadows said. 'Why didn't you tell me?'

'Because your father didn't want you to know his identity. Jerome wanted to keep his secret. He promised your father.'

'I need a drink,' Cosmo said. He unscrewed a bottle and poured a large glass of wine. 'Anyone w-want one?'

'I will,' Jenny said.

'I don't think anyone should be sharing,' Meadows said.

'I don't care what you think,' Jenny said. 'I happen to trust my family. If I do drop down dead, then you'll have your answer.'

'I haven't… I didn't…' Cosmo shook his head his eyes wide in horror at the suggestion.

'I know, Cosmo.' Jenny squeezed his hand. 'Drink your wine. You have nothing to worry about.'

'Why the swap?' Meadows asked.

'You'll know by now they served time together,' Iggy said. 'During that time they became friends, well, more like brothers. Phillip was consumed with guilt for what he had done and so was Kern.'

'What had they done?' Jenny asked.

'Kern, or Jerome as you knew him, caused the death of four people by drink-driving. One of them was his brother. Phillip, who you knew as Kern, I don't know. He never talked about it. As for me, I caused an explosion in a lab, a security guard died. I never meant for anyone to get hurt. I had a hard time inside. I was referred to as the rich kid and was a daily target. Kern and Phillip looked after me. When the time came for our release Phillip tried to take his own life.'

Meadows remembered the scars his mother had talked about on his father's arms. 'Was he frightened of what would happen to him when he left prison?' he asked.

'Yes, I knew he'd been inside since he was eleven years old. Moved from a secured adolescent unit to adult prison. He knew nothing of the outside world. He said he'd been called a monster most of his life and he believed he was. He didn't think he deserved to be released. He thought everyone on the outside would hate him. He had no concept of people moving on with their lives and forgetting. His world was confined to the prison walls. You have to understand, when you go to prison you lose your identity, you're just a number and the lowest in society. People think you are worthless, and you believe it. Phillip more so.'

'That's sad,' Cosmo said. 'He was... a g-good guy... nice man.'

Iggy nodded. 'Phillip's grandfather had left him this place and Kern tried to persuade him it would be a fresh start, far away from people. Phillip had been granted a new identity for his own protection but even with that he was terrified. There were still men inside who knew who he was, his real name.' He looked at Meadows. 'I'm guessing the police also knew his identity.'

Meadows nodded. 'Only a small group though. A designated police officer, high rank, who worked in the area would need to know. Then there's probation. His identity would have been secure, this would have been explained to him.'

'That may have been the case but he felt like he would never be free. Kern talked him around. He told him he had an opportunity to be a new person and he should grasp it with both hands.'

'But he couldn't just run away,' Meadows said. 'He would have been on life license.'

'That's right,' Iggy said. 'We all ended up in the same halfway house. It was only me and Kern who knew Phillip's real identity, but he was still wary of people. We all did volunteer work, a part of being reintroduced to society. Phillip kept close and only ever spoke to us. Kern was worried that Phillip would try to end his life again. He was just existing. He tried again to get him to come here and see the farm and land, but he was still afraid. He thought people would connect him to his grandfather and he wouldn't be safe. Kern offered to pretend to be him so

211

if there was any trouble it would come back on him. So they came here, and Phillip loved the place and he thrived. Pretending to be Kern Meadows gave him freedom. He was the man who had made a stupid mistake. Not the monster anymore.'

'Is that it?' Meadows asked. 'You're telling me the only reason they swapped identities is because my father was afraid he'd be found out. There wasn't some other motive.'

'Yes,' Iggy said. 'That's the only reason. I suppose it gave him another level of protection. The name Kern Meadows couldn't be linked to Phillip Carew.'

'What did Kern Meadows get out of it? I suppose becoming Jerome gave him ownership of the land.'

Iggy shook his head. 'You know better than that. Jerome never claimed the land as his own. Kern said he was happy to become Jerome Gwyn. He did it for his friend, to give him a chance of happiness. It also gave him an opportunity to escape his own past.'

'I guess that makes some sense but why keep their own date of birth?'

'I can't answer that,' Iggy said. 'Perhaps Jerome wanted to keep one small part of himself. Maybe Phillip didn't want to be older. Who knows?'

'How did they get away with it for so long?'

'It wasn't difficult. They asked me to join them here and after a while Phillip became Kern Meadows to me and Kern became Jerome Gwyn and that's how I saw them from then on. Your father was happy here, and he gave others the chance to escape their past and rebuild their lives. They even managed to fool probation. When the old officer retired and they got a new one, they swapped places and it was never picked up. The probation officer would even contact Jerome and ask him for help with people struggling to adjust after release. That's how Haystack came to live here. I haven't a clue what he was inside for, but he's never been any trouble.'

'So you're telling me that this place is full of ex-cons?'

'No,' Iggy said. 'It's only a few of us. The rest just came, mainly to escape mainstream society. This is my home. I've been happy here. Just because some of us have a past doesn't make our values and beliefs any less valid.'

Meadows nodded.

'There were never any problems until Jonah came along,' Jenny said. 'I told you what he did to me, so I imagine that he tried to interfere in Kern's and Jerome's lives.'

'I don't want to talk about J-Jonah,' Cosmo said.

Meadows wondered what it was that Cosmo had done in the past. He was clearly distressed by the idea of anyone knowing. Perhaps Jonah found out, he thought.

'I'm sorry, we have to talk about Jonah if I'm going to have any chance of saving Rain,' he said. 'I need to know who killed Kern, Phillip, or whatever you want to call him.'

'Phillip became Kern Meadows, it's who he was, who he wanted to be so that's what I will call him,' Iggy said.

'So who killed him?' Meadows asked.

'Steven Parry,' Iggy said.

'You saw this?' Meadows asked.

'No.'

Meadows looked at Jenny and Cosmo who both shook their heads.

'But you all knew.'

'None of us knew until the remains were found,' Jenny said.

'Then how do you know it was Steven Parry who killed Kern?'

'Jonah was on at Kern and Jerome to join his stupid counselling sessions,' Iggy said. 'Kern was worried about it. Jonah had a way of finding out information. He would disappear for a few days then come back asking questions. In the end Kern took Fern and you boys away. Jerome just stayed out of Jonah's way. He was always stronger than Kern.

'Anyway, as you know, things didn't go too well for your mum and dad when they left here. This had been Kern's safe haven and he struggled. Then after they had that awful fight Kern came back here. He started talking to Jonah, spending time in the big tent with him. Jerome was concerned about it. Kern kept saying he was a monster and needed to make amends for what he had done.' Iggy sighed. 'It wasn't that Jerome was worried for himself, his concern was that Jonah would find out who Kern really was and give away his identity. He knew that would break Kern. Kern was becoming withdrawn and Jerome couldn't get through to him. Then Kern and Jonah had an argument. Jonah took off for a few days. He came back in time for the summer solstice. There were a lot of people there that night. Steven Parry turned up. I swear I didn't know who he was at the time. He seemed friendly, he asked me where Kern was and I pointed him out. I would never have done if I'd known.' Iggy shook his head.

'It's not your fault, Iggy,' Jenny said.

'The only one to… to… blame is Jonah,' Cosmo said.

'What happened then?' Meadows asked.

'I don't know,' Iggy said. 'A little while later Jerome asked me if I'd seen Kern. He said something about Jonah having done something stupid and he was worried about Kern. I said the last time I saw him he was talking to Steven Parry, I didn't know that was his name at the time. I offered to help look for him. Jerome said to check Kern's tepee and down the fields. If I found him to bring him back to the bonfire. He said he would check the woods. I'd had a fair amount to drink so I suppose it must have taken me longer than usual. I stumbled on some people, you know, having fun. No one had seen Kern. I walked down the fields and back to the bonfire. There was no sign of Kern, Jerome, or Jonah so I decided to go to the woods to check on them.'

'What time was this?' Meadows asked.

'I don't know. It was getting dark. As I got to the edge of the woods I heard voices so I called out. Jerome came out. He was in a state. He said there had been an accident. I said I would go for help but he said no. He told me to go back to the party and make sure that no one came to the woods. That's what I did. Not long after Mina came to me. She said she had seen Jonah come out of the woods with blood on his clothes. I thought that it was likely that Kern or Jerome had given Jonah a thumping so I didn't think any more about it.

'The next morning everyone was hungover, and I didn't see Jerome until later that afternoon. He said Jonah had invited Steven Parry to the party. That's when I realised what I had done. I had given Kern away. Jerome said that Steven Parry and Jonah both now knew Kern's real identity, so Kern had to go away. I didn't know Kern was dead until the remains were found.'

'So when did you know the remains were Kern's?' Meadows asked.

'I talked to Jerome. He said Steven Parry had killed Kern that night.'

'Why didn't he call the police?' Jenny asked.

'Because he wanted to protect…' Cosmo twisted his hand as if turning a cog. 'Protect them.'

'Who?' Meadows asked.

'You,' Iggy said. 'You, Rain, and Fern. If the police had been called then the secret would've come out. Kern never wanted you to find out about his past. Jerome wanted to do that one last thing for his friend. All this time I thought Kern was in hiding. You thought he'd left you. Walked out on your mum. Fern tried to pretend like she wasn't hurt and she could manage but you were all struggling, emotionally and financially. All these years I blamed myself because I had pointed out Kern. Still, if I had realised then none of this would have happened.'

'This isn't your fault, Iggy,' Meadows said. He thought back on those times. Things had been hard for them. He remembered Jerome and Iggy visiting. They brought food. Vegetables and fruit they had grown on the commune. Jars of honey and pickles. Then the mortgage had been paid off. He looked at Iggy.

'It was you,' Meadows said. 'You paid off the mortgage on the cottage.'

Iggy nodded. 'I wanted you to have a home and Fern not to have to worry. I knew she wouldn't take the money from me. Besides no one knew of my background. I never wanted all that money, and it didn't even dent what I had in the bank, so I don't want you to think on it.'

'I can at least say thank you for what you did,' Meadows said.

'And that will do,' Iggy said. 'We never mention it again. So now you know everything.'

'I wish I did,' Meadows said. 'I don't know who the other poor soul is we found in the woods.'

'I'm guessing that's Steven Parry,' Iggy said. 'Jonah came back after that night so it can't be anyone else. Maybe Jonah killed him. I guess we'll never know. By the time you dug up the remains Jerome was gone so I couldn't ask him.'

'When did Jonah leave for good?'

'I don't know,' Iggy said. 'He left after that night with Kern then came back a few months later. He stayed a while then was just gone one morning.'

'Are you all positive that you saw Jonah after the summer solstice?'

'Yeah,' Cosmo said. 'No-nobody wanted him around.'

'I remember Jerome being upset when he came back. Now we know why,' Iggy said. 'Yes, that's right, we talked about asking him to leave. Jerome didn't want him around for the winter solstice.'

'Did he stay for the celebrations?'

'Erm, I'm not sure,' Iggy said. His forehead creased in concentration. 'The years just blend into each other. I'm sorry I don't remember exactly when he left.'

'And now J-Jonah is back,' Cosmo said. 'He killed Jerome and... and... he's going to kill all of us.'

'Jonah is not back,' Jenny snapped. 'We would have seen him. Besides, what possible reason could he have for killing us?'

'Well if he did kill Steven Parry you were the only people who would know,' Meadows said. 'The discovery of the remains was on the news. He may have come back to make sure no one talked.' He turned to Cosmo. 'That night you and Jerome found me in the woods. Did you see anyone else? Hear anything?'

'No,' Cosmo said. 'I told you I went for a pee, and I saw you running. I didn't see anyone else other than you and Haystack.'

'What about any other night? Have any of you seen anything unusual, heard noises or felt like someone had been in your home?' Meadows asked.

'No, nothing,' Jenny said. 'But when I go to sleep that's it until I wake. You could have a party around me and I wouldn't notice.'

'Cosmo?'

'No, well s-someone made a mess in one of the polytunnels.'

'I think that may have been me,' Meadows said. 'I thought there was someone inside. You've been growing violets.'

'Yeah,' Cosmo said. 'I always g-grow them. Sell them to the locals.'

'There were violets in the woods,' Meadows said.

Cosmo shrugged. 'I don't grow them in there. They've b-been there for years.'

Meadows thought it was pointless to try and work out who had put the flowers in the woods. They were easy to access, it could have been anyone of them marking the grave. Even Jerome, as he knew Kern was there, he thought.

'What about you, Iggy?' he asked. 'Have you seen or heard anything out of the ordinary?'

'Well it's probably nothing but the night you were all in the woods there were lights on in the distillery cabin.'

'Mina,' Jenny said.

'It was the middle of the night,' Iggy said. 'Maybe she couldn't sleep.'

Or maybe she was mixing up something, and didn't want anyone to know, Meadows thought. He drank down the last of his cold tea and stood up. He now had more information but none of it was going to help Rain. He wanted time alone to think.

He looked at Cosmo and Jenny. 'One more thing, where were you two when Steven Parry and Kern were together in the woods?'

'I don't know,' Cosmo said. 'I d-don't remember.'

'You know what the celebration is like,' Jenny said. 'Music playing, people dancing, and lots of drinking. I expect we were all near the bonfire like we usually are. You're talking years ago, none of us could tell you where we were at a specific time. Even Iggy can't tell you what time he went into the woods.'

'No time of death, no witnesses, and no evidence,' Meadows said. 'That's what you are all telling me. It's all very convenient.'

'Are you accusing us of being involved?' Jenny asked. 'Iggy already told you what happened.'

'No, he didn't,' Meadows said. 'He said that Jerome told him there had been an accident. Did Jerome specifically say that Steven Parry had killed Kern?'

'Not exactly, no,' Iggy said. 'When I asked him about the remains that had been found he said that Kern had died that night and there was nothing he could do. I said it was because I had pointed out Kern to Steven Parry. All he said was it wasn't my fault, that I wasn't to know that Jonah had invited him. It had to have been Steven Parry, otherwise Jerome would have said so.'

Unless he killed him, Meadows thought. 'I'll speak to you all in the morning.'

Meadows walked back to his tepee, picked up another bottle of cold tea and walked up the field to call Blackwell.

'How are you getting on with Mina?'

'Still waiting for the solicitor to arrive,' Blackwell said. 'If it's the same one that came for Iggy then we've got a long wait. How did you get on with the others?'

Meadows filled him in.

'Well, if Steven Parry did kill Phillip Carew then I'm guessing one of the other two offed him. The likelihood is that the second remains we found are going to be those of Steven Parry.'

'It still doesn't answer who poisoned Jerome and Rain,' Meadows said.

'I'll ask Mina about her being in the distillery cabin that night. At the moment she isn't saying anything.'

'I can't see a motive for her killing anyone,' Meadows said. 'She was close to my father years ago so if she thought Jerome killed him then I guess she may have taken revenge. Still doesn't explain why she would try and kill Rain.'

'I'll bring the lot in for formal questioning in the morning,' Blackwell said. 'See if we can find any inconsistencies in their stories.'

'Yeah, that's what I would do,' Meadows said.

He ended the call and talked to Daisy and Fern for a few minutes. Rain was responding to the treatment. His vitals were improving which gave Meadows some encouragement as he went back to his tepee. He took out all the notes he had made and laid out his incident board. He added the new information. By the time he finished writing his head ached and his mouth was dry. He made a cup of peppermint tea and looked at a spiderweb diagram he had drawn. No matter how hard he looked at it, he couldn't come up with a logical explanation.

Jonah left that night. If he killed Steven Parry then why come back a few months later? If it had been Jerome who killed Steven then Jonah would have had a hold on him and most likely have taken head position in the commune, he thought. But Jerome had no motive other than the new identity and the land. In either of these scenarios, it didn't explain the poisoning of Jerome and Rain, unless… He looked again at the lines linking the names and thought back to that last night with Jerome. They had been drinking the tonic Mina had made. He and Rain had only had a small glass, they had given the rest to Jerome. The poison had been meant for me and Rain, he realised. The jugs of lemonade and the tonic that Mina brought them. Why didn't I see this before? he thought. All those days feeling sick. He ran his hand through his hair. He knew the answer. All the emotions, feeling unwell, the virus going around the commune, and the confusion with his father's identity. No wonder I haven't been thinking straight, he thought.

He added this new scenario to his notes with the word "Why?" underlined. He checked the time. Another fifteen minutes until he was due to call Daisy. His head was pounding now so he took two paracetamols and turned off the lamps before lying on the bed. He just wanted to lay quietly for a few moments but his thoughts wouldn't still. It's about my family, he thought. Punishment, revenge, for what his father had done. But punishment for what Kern Meadows had done or what Phillip Carew had done? These were his last thoughts as he fell asleep.

A piercing cry awoke him. He sat up and pain, like a lightening fork, tracked down the nerves in his head. His T-shirt was soaked with sweat and his mouth so dry he couldn't swallow. He grabbed a bottle from the side of the bed and glugged it down. He picked up his phone to check the time but the screen was blurred. He blinked a few times but still couldn't focus. He tried to get up but his legs felt too weak to hold him. I need help, he thought. He knew he couldn't make it to the top field to get a signal, so his only option was to get outside and shout for help. He started to crawl towards the entrance.

'Don't go out there,' a voice said.

The voice startled Meadows and he dropped his phone, the little light he had from the screen vanished. He turned his head, but he couldn't make out any shapes in the darkness.

'Who's there?' Meadows asked.

There was nothing but the sound of his own laboured breathing and the thudding of his heart which seemed to be growing louder. He put his hand to his chest and felt the palpitations. It was as though his heart had risen to the surface and was trying to break through the skin.

'It's the cry of winter,' the voice said. 'Your time has come.'

Meadows tried to scramble to his feet but fell. Panic blinded his thoughts and every muscle felt like it was going into a spasm. He sucked in the air.

'You're dying,' the voice said.

He tried to crawl while moving his hand around the ground to locate his phone. Then the pain came, razor-sharp fingers squeezing his stomach until he heaved. Time after time he kept retching. Around him the darkness closed in, and he felt himself falling into the blackness.

Chapter Twenty-eight

Iggy sat in his caravan drumming his fingers against his leg as he waited for news of Mina. He couldn't settle. After Meadows had left them he had listened to Cosmo and Jenny discussing the reasons why Mina may have poisoned Jerome and Rain. Jenny had even suggested that one of them should go and persuade her to identify the poison. He was certain Mina wasn't responsible and he wouldn't let her take the blame for it. Then again, she had offered him an alibi. Did it mean she knew something? The other reason he was unsettled was that he had lied to Meadows or rather he'd omitted certain things.

He stood up and paced the caravan. There wasn't much room and it only took a few paces to reach the end. How long would it take the police to find out? Was an omission as damaging as an outright lie? These thoughts caused a knot of anxiety in his chest. He felt like a tightly coiled spring with no way of getting release.

When he could stand it no longer, he left the caravan and walked down to the old farmhouse where the communal car was parked. The keys were behind the sun visor where they were always kept. Feeling action was better than waiting around, he started the engine and drove away from the commune. He found the police station easily, having only been there a couple of days ago.

He wasn't given any information at the reception desk but was told he could wait. More pacing and what felt like hours later Iggy saw his solicitor, Mr Finch, who was on his way out of the police station.

'Mr Sealy, I didn't expect to find you here again so soon,' Mr Finch said.

It was strange for Iggy to hear his surname being used. 'I've come for Mina. Is she OK?'

'Yes, she'll be along shortly.'

Iggy felt the anxiety leave his body. 'Thank you.'

Mr Finch smiled. 'Pleasure. Any more problems just call.'

A few moments later Mina came out. Her face lit up when she saw Iggy. She rushed forward and threw her arms around him. Iggy felt a warmth spread through his body before she released him.

'Thanks for coming. I didn't know how I was going to get home,' she said.

The thought of her being stranded hadn't entered Iggy's mind. He'd been more concerned that she would be charged with murder and kept in a cell. 'Well, I couldn't let you walk,' he said. 'Come on, the car's outside.'

'Mr Finch was wonderful,' Mina said as soon as they stepped outside. 'He dealt with all the questions.'

'Let's talk in the car,' Iggy said and opened the door for her then settled in the driver seat. 'So what did they ask you?'

'About my relationship with Kern, who was not Kern.' Mina shook her head. 'What a mess. Then they asked about Jonah, wanted my movements today, and then a lot of questions about the oils and tonics I make.'

'What did you tell them?'

'There wasn't much to say about it. I kept my answers brief like Mr Finch advised. You know I've been making those tonics for years. No one has ever got ill. You do believe that I didn't try to hurt Rain or Jerome?' she asked.

Iggy was quiet for a moment. He thought of the lights on in the cabin when she should have been asleep. Then there was her relationship with Jonah. Would she poison Jerome if Jonah asked her to, even after all these years?

'Iggy?'

'Yes, I want to believe you, but I saw you in the cabin in the middle of the night.'

'When?'

'That night Winter said he followed someone into the woods. Erm, Sunday night.'

'I haven't been in there late at night. You can't have seen me, it must've been someone else. Was it definitely a woman you saw?'

'No, I mean I didn't actually see anyone. Just the lights on.'

'I thought someone had been in there. Things had been moved. Then I went in early one morning and the copper pot was warm.'

'Did you tell the police this?' Iggy asked.

'No, Mr Finch said not to offer information.'

'I need to ask you something. Why did you offer to give me an alibi for the summer solstice? You and I both know we weren't together.'

Mina sighed. 'Because I thought the others were up to something. I didn't want you caught up in it all and, well, I don't know how more obvious I can make it. I like you.'

'I like you too,' Iggy said. 'You've always been a good friend.'

'That's it? A friend?'

'Oh.' Iggy felt a fluttering in his stomach. 'You mean, well, you and me?'

'We're too old to play games,' Mina said and touched his cheek.

'I've always liked you,' Iggy said. 'But look at me.'

'I am.' She smiled. 'You are the kindest, sweetest, and most generous man I have ever known.'

Iggy leaned in and kissed her, and all his concerns melted away. He still felt his lips tingle when they drew apart.

'Is there any news on Rain?' Mina asked.

'No, I saw them taking boxes from the cabin. I guess they are hoping to find something there. You could help,' Iggy said.

'The police?' Mina's eyes narrowed. 'No.'

'Think of it as helping Rain, not the police.'

'I don't see how I can.'

'Think about all the stuff you keep in the cabin. It's going to take them a long time to identify the different herbs and plants. If you were to look, you might find something that shouldn't be there.'

'Yeah, and then I'll get the blame.'

'If they do find anything you'll be blamed anyway so what difference does it make? It will look better for you if you help, and it will speed things up.'

'OK, but you're coming with me.'

They walked into the station and asked to see Blackwell. At first Iggy thought that he wasn't going to allow Mina to help but after some phone calls he agreed.

Dressed in protective clothing they followed Blackwell into the laboratory.

'This is Mike Fielding, our forensic officer,' Blackwell said.

Iggy nodded a hello.

'Come with me,' Mike said. 'We've been trying to contact a botanist but at this hour it's not easy. Just now we could use all the help we can get. We are looking for anything that could've been used to poison Rain. As you know the area I assume you know which poisonous plants can be found.'

'Yes,' Mina said.

'So the question is, if you were going to poison someone, what would you use?' Blackwell asked.

'I don't think I want to answer that,' Mina said.

'Put it another way, what are we looking for?' Mike asked.

'Well, I wouldn't keep anything dangerous in the cabin. When I make up cough mixtures and any stronger tonics, I do lock them away. It's just for the safety of the children but I haven't made up any batches recently.'

They stopped by a long table where there were trays of evidence bags.

'These are just common herbs,' Mina said pointing to the various bags as she named them. 'I guess you could be looking for some sort of fungi. You've got the well-known ones, *Amanita bisporigera* and *Amanita phalloides*; you'll know them as destroying angels and death caps. They would cause vomiting, convulsions, and delirium. If it's not treated promptly, it's fatal.'

Iggy saw tears gather in Mina's eyes and he gave her arm a gentle squeeze. 'I'm sure they would've considered those at the hospital,' he said.

Mina nodded. 'There's lots of toxic plants, like *Aconitum*; you'd know it as monkshood but it's not wild. It would have to be grown and I haven't seen any in the commune polytunnels. I suppose someone could have grown it in their garden.'

'Aconite,' Mike said.

Mina nodded. 'What else? Erm… You can make cyanide from laurel leaves but he would have died in a matter of minutes.' She continued to look at the bags. 'I'm sorry, there are so many possibilities.'

'You're doing great,' Mike said. 'We can at least give a list to the hospital so they can test Rain. We'll also run tests here on the blood taken from Jerome Gwyn. With a bit of luck, we'll get a hit.'

Mina stopped and picked up a bag. She looked at Iggy. 'This looks like the root of *Atropa belladonna*.'

'Deadly nightshade?' Mike asked.

'Yes, I do use it in cough mixtures. You have to be very careful with the doses. I use the berries as well as the root. The whole plant is poisonous.'

'So you've been using the root?' Blackwell asked.

'No,' Mina said. 'I've been making oils. I'd never keep this among the other herbs. It would be too risky.'

Blackwell nodded. 'It looks like we've found our culprit.'

Chapter Twenty-nine

Meadows didn't want to open his eyes. He was no longer in pain or afraid. In fact he felt comfortable. The last thing he remembered was being sick, the horrendous pain in his stomach and head, and someone standing over him. They were watching me die, he thought. Maybe I am dead. If I am then it's peaceful. With that thought he opened his eyes. The first thing he saw was the bottom rail of a hospital bed.

'You're awake.' Daisy leaned over him.

'We were so worried about you.' Fern's face came into view.

'How did I get here?' Meadows asked.

'You didn't call us,' Daisy said. 'We knew something was wrong. You wouldn't have gone to bed without first checking on Rain. I called Blackwell. He found you unconscious on the tepee floor.'

'Rain?' Meadows sat up and his head spun.

'Take it easy,' Fern said. 'Rain is fine. I'll go and get him.' She kissed Meadows on the forehead and left the room.

Meadows picked up the glass of water from the bedside and took a sip. 'I don't understand. I was careful.'

'It was deadly nightshade,' Daisy said. 'It must've been in something you ate or drank.'

'No, no one had the opportunity to put anything in my water. I carried it with me at all times.'

'You're with us at last,' Rain said as he came into the room. 'Man, I've tried some shit in my time but that stuff has to be the worse trip I ever had.'

Meadows laughed. 'Yeah, I second that. Still can't work out how.'

'Me neither,' Rain said. 'I drank water, or the dandelion cordial which we had the whole time we were there.'

'I guess someone could've gone into the tepee when we were out and tampered with the bottles,' Meadows said. 'I sterilised everything that was left and made my own drinks. Mostly cold tea I'd brewed myself.'

They were interrupted by the appearance of Blackwell, Valentine, and Edris who all gathered at the bottom of the bed.

'If I'd known we were having a party I would have dressed for the occasion,' Rain said.

Blackwell smiled. 'Valentine and me are just here to question the victim.'

'I just wanted to tag along to see how you were doing,' Edris said.

'I feel pretty good,' Meadows said.

'That will be the drip,' Rain said. 'I don't know what they put in it but it's good stuff.'

'I'm just glad to see you're better,' Valentine said. 'You gave us all a scare.'

Meadows looked at Blackwell. 'I guess I have you to thank for finding me.'

'It was Daisy that alerted us,' Blackwell said. 'I'm going to need to ask you a few questions.'

'I'll leave you to it,' Rain said.

'You may as well stay, we need to speak to you as well.'

'Shall we go and get a cuppa, Fern?' Daisy asked.

'Yes,' Fern said. 'I don't think I want to hear the details. I've seen enough for the last couple of days.'

Blackwell plonked down in the seat Fern had been using and Valentine sat on the opposite side. Rain sat on the end of the bed leaving Edris the only one standing.

'Have either of you any idea how you managed to ingest the poison, which we now know was belladonna?'

'We we're discussing it before you came in,' Rain said. 'Neither of us accepted any food or drinks from anyone. We used only the ones that were in the tepee.'

'Traces of belladonna were found in the bottle we found next to you. Also in the contents of another bottle. Whatever it was you were drinking.'

'Tea,' Meadows said. 'It was just mint and ginger. I made it myself in a large pot then cooled it in the bottles. It must've already been in with the tea.'

'So it could have been put in at any time,' Blackwell said.

'Yeah,' Meadows said. 'There are several canisters with different teas.'

'We think the root of the plant was used and possibly juice from the berries,' Valentine said. She looked at Rain. 'You wouldn't have tasted it in the dandelion water, apparently it has a sweet taste.'

'I saw your notes,' Blackwell said. 'Well a lot of them didn't make much sense but I took them back to the station hoping that you'd left some clue as to what happened. There were some interesting points. You seemed to be suggesting that you and Rain were the targets and not Jerome. Why?'

'Jerome was with us the night before he died,' Meadows said. 'We had a jug of tonic. We only had a small glass each, we gave the rest to Jerome. Then I started to think about how sick both Rain and I had been since we arrived at the commune. Headaches, sickness, and cramps. We thought we'd caught the virus that's been spreading through the commune. There were a few people sick with it. Then Rain got poisoned. I figured the killer was trying again.'

'And it was Mina that gave you the tonic,' Blackwell said.

'Yes, but she made it for us most mornings,' Rain said. 'It was making me feel better.'

'If it was Mina giving us the poison then why give us something to counteract it,' Meadows said.

'Perhaps she got the dose wrong, and you weren't given enough to make you seriously ill,' Edris said. 'So she gives you something to make you feel better, so you don't get suspicious, then tries again.'

'When did you first notice you were feeling unwell?' Valentine asked. 'Maybe if you can pin down what you drank you can work out who spiked your food or drink.'

'I was sick after the memorial evening,' Rain said.

'Yeah, but that was Cosmo's brew,' Meadows said. 'Iggy was ill the next day too.'

'Yeah exactly, I told you I don't get hangovers like that. If you remember Cosmo brought you a bottle.'

'And I gave it to Iggy,' Meadows said.

'Interesting,' Blackwell said.

'Yeah, but Cosmo didn't bring us the tonic that we gave to Jerome,' Rain said. 'Mina did.'

'Did she hand it to you?' Edris asked.

'No,' Meadows said. 'She left it in the tepee.'

'Easy to tamper with,' Valentine said.

'After that I was drinking water, the dandelion water or tea,' Rain said.

'Same here,' Meadows said. 'All which were left unattended.'

'So Cosmo could've taken the opportunity to go into your tepee and doctor your water and tea,' Blackwell said.

'But why?' Meadows asked.

'We still don't know who Cosmo is,' Blackwell said. 'How long have you known him?'

'All my life,' Meadows said.

'He's always just been Cosmo,' Rain added.

'Probably another one with a past to hide,' Blackwell said.

'He has got a temper,' Meadows said.

'Yeah, but angry is his default mode,' Rain said.

'I guess it's more like frustration,' Meadows said. 'Besides, he wasn't in the woods the night my father was murdered. Iggy said it was Jerome, Kern, Jonah, and Steven Parry.'

'Yeah, we saw that on your rambling notes,' Blackwell said. 'The other thing you should know is that the second remains we found were not those of Steven Parry. Male, mid to late thirties, that's all we know.'

'I don't understand, there was no one else with them,' Meadows said.

'According to Iggy,' Edris commented.

'If it's not Steven Parry then who is it?' Rain asked.

'If Jonah invited Steven Parry, then he could have invited someone else,' Blackwell said. 'Craig Wilson had a brother. Gareth.'

'Who is very much alive,' Meadows said.

'Don't tell me you went to see Craig Wilson's family,' Blackwell said.

'I did. I told them who I was. I didn't go in any official capacity if that's what you're worried about.'

Blackwell huffed. 'The only reason I haven't been to see them yet is that you got yourself poisoned, added to that, Phillip Carew's new identity also covered his family, namely yourself and Rain. This was supposed to be handled sensitively. Well you fucked that up.'

'You did say that you thought you and Rain were the targets,' Valentine said. 'Is it possible that Craig Wilson's family took revenge on your father and want to make you suffer as well?'

'There is no way that Gareth Wilson has been creeping around the commune,' Meadows said. 'Any stranger would stand out.'

'You said yourself that someone was in your tepee at night, then in the woods and fields. If he only came at night, then he wouldn't have been seen. He could've poisoned your tea when you were asleep.'

'Maybe there is a member of the commune who is related. They could have integrated themselves and waited for the opportune moment,' Edris said.

Meadows thought of all the families in the commune. No one stood out. 'Why wait thirty years to take revenge?' he asked. 'It doesn't make sense. I don't think this has anything to do with the Wilsons.'

They were all quiet for a few moments. Meadows' head was the clearest it had been for days and still the whole thing didn't add up. Now there was an unidentified male. Two murders, and years later another murder and two attempted murders.

'Is there anything else you can think of, or anyone that is missing?' Valentine asked.

'Jonah came out of the woods that night,' Meadows said. 'We know he came back sometime close to the winter solstice, well that's what Iggy told me.'

'We still can't find Jonah,' Edris said.

'What about Lee Morris? He was the only one, other than Iggy, who knew that Jerome and Kern were not who they said they were. What if Jonah invited Lee Morris that night to identify the real Kern Meadows. Iggy said that Jerome had told him that both Steven Parry and Jonah knew his identity. That's one way Jonah could've been certain – he used Lee Morris.'

'That fits,' Blackwell said. 'We've been trying to trace Morris. He was badly injured in the car crash and had a bleed to the brain. He spent months in hospital and then rehabilitation learning to walk again. He wasn't fit for work so was claiming disability payments. He hasn't attended a payment review, hospital appointment or touched his bank account since the late 1990s.'

'Let me guess,' Meadows said. '1999. It has to be Lee Morris' remains we found in the woods.'

'Steven Parry kills Kern Meadows and Lee Morris, then Jonah and Jerome cover it up,' Edris said.

Meadows shook his head. 'I can't see that happening but then again Lee was in the car with Kern. So Steven kills Kern not knowing his true identity, Lee tells him that he's made a mistake, so he turns the knife on Lee.'

'Except there is no evidence of a knife wound on victim number two,' Blackwell said.

'Wouldn't necessarily leave a mark,' Meadows said. 'If he hit an artery.'

'That would mean that Jerome and Jonah buried the evidence and just let Steven Parry walk away,' Rain said.

'Yeah, that doesn't make much sense,' Valentine agreed.

Meadows nodded. 'Jerome would've just witnessed the murder of his best friend. He would be afraid of Steven. Put yourself in Steven's position. Two witnesses. Would you let them walk away?'

'I think it's time to organise a search of the woods,' Blackwell said.

* * *

Meadows and Rain stood at the edge of the woods watching. The dog handlers had gone in and were walking the grids that had been marked out on a map. There were officers with metal detectors and specialist equipment that could detect subtle changes in the earth.

'Do you really think they are going to find Steven Parry's remains?' Rain asked.

'Yeah, I think it highly likely. We know that Steven was present the night our father was murdered. The question is which one killed him? Jonah or Jerome? Jerome told Iggy there'd been an accident. Maybe it was just that. One or both of them tried to wrestle the knife from Steven and he was fatally injured. That's the simple answer.'

'Which doesn't answer the question of who poisoned Jerome and us,' Rain said.

'The only conclusion we can draw from that is Jerome was only a witness to what happened and someone didn't want him talking, or us asking questions.'

'So that leaves Jonah,' Rain said.

The arrival of Jenny and Mina interrupted their conversation.

'We thought we'd come and see how they were doing with the search,' Mina said. 'Do you think it will take them a long time?'

'I don't know,' Meadows said. 'There's a lot of ground to cover and they have to be thorough.'

'I wouldn't worry,' Rain said. 'There's plenty of wood in the stock shed and you won't need any for heat for a while.'

'It's not that so much,' Jenny said. 'It's having all these police officers traipsing back and forth. No one can relax.'

'I'm sure you can nip down the field for a quick smoke. That's what I've been doing,' Rain said.

Jenny tutted. 'I've no interest in smoking that stuff.'

'What are they hoping to find?' Mina asked. 'Not another body, surely.'

'Possibly,' Meadows said. 'They will also be looking for any weapons. Chances are the perpetrator would've wanted to get rid of a knife, or anything else like clothing, quickly. The likelihood is they buried it in the woods.'

'What good will that do?' Jenny asked. 'They won't be able to get any evidence from it, will they?'

'You'd be surprised,' Meadows said. 'Forensics is so advanced now. A minute drop of blood, a hair, something is always left behind.'

'I wish things would just go back to normal,' Jenny said. 'I guess that's never going to happen.'

Meadows saw tears fill Jenny's eyes before she walked away.

'Is she OK?' Rain asked.

'No,' Mina said. 'She's struggling with Jerome's death. I'm just so happy you two are OK.'

'We have you to thank for that,' Rain said.

'Yes,' Meadows agreed. 'If you hadn't helped identify the belladonna, we could've been looking at a different outcome.'

'I just got lucky,' Mina said. 'It could have been any number of things. You should really be thanking Jenny. She taught me everything I know. She trained as a chemist. Such a shame that she married a dick and didn't get to use her skills.'

Meadows looked at Mina, she didn't seem aware of the implications of the information she had just given. 'Jenny would know how much belladonna would be needed to be a lethal dose.'

Mina shook her head. 'No, Jenny would never try to harm you two and she adored Jerome. She was the closest to him, I guess because she knew him longer than any of us.'

'I thought Jenny came to the commune after you,' Rain said.

'Yeah, but Jenny knew Jerome before she came to live here,' Mina said. 'They went to school together. I heard them talking about their old headmaster, and some of the tricks they used to get up to.'

Meadows thought back to the conversation he'd had with Iggy, Cosmo, and Jenny the night he was poisoned. Jenny had acted surprised by the swap of Kern's and Jerome's identities. Why act surprised if she knew? he thought. Then there's the violets outside her yurt, she was the one to tell me the meaning of the plant, and now her knowledge of plants and medicines.

'What is it?' Mina asked.

'I'm going to speak to Jenny,' he said. He looked at Rain. 'Come and get me as soon as they find something.'

Rain nodded.

Meadows walked back to Jenny's yurt with a heaviness in his heart. Why? he thought. He could think of no reason, but it all started to make sense. Mina told the group she had left tonic in the tepee the night Jerome died, then Jenny had left the group claiming to look for Cosmo when he'd told them all that he and Rain were going to dig the woods. Plenty of opportunity to slip the belladonna into the tonic. He stopped outside Jenny's yurt and looked once more at the violets before calling out.

'Are you home?'

'Yes, come in.'

Meadows stepped into the yurt. Jenny was sitting on a purple cushion, cradling a frosted glass of liquid.

'You know, don't you?' she said.

Chapter Thirty

Meadows looked at Jenny, for a moment he didn't speak. He was taken by surprise. He thought he would have to challenge her, but she seemed calm, almost resigned. It was as if she had been expecting him.

'You better sit down,' she said. 'I won't offer you a drink.' There was a hint of a smile on her lips.

Meadows took a cushion from the pile, placed it on the floor and sat, but not too close. He didn't want to make her feel intimidated. Her yurt was homely with most of the lattice walls covered in her paintings and pictures of her late partner, Mags. The bed had a purple throw and the two long shelves held earthenware crockery. Everything was neat and ordered. It almost looked unlived in, as if the contents had been neatly packed away. Was she planning on running?

'So how did you work it out?' Jenny asked.

'The violets, your knowledge of poison, and the fact you went to school with Jerome. You knew all along that he was Kern Meadows. The poison wasn't meant for Jerome. You said it was my fault he died, and I guess you were right on that point. I did give him the tonic.'

Jenny nodded. 'If you were still in my class I would give you top marks. I knew you wouldn't be able to let things go, that you would keep asking questions. I expect Mina told you about my skills. I felt so bad when the police took her. If they had charged her, I would have owned up. I prepared myself, put everything in order. I would never have let her take the blame. You must make sure she knows that.'

'I'm sure you'll get a chance to tell her yourself,' Meadows said. 'Why? What did Rain and I do to you that was so bad that you tried to kill us?'

Jenny shook her head. 'I wasn't trying to kill anyone. I didn't mean for any of this to happen, well apart from Jonah, which was different.'

'What do you mean?'

'That night at the summer solstice when Steven Parry turned up, I saw him talking to Kern, that is your father, not Jerome. They went off together. Apparently Jonah was supposed to organise the meeting between them but Steven had asked around and Iggy had pointed out Kern, not realising. Jonah knew by then who Kern really was and he was going to drag Jerome into it so he'd be forced to face up to his past or let Kern take the blame. When Jonah saw that Kern and Steven were missing, he told Jerome. They asked me if I'd seen Kern and Steven. I could see by Jerome's face that he was worried, so I went with them to look.'

'Just you, Jonah, and Jerome?'

'Yes, when we got to the woods Steven was shouting at Kern. He was in such a rage. You can't blame him, he was damaged. Not enough help was given to trauma victims back then. Imagine being trapped in a car with your dead mother and sister. Kern just stood there, he didn't defend himself, just said how sorry he was for what had happened to Steven's family. Then Steven pulled a knife from his jacket – it was some sort of hunting knife. Jerome tried to intervene. He told Steven that he was Kern Meadows and that any revenge Steven sought should be taken out on him.' Jenny shook her head and wiped away a tear that had escaped from her eye.

Meadows could imagine the scene easily. A warm summer's night with the smell of the bonfire in the air. Laughter and singing in the distance and his father facing a knife. The shock they all must have felt at seeing a weapon in their peaceful home, the fear his father must have felt, and the guilt Jerome carried all those years manifested in Steven Parry.

'I'm not certain what happened next, it was all so quick,' Jenny said. 'Steven turned on Jerome and Kern tried to stop him. Then Kern crumpled to the floor. Blood coming from his chest. Jerome tried to go to Kern to help him, but Steven still had the knife. He was in a frenzy. Jonah just stood there watching. I thought Steven was going to kill Jerome. We were close to the border of the woods where we'd been felling trees. There was an axe in one of the stumps. I grabbed it and swung it at Steven. I hit him in the head. I never meant to kill him.

'We all just stood there for a moment, we were in shock. Then Jerome knelt down next to Kern, but he was gone. We buried them. Iggy was right when he told you why he thought they didn't call the police. Kern's identity would have come to light. You would've lost your father and found out about his past. Jerome didn't want to do that to you. He kept quiet to protect you. Kern never wanted you to know what he had done. We told Jonah if he didn't leave then we would call the police and tell them that he had killed Steven. He left the next morning and we let everyone think that Kern had left too. I put the flowers on the graves as I didn't think it was right for them not to be marked.'

'But it wasn't Steven Parry's body that Rain and I found.'

'No, it was Jonah,' Jenny said.

'You said he left. He was seen after the summer solstice.'

'Yes, he came back just before winter solstice. He hadn't changed. He was back to his old self interfering in peoples' lives. He was badgering Iggy. He had ideas on how the commune should be run. He said it needed a leader. He brought people with him, followers he called them. Jerome couldn't stand up against Jonah, he had too much to lose, and Jonah wouldn't hesitate to use what he knew about him and your father. Iggy, well, he doesn't do confrontation, he never has. Cosmo would have no chance against Jonah. Jonah would have turned this place into some sort of cult with him dictating. I couldn't let that happen. I had to stop him.

'You know us olds take it in turns to collect the mistletoe for the winter solstice. That year it was my turn but a few days before Jonah said it should be him. I used laurel leaves to make cyanide, it's a bit tricky but I knew how to do it. When Jonah went into the woods that day to collect the mistletoe, I followed. Everyone was busy with the preparations. I took a small bottle of elderberry port laced with cyanide. I told him I wanted to talk to him alone. I gave him a load of bullshit about supporting him as leader, that I would persuade the others to follow. I poured the drinks and said we should have a toast to new beginnings. He didn't suspect a thing. He drank down his port in one go. I only raised mine to my lips. It didn't take long to work, a minute or two at the most.

'I'd started digging the grave over the two previous nights. It was a risk, but no one stumbled upon it. I dragged his body to the hole and rolled him in. Covered him up and that was the end of that. I did go back, though, and plant some violets.'

'His absence must've been noticed,' Meadows said.

'Yes, but I don't think anyone was bothered. His followers left not long after and things went back to normal.'

'Did Jerome know what you had done?'

'No, I didn't tell anyone. It was better that way.'

'So, it was really just Rain and me you wanted to kill.'

'No, I didn't want to kill you. If that was the case, I would have used cyanide. I just wanted to make you ill. I got the idea when Martin's girls went down with a virus. I also had to make a few more people sick so you wouldn't get suspicious. I put juice from the belladonna berries into Cosmo's wine, and in the tonic Mina gave you in the evenings. Then I grated the root and put it in among your tea. If I thought you had taken too much I would doctor Mina's tonic with carbonated charcoal. Then you gave Jerome the tonic, it was meant for the two of you and he drank the lot. It was too much.'

'But why?' Meadows asked. 'Why would you want to make us so ill?'

'I just wanted to stop you asking questions. I needed time to figure out what I was going to do. None of us wanted you to find out about your father's past so it was easy to persuade them to keep quiet about Jonah and the things that had gone on. I wanted to keep you distracted. I knew you wouldn't be able to stay for too long. If you were unwell you wouldn't be thinking straight. I thought the investigation would be fruitless, the case would be closed, and you'd go back to work. Another case would come along to take up your time. You could give your father a proper burial and move on. Maybe you'd keep up the search for Jonah for a while, you'd blame him for your father's death. It was his fault after all. The poison was just supposed to slow you down. You were never meant to get seriously ill. I was sure Mina would help identify the belladonna. I wouldn't have let you or Rain die.'

'Someone wanted me to know the truth,' Meadows said. 'They led me into the woods.'

'There was no one who could've done that. No one knew about Jonah and where he was buried. I should have guessed you'd figure out the significance of the violets. I thought about moving Jonah but digging up the grave was too risky. I moved the plants but left a few in a spot where I knew you wouldn't find anything. I thought you'd just dig there and that would be it. I didn't expect you to keep digging, especially as you wouldn't be thinking straight with the belladonna in your system. It can cause all sorts of symptoms. Hallucinations and loss of memory being just a couple. It should've been enough to keep you away. I suppose it's my own fault. I shouldn't have planted the flowers but even Jonah deserved some respect in death. I am sorry about Steven, that was an accident and I don't blame him for what he did that night. He must have suffered years of torment, then Jonah came along and stoked the fire. As for Jerome, I will never forgive myself for his death.'

'You know I'm going to have to tell Sergeant Blackwell. I don't have a choice.'

'I know and I understand. I don't want you to feel guilty. There's just one thing I'd like you to do for me.' Jenny took an envelope from her pocket. 'Like I told you, I prepared myself. Please give this to my daughter, Clover. Her address is on the front. She will be expecting bad news.'

'What do you mean?' Meadows asked.

'I'm dying. Cervical cancer. It spread and there is nothing they can do now. I want it to be in my own home on my own terms.' She looked down at the glass she'd been cradling.

'No.' Meadows pitched forward and tried to knock the glass away but Jenny twisted her body and gulped down the liquid.

There was no time to save her and as Meadows cradled her in his arms, she took her last breath.

Chapter Thirty-one

Meadows walked into the office clean-shaven and dressed in a suit. He smiled as his team broke into a round of applause.

'It's good to have you back,' Valentine said. 'It hasn't been the same without you.'

'Yeah, we missed you,' Paskin said. 'Not as much as Edris has.'

'Yeah, any longer and I would have packed my desk up,' Edris said.

'Not before I booted you out,' Blackwell said. 'You've done nothing but whine the whole time.'

'Yeah because you've had me stuck in the office or traipsing through fields looking for a dead person.'

'Well, we didn't know he was dead,' Blackwell snapped.

'Glad to see nothing's changed in my absence,' Meadows said. 'It's good to be back. Did you have a good holiday, Paskin?'

'Feels like it was months ago now, but yeah, it was great.'

Meadows looked at the incident board which still displayed all the information from the investigation. It was a strange feeling to see his father's name up there, and the picture of Jerome brought a fresh wave of pain.

'We were going to clear all that away before you got back,' Blackwell said. 'It's just we had a shout and things got busy. Just so you know, all the information we gathered about your father is only known by the team and DCI Lester. No one else knows and it will stay that way.'

The team all nodded their heads in agreement.

'Thank you, I appreciate your discretion,' Meadows said.

'Edris, you can pack it all away now. The case is closed,' Blackwell said.

There were still a lot of unanswered questions, some they would probably never find the answers to. Meadows didn't like loose ends and there was something troubling him, but he couldn't work out what is was.

'Did you manage to track down Lee Morris?' he asked.

'No, but we do have a confession so there is nothing left to do, and, well, there will be no trial,' Blackwell said.

Meadows nodded. 'I'll give you a hand to file this lot.' He stepped up to the board and looked at the last remains that were found. 'Steven Parry?'

'Yeah, we found him close to where your father was buried. DNA was a match to his sister. Cause of death is consistent with a blow to the head with an axe, as Jenny described. We found the axe buried along with a hunting knife. Everything she told you tallies,' Blackwell said.

'You put up my notes?' Meadows said.

Edris laughed. 'Yeah, the ones we could make sense of.'

Meadows took them down and read through what he had written. Among them were the initial notes he had made when he first spoke to the olds. 'This isn't right,' he said.

'What?' Valentine asked.

'Jenny wasn't at the summer solstice in 1999. I made a note of it.'

'Well of course she would've told you that,' Blackwell said. 'Distance herself from the crime. It's only because she thought we would find the weapon and be able to get DNA that she confessed.'

'I don't think so,' Meadows said. 'Her son died that year. I remember because it was not long after my father left.'

'Yeah, but it could have been any time before or after the murder,' Valentine said.

'Paskin, could you check birth and death records please. Look for Carl erm… I wrote down Jenny's married name somewhere. Ah here it is, Jones.'

'I think you're looking at problems that aren't there,' Blackwell said.

'What if she was protecting someone?' Meadows asked.

'Take her own life to stop someone getting caught,' Valentine said. 'It would need to be someone that was more than just a friend. You said her partner died.'

'Yes, she did, she has a daughter, Clover, she's a bit older than me. She visits the commune, but she left to study before we left. Then she worked and lived up in York. I can't see that she would be involved. Jenny was dying and it doesn't sound like she had long left. The people in the commune were her family. I don't think it's such a stretch that she would take the blame for one of them.'

Meadows continued looking through all the notes and information on the incident board, Blackwell returned to his desk and Valentine went off to make tea, leaving Edris standing next to Meadows looking at the notes.

'Found him,' Paskin said. 'Carl Jones. Death registered on the 25th of June 1999, he died on the 22nd.'

Meadows did a quick Google search. 'Summer solstice fell on the 21st of June that year. She wouldn't have left him. She was with him when he died.'

'How can you be certain?' Blackwell asked.

'Her daughter would know,' Meadows said. 'I think it's worth talking to her.'

'Do you want me to put the information back on the incident board?' Edris asked.

'No,' Blackwell said. 'The case is closed.'

'Put it all back,' Meadows said. 'Until we are sure.'

'Fine.' Blackwell huffed.

Once all the information was pinned back Meadows stood back and looked. Now he had a clear head it was easier to process the information. 'The disappearance of Lee Morris is troubling. Particularly as the last trace of him was 1999.'

'I hope you are not suggesting we search the woods again,' Blackwell said.

'He could be there,' Paskin said.

'We did stop digging after Jenny's confession,' Valentine said.

'Yeah, because we had already found Steven Parry's remains. We had no reason to believe anyone else would be buried there. We still don't,' Blackwell said.

'Maybe that's why she confessed,' Paskin said. 'To stop us finding more bodies.'

'She confessed to killing Steven Parry and Jonah, why not confess to Lee Morris if she killed him?' Edris asked.

'Because I don't think she killed them,' Meadows said. 'Maybe she didn't know about Lee Morris. The only ones left that she would be protecting are these.' He pointed to the board. 'Iggy, Cosmo, and Mina.'

'What does it matter?' Blackwell asked. 'Even if she is protecting one of these people, we have no proof. There's no evidence to use in a conviction. The only way we would get anywhere is if they confessed. I can't see that happening.'

'You're right,' Meadows said. 'But we'll know the truth. Clover is staying with her aunt, Jenny's sister, until the funeral. My mother went to see them yesterday. We need to speak to her to confirm her mother wasn't at the summer solstice that year. If the only thing we achieve is that Clover's memories of her mother are not tainted by her killing three people, then I'll be happy with that. I know how it feels to carry that knowledge.'

Blackwell looked like he was about to protest then he shrugged his shoulders. 'Your call.'

Meadows looked at Edris. 'Come on, let's go.'

Edris' face lit up and he grabbed his jacket.

* * *

Clover answered the door and her eyes filled with tears when she saw Meadows.

'Winter, it's so good to see you. It's been a long time.' She hugged him tightly then drew back and brushed her tears away with her fingers. 'Come in.'

'This is Sergeant Edris,' Meadows said as he followed her.

'Is this an official visit?' Clover asked.

'Yes and no,' Meadows said. 'I wanted to come and see you, but I also need to ask you a few questions.'

They entered the sitting room and a woman who looked remarkably like Jenny rose from an armchair.

'This is my auntie Laura,' Clover said and introduced Meadows and Edris.

'I'm so sorry for your loss,' Meadows said. 'Jenny was a lovely woman.'

'Thank you,' Laura said. 'Please have a seat. Can I get you anything to drink?'

'No we're good, thanks,' Meadows said as he sat down on the sofa.

'I heard you were with Mum when she died,' Clover said. 'Did she…?'

'It was very quick,' Meadows said. 'She didn't suffer.'

'I'm just glad she wasn't alone.'

Meadows could sense an awkwardness in the two women, and he guessed it had to do with Jenny's confession. There was no way to avoid the subject, so he thought it best to just bring it out rather than try to mask it with polite talk.

'I wasn't officially investigating the case at the commune because of my personal involvement,' he said. 'I understand that Sergeant Blackwell talked you through what your mother told me before she died.'

'I still can't believe it,' Laura said.

'She said in her letter that she was sorry, and that she hoped I understood,' Clover said. 'I'm trying. She did those things to protect the people she loved. Faced with a man and a knife, who knows how any of us would act? The poisoning, well that's different. She planned it, and she nearly killed you and Rain. It doesn't tie with the woman I knew, not my mother.'

'There are some things that are unclear,' Meadows said and looked at Edris.

Edris opened his notebook. 'Your brother, Carl, died on the 22nd of June 1999, is that correct?'

'Yes,' Clover said.

'Your mother was with him when he died?'

Clover looked alarmed. 'You don't think that she… no, there is no way, she wouldn't…'

'It's nothing like that,' Meadows said. The thought hadn't occurred to him that she may have eased her son's passing. It wasn't a line of enquiry that he wanted to go down. It's too late now, he thought. 'We just need to establish your mother's whereabouts at the time.'

'She was with Carl,' Laura said.

'The whole time?' Edris asked.

'Yes, for about two weeks. He died here. She didn't want him to die in hospital, so we made arrangements for him to come here. We had help, the Macmillan nurses were fabulous, but Jenny never left his side. He died in the early hours of the morning with her holding his hand.'

'Why is this important?' Clover asked.

'The night your mother said she hit Steven Parry in self-defence was the 21st of June 1999,' Meadows said.

'If, as you say, she was here the whole time, then she can't possibly have killed Steven Parry,' Edris added.

'Why would she say she did?' Laura asked.

'That's what we are trying to find out,' Meadows said. 'Who did Jenny care so much about that she would let you and Clover believe she had killed a man rather than let that person face the consequences?'

'There is no one,' Clover said.

'Other than us, and Lee, no, we're all the family she has,' Laura said.

'Lee? Lee Morris?' Meadows asked.

'Yes, Lee is our brother. Morris was my maiden name. Jenny is the oldest, Lee is our younger brother.'

'We've been looking for him,' Edris said.

Both Laura and Clover looked puzzled. 'Has something happened to him?' Laura asked. 'I haven't seen him in a while. I thought he would come here after Jenny died.'

'Could you give us his address?' Edris asked. 'He's not in any trouble. We just need to speak to him.'

Clover looked at Meadows. 'Is he not living in the commune anymore?'

'Lee lived in the commune?' Meadows asked.

'Yes, he went there years ago,' Laura said.

Meadows tried to think through all the people that had lived there when he had been a child. He couldn't remember Jenny having a brother. 'Your brother had an accident when he was younger,' he said.

'Yes, when he was fifteen. He was in a stolen car with Patrick and Kern Meadows and, what was the other boy's name, Nicolas I think.'

'Kern Meadows was your father,' Clover said. 'Mum never told me this.'

Meadows didn't want to correct her. It was too complicated. 'Yes,' he said. 'I only just found out myself.'

'Lee was badly injured,' Laura said. 'It took months of rehab for him to be able to walk and talk. He was never the same. Jenny took him to live in the commune with her.'

'You know him,' Clover said. 'Oh, probably as Cosmo.'

Chapter Thirty-two

Steel-grey clouds met with the mountaintop and sheep huddled together as Meadows steered the car around the winding mountain road.

'Looks like a storm is coming,' Edris said. 'At least it will cool things down.'

Meadows nodded. The weather was the least of his concerns. If he was right, then Jenny's efforts to protect her brother were in vain.

'Are you OK?' Edris asked. 'You're very quiet.'

'I'm fine,' Meadows said. 'I just didn't expect to be going back to the commune so soon. They're all still in mourning and I'm not sure of the welcome I'll get.'

'None of it is your fault,' Edris said. 'I'm sure no one there blames you for what happened to Jenny. If they hadn't kept secrets, it could have been a different outcome.'

'There still would've been an arrest, maybe two.'

'Why two?'

'I'm not sure about Jonah's murder. Every one of them knew about the swap, they also knew that Cosmo was Lee Morris. It's going to be hard to trust anything they say. I've been thinking back to the conversations I had with them all. I don't think I spoke to Cosmo alone. I think they made sure that someone was always with him because if anyone was likely to blurt out the truth it would have been him. It's the poison that concerns me. I'm not sure Cosmo would know how to make cyanide.'

'We'll just have to see what reaction we get when we ask him,' Edris said. 'I still can't believe Lee Morris was at the commune the whole time. At least we won't have to go digging for any more bodies.'

They arrived at the commune to find life going on as normal. Meadows guessed there wasn't time for people to wallow in grief. He saw several of the men carrying sandbags, they greeted him with the usual smiles and stopped to chat for a moment. They saw Martin, who seemed to be organising the group.

'What's going on?' Edris asked.

'Storm is coming,' he said. 'We need to weigh down any of the homes that are at risk from high winds.'

'I haven't seen the forecast,' Edris said. 'Is it going to be a bad storm?'

Martin laughed. 'We don't need a forecast, you can smell it in the air.'

Edris looked amused but didn't comment.

'We better get on,' Martin said.

'You seen Cosmo around?' Meadows asked.

'Probably checking on the hives,' Martin said.

'Thanks,' Meadows said.

They walked through the lavender field and into a meadow that was speckled with wildflowers. Cosmo could be seen moving between the hives.

'Shouldn't he be in protective clothing?' Edris asked.

'He's never bothered,' Meadows said. 'He talks to them, says they understand each other.'

'Don't come any closer,' Cosmo called out. 'You'll upset them.'

'We need to talk to you,' Meadows said.

'I'm busy.' Cosmo turned his back on them.

'It's important,' Edris shouted.

Cosmo turned around and stomped towards them. 'I'm not in the… in the… mood for t-talking.'

'Do you think he's dangerous?' Edris whispered.

'Nah, he's just like his bees,' Meadows said. 'Angry buzzing, that's all it is. It's his nature, probably a result of the accident.'

'I'm sorry,' Meadows said to Cosmo, 'but this can't wait.'

'Fine, what d-do you want?'

'Maybe it's better if we talk indoors,' Meadows suggested.

Cosmo looked at Edris. 'Does he have to c-come?'

'Yes,' Meadows said. 'We need to speak to you officially.' He saw a flash of fear in Cosmo's eyes and thought he was going to take off, but he just sighed, and his shoulders slumped.

'OK,' Cosmo said.

They didn't talk until they got back to Cosmo's yurt. Meadows didn't want anything they said to be overheard. He thought Cosmo deserved their discretion no matter what he had done.

Inside was a mess. Piles of clothes and unwashed dishes. Cosmo moved around some things then sat on the floor and started drumming his fingers on his legs. Meadows grabbed a cushion and handed it to Edris before sitting down.

'Edris needs to ask you a few questions,' Meadows said.

'G-go on then,' Cosmo said.

'During our investigation into the death of Kern Meadows we interviewed people who were involved in the car crash and their families,' Edris said.

'Which K-Kern Meadows are you talking about?' Cosmo asked.

'The real Kern Meadows, Jerome,' Meadows said.

'One of the people we were trying to contact was Lee Morris,' Edris continued.

Meadows watched Cosmo's reaction. He shifted, then jiggled his legs in time with the drumming of his fingers. He made no comment.

'We know you are Lee Morris,' Meadows said.

Cosmo's eyes narrowed. 'Who t-told you that?'

'We spoke to your sister, Laura,' Edris said.

'Who else knows?'

'No one,' Meadows said. 'Why didn't you tell me?'

'I left Lee b-behind a long time ago. I'm Cosmo.'

'I understand,' Meadows said.

'No you d-don't. You've no idea what it's like.'

'Then tell us,' Meadows said.

'The night of the c-car crash, it wasn't Kern… not…'

'Driving?' Edris offered.

Cosmo shot him a look and shook his head. 'Fault,' he said. 'His brother P-Patrick and Nicolas were always in trouble. They were in the same c-class as Jenny. I was with Kern but the… youngest. Kern and m-me were hanging around that night, bored. We went to the p-park and Patrick and Nic were there drinking. They gave us some cider. It went st-straight to our heads. They thought it was…' Cosmo hit the side of his head.

'It's OK, take your time,' Meadows said.

'Funny, yeah, they laughed. Then one of them ro-rolled a joint and handed it around. It made me feel…'

'Stoned?' Edris asked.

'Grown up. It was P-Patrick's idea to steal the car. He'd done it before. They took it in t-turns to drive. Patrick and Nick. Then they got b-bored. They wanted us to have a go. Kern didn't w-want to but I was up for it. The car was an… an automatic so it was easy, like a b-bumper car. I drove around for a while then w-we all sort of pushed Kern into doing the s-same. We went on the backroads. Patrick was telling Kern to go faster, he took the… took the… bend too fast, then it was j-just lights and crunching metal.' Cosmo put his hands over his ears as if he could still hear the noise. 'The last thing I r-remember was that boy screaming. Kern never said a w-word about me driving, he took all the blame. He was in p-prison by the time I was... after hospital.'

'You went to visit him,' Edris said.

'Yeah, a few t-times. Jenny took me on the bus. I couldn't get in a car. I went as often as I could. No one else v-visited him. His parents blamed him for Patrick dying. Phillip didn't have any visitors so K-Kern asked me to request a visit with him. After that the three of us would spend visiting time together.'

'Did you see them when they got out?'

'Yeah, a few t-times and I met Iggy. You know the rest. Jenny came to live here and then I came. I've been here ever since. I got used to calling Phillip K-Kern, and Kern Jerome. Sometimes I would m-mess up but no one took any notice. Everything was good. Jenny looked after me, they all did. I would never have had this life if the p-police knew I had been driving that night.'

'You were only fifteen at the time. I doubt you would have got a sentence even if the police knew the part you played,' Meadows said. 'You shouldn't feel guilty. Is that why Jenny took the blame for what happened to Steven Parry that night? She knew how you felt about the accident. Knew you were afraid of people finding out. She didn't want you to go to prison.'

Cosmo looked at the floor.

'Clover will believe that her mother did those things. Is that how you want Jenny remembered? There has been enough blame and guilt.'

'I d-don't want that,' Cosmo said.

'I know,' Meadows said. 'You hit Steven Parry because you were afraid. Is that what happened?'

'He k-killed Kern, he was going to k-kill Jerome, and then he would have killed me. I just wanted to stop him.'

'You told Jenny what had happened.'

'Yeah, she knew s-something was wrong. I told her that Jerome had made Jonah leave but I d-didn't feel safe. She told me to leave Lee b-behind, no more hospital check-ups, no more using my b-bank account. She said if anyone came looking for Steven Parry then there would be no connection to me.'

'And then Jonah came back,' Edris said.

'Yeah b-but not for long. He went away again. Jenny said he wouldn't bother us again but she was wrong. He came b-back.'

This was what worried Meadows. He saw the look of confusion on Cosmo's face.

'What do you mean, he came back?' Edris asked.

'He p-poisoned Jerome.' He looked at Meadows. 'And you and Rain. He led you into the woods to sh-show you where Steven Parry was buried.'

'No,' Meadows said. 'Jonah has been dead a long time. That last time he came back Jenny poisoned him and buried him in the woods. They were his remains that me and Rain found.'

'No,' Cosmo said. 'Jenny wouldn't h-hurt anyone.'

'She wanted to make sure you were safe,' Meadows said. He didn't want to tell him that she was the one to poison Jerome.

'What's g-going to… to happen to me now?'

'Honestly, I don't know. I will have to call Detective Blackwell. He'll take you to the station to give a statement. There will likely be a trial, but you may get a lenient judge. You did act in self-defence. I'll do all I can to help you and I'm sure Iggy and Mina will do the same.'

'Do I h-have to go with you now? I need to f-finish checking the bees.'

'I'm sure that will be OK. Just don't leave the commune.'

Meadows stepped out of the yurt as the first drops of rain fell.

'Do you think it's OK to leave him?' Edris asked.

'Yeah, he's not likely to do a runner. Even if he did, he won't get far. He can't drive and you heard what he said about getting in a car.'

'Yeah.' Edris pulled up his hood. 'There's still one thing I don't understand. If Jenny was the only one who knew about Jonah being buried in the woods, then who was creeping around? Someone was in your tepee, someone led you to Jonah's body.'

'I don't think there was anyone,' Meadows said. 'Jenny said that belladonna poisoning can give you hallucinations. I think it was my mind's way of processing what I had seen. I've been in those woods near the old sycamore tree countless times over the years. The violets must've been there the whole time. I just didn't remember and make the connection. Then again in the polytunnel, I knocked over the violets.'

'Nah, I don't see it,' Edris said.

'Then what's your theory?'

'Well, it's obvious. You saw a ghost.'

Meadows laughed and it felt good. 'I wonder how you ever passed your sergeants' exam. Come on, let's go and see Iggy before it chucks it down. I want him to keep an eye on Cosmo.'

They found Iggy sitting under the awning of his caravan holding hands with Mina.

'Hello, kiddo,' Iggy said. 'How are you doing?'

'I'm OK,' Meadows said. 'I've just been having a talk to Cosmo. You knew he was Lee Morris?'

'Yes, I did.'

'What are you talking about?' Mina asked.

'I'll explain later,' Iggy said.

'Why didn't you tell me?' Meadows asked.

'It wasn't my story to tell. Besides, it wouldn't have made a difference.'

'It may have,' Meadows said. 'Cosmo was in the woods that night with Steven Parry. I'll let him tell you but he's going to need a lot of help and support. I hear you have a good legal team.'

Iggy nodded. 'I'll get on to it. I was hoping to see you before the funeral. I have something for you. Hold on.' Iggy went into the caravan and came out a few moments later with an envelope. 'Jerome asked me to look after this and give it to you if something happened to him.'

'When?'

'Oh years ago.' He handed the envelope to Meadows.

Meadows sat down on one of Iggy's chairs, opened the letter and read.

> *Dear Winter*
> *There are so many things I need to tell you but now it comes to it I find I don't have the words. Instead I'll just stick to the things that are important. You have been like a son to me and I am so proud of you and your brother, as I know your father would've been.*
> *There may be things you find out about me after I'm gone. I hope you won't think any less of me. The commune land now belongs to you. I know you will take care of the place and the people that live here.*
> *A man left this land to his grandson. He wanted him to have a second chance. That grandson grasped it with both hands and in turn allowed others the chance to do the same. The land is his legacy and your home always.*
> *With all my love*
> *Jerome*

Meadows folded the letter and put it in his pocket. He knew exactly what to do. The same as Jerome had done. The commune was for people who needed it, the land owned by those who worked it. Like Jerome, he would never lay claim to it.

List of characters

Police:

DI Winter Meadows
DS Tristan Edris
DC Rowena Paskin
DS Stefan Blackwell
DC Reena Valentine

Others:

Daisy Moor – pathologist
Mike Fielding – SOCO forensic
Chris Harley – forensic tech
Fern Meadows – Winter's mother
Kern Meadows – Winter's father
Rain Meadows – Winter's brother

The Commune:

Jerome
Mina
Jenny

Cosmo
Iggy
Haystack
Jonah
Martin

Others:

Craig Wilson – victim
Phillip Carew – victim
Anne Parry – car crash victim
Ray Parry – Anne's husband
Donna Parry – car crash victim
Christine Parry – car crash survivor
Steven Parry – car crash survivor
Patrick Meadows – car crash victim
Nicolas Llewellyn – car crash victim
Lee Morris – car crash survivor

If you enjoyed this book, please let others know by leaving a quick review on Amazon. Also, if you spot anything untoward in the paperback, get in touch. We strive for the best quality and appreciate reader feedback.

editor@thebookfolks.com

www.thebookfolks.com

Also in this series:

THE SILENT QUARRY (Book 1)

Following a fall and a bang to the head, a woman's
memories come flooding back about an incident that
occurred twenty years ago in which her friend was
murdered. As she pieces together the events and tells the
police, she begins to fear repercussions. DI Winter
Meadows must work out the identity of the killer before
they strike again.

FROZEN MINDS (Book 2)

When the boss of a care home for mentally challenged
adults is murdered, the residents are not the most reliable
of witnesses. DI Winter Meadows draws on his soft nature
to gain the trust of an individual he believes saw the crime.
But without unravelling the mystery and finding the
evidence, the case will freeze over.

SUFFER THE CHILDREN (Book 3)

When a toddler goes missing from the family home, the police and community come out in force to find her. However, with few traces found after an extensive search, DI Winter Meadows fears the child has been abducted. But someone knows something, and when a man is found dead, the race is on to solve the puzzle.

A KNOT OF SPARROWS (Book 4)

When local teenage troublemaker and ne'er-do-well Stacey Evans is found dead, locals in a small Welsh village couldn't give a monkey's. That gives nice guy cop DI Winter Meadows a headache. Can he win over their trust and catch a killer in their midst?

LIES OF MINE (Book 5)

A body is found in an old mine in a secluded spot in the Welsh hills. There are no signs of struggle so DI Winter Meadows suspects that the victim, youth worker David Harris, knew his killer. But when the detective discovers it is not the first murder in the area, he must dig deep to join up the dots.

RISE TO THE FLY (Book 6)

When the bodies of a retired couple are found by a reservoir, the police are concerned to discover fishing flies have been impaled on their tongues. After they find nothing in the couple's past to indicate a reason for the murder, they begin to look local. What will they turn up in this dark and secluded corner of Wales?

All available FREE with Kindle Unlimited and in paperback.

Other titles of interest:

NO REFUGE by Nicola Clifford

Reporter Stacey Logan has little to worry about other than
the town flower festival when a man is shot dead. When
she believes the police have got the wrong man, she does
some snooping of her own. But will her desire for a scoop
lead her to a place where there is no refuge?

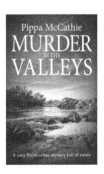

MURDER IN THE VALLEYS by Pippa McCathie

Having left the police following a corruption investigation,
ex-superintendent Fabia Havard is struggling with civilian
life. When a girl is murdered in her town, she can't resist
trying to find the killer herself.

Sign up to our mailing list to find out about new releases and special offers!

www.thebookfolks.com

Made in the USA
Monee, IL
08 December 2022

20206989R00163